TRADE
Me

COURTNEY MILAN

For CW, CJ, and MT
I would say why I'm dedicating this book to you.
But there's an old Russian proverb:
One never speaks of rope in the house of the condemned...

1.

TINA

*T*oday is going to be a good day.

There is little outward evidence of this. Ragged, gray clouds skittered in overhead during my morning bus ride. By the time I got to my stop a few blocks from the edge of campus, rain was coming down in earnest. Now, passing cars send up a fine spray of droplets. The umbrella in my backpack gave up the ghost as soon as I pulled it out, and I haven't had a chance to duct tape the fabric to the spines yet, because I'm about fourteen minutes away from a class that starts in eleven minutes and twenty-nine seconds.

Today hasn't started particularly well, and my schedule only forecasts worse. I have five hours of work this afternoon and several projects due in the next two days. Before I can tackle any of that, there's the pesky issue of three hours of morning classes. I'll be lucky to sleep before midnight.

But counterbalancing that undoubtedly depressing list is one bright beacon: I'm wearing my favorite sweater.

I know. It doesn't sound like much. But here are the facts: My favorite sweater is white cashmere. It's soft and warm. I found it in a Salvation Army in Alhambra when I was buying clothes for college two and a half years ago, tagged with the ridiculously low price of $3.79 even though it looked like it had never been worn.

I argued with myself—and my mom—for twenty minutes about buying it. On the one hand, it was a mint-condition cashmere sweater for under five bucks. On the other hand, it was cashmere. And white.

And that's why I'm positive that today will be a good day. Twenty-nine months after that purchase, I still have that sweater and it's still unstained. And let me tell you, Tina Chen is *not* usually that graceful on her own. That's two and a half years of no dropped coffee cups or sliding spaghetti strands. It's twenty-nine months of no toner spills at work, of nobody bumping into me holding a slice of pizza at the wrong time.

My life usually feels like a living illustration of Murphy's Law. But when I wear my favorite sweater, somehow everything that can go wrong magically doesn't.

So yes, today *is* going to be a good day. I'm not generally a superstitious person, but I don't have to imagine my stars aligning. The rain slows and the clouds begin to thin as I make my way to the forested edge of campus. The pedestrian signal magically changes at the exact moment I come to the intersection. The campus bell tower is playing an arrangement of "Take Me to the River," and even though I'm breathing fast by the time I make it to Dwinelle, where my class is, I've made up for lost time. All I have to do is cross one last expanse of wet asphalt and painted white lines.

The lot is filled with gleaming wet cars, and I pick my way through it, navigating around dirty puddles of rainbow-hued water. I check my watch one last time.

Three minutes to go. One minute to get to the building, two to dash up the stairs. I'm going to make it.

One minute, I'm stepping out from between two cars, looking at my wrist. The next, a silent blur of glistening black engineering going way too fast for a parking lot cuts by. The car sweeps beside me and muddy, oily water sheets up in a wave. I don't have time to move away. I barely even have time to turn my head. Water flies everywhere, drenching me.

The wind picks up—or maybe I only feel its chilled fingers against my arm because I'm wet through. I wipe my face, glaring at the car ahead of me. It takes me a moment standing frozen in the parking lot to understand what just happened. I'm cold. I'm wet. And that means…

I look down, and it's not just my arm that feels cold. The whole world seems to turn to ice around me, shivering and shaking.

My sweater.

That asshole just splashed muddy water all over my sweater. Dark flecks mark the once-bright white sleeve.

For a moment, I can't even believe it. It's not possible.

Oh, trust me. This kind of thing happens all the time. But it's not supposed to happen to my sweater.

Fuck. Fuck, fuck.

I glare at the car. It turns smoothly and pulls into a space marked with a sign proclaiming that the spot is reserved for visitors of the chancellor's office. Whoever's inside, whoever is driving, is already off-limits. My fists clench, but what am I supposed to do? Yell at some visiting official?

Then the car door opens and the driver gets out. He's tall and thin with sandy-blond hair. He reaches back into the car for a messenger bag and then slams the door.

He's not the chancellor. He's not even a visitor to the chancellor's office. And I don't need to be psychic to know that, because I recognize this driver. For one, he's in my next class.

For another, he's Blake Reynolds. Yes, *the* Blake Reynolds—he of the adorable childhood commercials, of Cyclone Systems fame.

Until now, I have had nothing against Blake Reynolds. He sits one aisle over in class. Our discussion section started two weeks ago, and we've made eye contact once or twice during class. He has a nice smile.

When I'm eighty, and I don't care about the truth anymore, I'll tell all the kids who will listen that yes, I knew Blake Reynolds, and you know, he kind of had a thing for me. You should have seen me back then. I was so cute!

But I'm twenty now and I don't have the luxury of lying to myself. So right now, watching him stride across the parking lot, the memory of his smile turns my stomach. Blake's smile is like a lottery ticket: It's the smile that a thousand people will use to construct impossible dreams. In reality, it's as indifferent as the weather. Good fortune; bad fortune. It doesn't matter. He's never really noticed I'm there.

I have nothing against Blake Reynolds, except that he nearly ran me over. Except that every time he's smiled at me, I've felt a little tickle of *something* in the pit of my stomach, and I don't have time for *something*, let alone harboring that *something* for Blake Reynolds. I have nothing against Blake, even though he's apparently been told he can park in the chancellor's spot, for God's sake. I have nothing against the fact that the Graduate Student Instructor who leads our section practically fawns over him, hanging on every word he says as if it were chiseled on stone tablets.

I have nothing against Blake except that I'm going to spend the next few hours freezing because of him. And he got oil stains on my lucky sweater.

Fine. I admit it. I have something against Blake Reynolds.

He lopes up to the building as I squeeze water out of my sleeve. He has an easy, smooth gait, and he disappears between the glass doors before I can say anything. I follow behind, grimly strangling the straps of my backpack and pretending it's his neck. But I don't have time to do anything except follow him into the building, dash up a few flights of stairs, find a bathroom, and rub hopelessly at my sleeve with whatever I can find. Thirty seconds convinces me that water and a swiftly eroding paper towel aren't going to solve the problem.

I'm two minutes late when I slide into my seat. The instructor—he's told us to call him Fred—gives me a dirty look. The girl behind me gives me an understanding smile as I sit down and brush at my sweater.

"Shitty weather, isn't it?" she whispers.

"Seriously."

Beside me, just two feet away, Blake glances my way. For a second, our eyes meet, and I imagine myself throwing my backpack at him. But he just smiles at me— that goddamned lottery ticket of a smile—as if nothing is wrong.

I gave him a dirty look, but he's already looked away.

Of course. He still doesn't notice.

I take my folder out of my backpack, set the week's reading on the desk next to it, and sit back.

This is not like my programming languages class, where I take notes constantly. This is a class for freshmen, a survey course where people just...talk about the reading. I have two majors, both with a huge slate of prerequisites. For scheduling reasons, I didn't end up getting all my required classes out of the way my first two years of college. Consequently, Blake and I are the oldest ones in the class.

This is just a discussion section, which means that people—*freshmen* people, to be exact—spend time expounding on their theory of the world. Since almost none of them have any experience to speak of, the discussions tend to be both heated and naïve. I'm not a big talker, so I normally don't say anything unless I'm prodded.

We've been talking about the politics of the safety net for the last week and a half. Today, we're talking about food stamps. Everyone speaks earnestly and academically about topics that have no effect on their daily lives. I don't know if I'm alone in my experience—I can't be the only one in here who doesn't come from money—but from the conversation, it sure sounds like it. I nod and pretend that these things don't matter to me, either.

I pretend it doesn't matter when the girl at the front of the class says that people on food stamps are lazy. I pretend I don't care when someone talks about how they saw someone buying a fifth of vodka and a bag of candy with EBT. I nod and I smile and I try not to shiver. I tell myself it's the draft, that it's my drenched, mud-stained, no-longer-lucky sweater.

And don't get me wrong. This is Cal, and the students here are not exactly known for their staunch conservatism, so there are even more people defending the concept of food stamps. Somehow, they still manage to imply that people on food stamps are an endangered species and that the smarter, better parts of society should extend a helping hand to those less-fortunate primates who can't take care of themselves. God save me from college students who think they can save a world they don't really inhabit.

I grind my pen into the desk and keep my mouth shut.

And then Blake raises his hand.

I've been trying not to look at him since class started. I've been trying not to *think* about him, because I'm already pissed off and I don't need to feel more pissed off. But he's the golden boy of the class, and when Fred gestures to him and he leans back in his seat, I can't *not* look at him.

Blake is tall and blond. He has a light dusting of facial hair—more than scruff, less than a full beard—that would look unkempt on just about any other student. On him, it looks distinguished. He started college a little later than most students would, and before he came here, he had a high-level position in his father's company. He glances around the room, smiling, supremely confident that whatever he's going to say will be brilliant. Everyone else seems to hold their breath, already believing the same thing.

Blake also wears a suit and tie to class. Let me be honest: Most college students who dress up look like douchebags playing at being adults. They look like they care so much about their appearance that they're afraid to relax. By contrast, Blake looks like he's got the money to dress well and then another million bucks on top of that. He doesn't have to give a shit about what anyone thinks of him.

I suppose he's good-looking, if you like the juxtaposition of sharp with slightly disheveled.

Which I definitely don't. Not today.

"Here's how I see things," Blake says. At the front of the class, Fred sets his hand on his chin and nods.

"We can discuss the effect that food stamps have." Blake has a trillion-watt smile, one that could power every computer that his father's company has ever produced. "We can argue whether policies like food stamps make people lazy. We can talk about incentives, and we can talk about money. And I understand those who say that all our good intentions do is create a permanent underclass that perpetuates the cycle of poverty, that people need to work for the benefits they're given, not just have them handed to them for doing nothing."

A tide of red anger fills me. My pen gouges the paper.

"But," Blake says, "let's say we grant all that is true for the sake of argument. What are the real alternatives? We've tried doing nothing, Dickens-style, and we know how that turned out. No matter what we do, we will have a permanent underclass. The only question we have is how we treat them, and what that says about us."

Oh, that's the only question, is it? Funny. *I* have other questions.

Shut up, I tell myself desperately, but it's too late. My mouth seems to work of its own accord.

"I see," I hear myself say. "So poor people are lazy and doomed, but we should help them anyway so that you can take the credit?" My face flushes as I speak.

Blake's eyes widen. Slowly—every second seems slow right now, drowned by the beat of my heart—he turns to me. He sits right across from me; our eyes meet, and I can see the astonishment in his gaze. I can almost feel him taking in my stained sweater, my fading jeans. I'm nothing to him.

"I'm sorry." He sounds honestly surprised, as if he can't imagine that anyone would disagree with him, let alone a nothing like me. "What did you say?"

I should put my head back down. I should go back to holding my tongue, watching other people talk about my life. But I can't. The only thing I've ever had to stave off the direst consequences of Murphy's Law was a sweater and superstition, and Blake destroyed my faith in both today.

"You heard what I said." My voice is shaking. "When have you ever been on food stamps? When have you ever had to work for anything? Who gave you the right to grant that poor people are lesser beings for the sake of argument? And who the hell are you to say that the only important thing is not whether people actually starve to death, but how the world will judge the wealthy?"

His face goes white. "I work," he says. "I work really hard. It's not easy—"

"It's not easy being Adam Reynolds's son," I finish for him. "We all know how hard you work. Your dad told the entire world when he put you in charge of his interface division at the age of fourteen. I'm sure you've worked a lot of hours, sitting at a desk and taking credit for what other people do. It must be really hard holding down the part-time job that your father gave you. I bet it leaves you almost no time to spend your millions of dollars in stock options. Hey, I guess I was wrong. You do know what it's like to get something in exchange for nothing. You're an expert at it."

His lips press together.

"But it doesn't make you an expert on poverty," I tell him. "I was up until midnight last night. I live five miles away, because I can't afford to live in Berkeley. It takes me forty-five minutes to get to class. How long did it take you to park your BMW in the chancellor's spot?"

He looks at me, his eyes wide. "It's…" He shakes his head. "It's not a BMW." As if that were the one salient fact in our prior discussion.

At the front of the class, Fred, the hapless instructor, is rummaging through his papers for the seating chart.

"It's really big of you to say it doesn't matter if people think my parents are lazy," I tell him. "But they're not *your* parents, and starting off your charitable statement by assuming that my family is subhuman is really, really crappy."

"Hey," Fred says. "Hey, uh…" He peers at the paper. "We don't need to engage in personal attacks, uh…" He squints. "Uh." Fred calls all the students by their first name, but my legal name has obviously stymied him. He shrugs and bulls on. "Let's keep this about the issues, Miss Chen."

"He got personal first." My voice trembles. "I *am* this issue. My dad lost his job when I first started college. If my family hadn't had food stamps then, I would have had to drop out." I'm not going to cry. Not in front of everyone, and especially not in front of Blake. "None of you have any idea what you're talking about. You don't know what it's like to go into a store and use EBT. You don't know what it's like to slink into a Salvation Army and hope that there will be something that will let you fit in with classmates whose weekly allowance would feed your family for two months." I glare at Blake again.

Blake looks away. On the plus side—and this is not a huge plus—it looks like I won't have to worry about Blake smiling at me anymore.

"And that's why this issue is personal," I say. "We're invisible to you, except when you want to tell us what to do. You know what, Blake? Nobody here would care about a word you said if your family was on food stamps. Try trading lives with me. You couldn't manage it, not for two weeks."

He looks away from me. The tips of his ears turn pink, though, and his lips press into an angry line.

Nobody is looking at me, for that matter. They're avoiding eye contact like I'm some kind of feral dog that needs to be put down. And that's when I realize precisely how many people are witnessing this. How many of my fellow students are tapping out distress signals on the phones they're cradling surreptitiously on their laps.

I can almost feel the Facebook posts springing up around me.

ZOMG. Some nobody just bitched out Blake Reynolds.

LOL did u hear she was on food stamps?

I look down at my stained sweater. *She was dressed like a homeless person. I shit you not.*

It's going to be all over the internet in a matter of minutes.

"Are you done, Miss Chen?" Fred asks sarcastically.

I'm almost hyperventilating in panic, but then I realize how ridiculous I'm being. The one good thing about being a Tina Chen at Berkeley is that I'm indistinguishable from any of the other dozens of Tina Chens around. I can be as inappropriate as I want. I'm not googleable. I bow my head, letting my hair fall around my face like a curtain.

Someone else's hand is in the air. "I think that's really unfair to Blake," someone in front pipes up. "We all know how hard he works, and how hard his dad works. They've definitely earned everything they have."

Fine. They don't want to acknowledge me as a person. Nothing's really changed. I don't have the time or the energy to care. But apparently, the class has turned into a referendum on Blake, and now everyone has to have their say.

"I really like the tap-to-call feature on my Tempest," another girl puts in. "It's genius. Blake deserves everything he has."

It goes on like that for a few minutes. I take copious notes throughout the entire debacle. *Fuck fuck fuck fuck fuck shit shit shit shit fuck fuck fuck,* I write in my notebook in my neatest cursive. Everyone—Fred included—falls all over themselves to say how great Blake is. And then the tone shifts.

"I think *some people* need to stop blaming others for where they are. If *some people* stopped wasting energy on playing the victim, and started doing something instead, they'd get a lot further in life."

I hunch in on myself, preparing for even worse.

"Hey," Blake says sharply.

He's just two feet away from me. I'm not going to look at him.

But his tone is icy. "This has gone on long enough. Come on, guys. Enough of this crap. She's right. We all know I won the nepotism lottery. I'm not an expert, and if I said something stupid, I'm glad she was willing to point it out."

Silence falls in response. At the front of the class, Fred clears his throat, maybe now remembering that he has a job besides savaging students. "Right. Let's…uh, let's move on."

And I? I do not want to feel grateful to Blake. I hate that nobody even recognized me as a person until Blake spoke up. And when I tilt my head to the side… I hate that he looks at me, that he gives me a silent nod, like he's granted me his permission to criticize him.

I didn't need his permission.

After class lets out, I take my time leaving so I don't have to fake nonchalance on my way out.

The girl in front of me stands and then turns to me. "You know," she murmurs in a low, furtive voice, as if wanting to make sure nobody else hears her, "I thought you had a good point. I'm glad you said it. I didn't want to."

"Thanks."

But I don't want to talk, so I wait until she goes. I consider whether my pen belongs in the front pocket or the side pocket of my backpack. I make sure my notebook is securely placed next to my textbooks. I check the zipper. Twice.

By the time I leave, the classroom is empty.

The hallway outside isn't, though. There's one person from class still there, and he's the last person—the very last person in the world—that I want to talk to at the moment. He's leaning against the wall, looking even more like a businessman than a student. He looks at me now. His eyes are the ridiculous blue of ocean waters on some tropical beach. They make me think of a spring break that I will never be able to afford.

"Hey," he says.

I'm not sure how to respond. My hands are still shaking. I don't think I can keep it together through a longer spat with him. I should have kept my mouth shut in the first place.

I give him the barest of nods and keep walking.

"Hey," he repeats. "Tina."

That does stop me. *Fred* didn't know what to call me. How does *Blake Reynolds* know my name?

Slowly, I turn to him. I've never talked to him before today. Maybe he emailed someone while we were in class? One of his…people. Someone like Blake has to have people, right? He parked in an official visitor's spot with impunity. Getting a class roster would hardly pose a problem.

But wait. Even if he got my name off the official class roster, he wouldn't know I go by Tina. He'd only know my legal name—Xingjuan Chen.

I swallow.

And then he does something I'm not expecting. He gives me a sheepish smile. It's so different from the cocky grin that he normally wears that I take a step back.

"I'm sorry," he says.

"For what?"

He shrugs. "You're right. It's not my place to say it doesn't matter what people say about you. And I should have stopped that before it turned into a pile-on." He indicates the room we just came from with a tilt of his head. "I was just taken aback."

He looks at me like he expects me to shrug it all off, like I'm supposed to pat him on the shoulder and say that it's okay.

But it's not. And the fact that he thinks it *can* be just makes me feel worse. Nothing about my life is okay right now, and he can't change that.

"Can I…" He takes a deep breath, and then that cocky smile is back on his face, like he's sure of himself again. "Can I get you coffee or something as an apology?"

He holds his hand out to me, like I'm supposed to shake it. When he does, his coat—impeccably tailored gray wool—pulls back from his sleeve. For a second, with his hand outstretched, I see dark ink against his wrist, the edge of a tattoo that seems completely at odds with everything I know about him.

For just that second, I wonder if I'm imagining it. His life has been an open book to the world ever since his father first put him in a television commercial at the tender age of twenty months.

Everyone knows everything about Blake Reynolds, boy prodigy, certain successor to Cyclone Systems. Everything…except I've never heard of that tattoo.

I take another step away from him, putting my hands behind my back.

"Let me explain something," I say. "You get to park in a spot reserved for the chancellor's office."

He grimaces. "Yeah. I usually don't. But when I started school, he…um." He trails off, as if realizing that now is not the time to remind me that the entire university administration is no doubt slavering over the potential endowment boost his attendance represents.

"By contrast," I say, "I have an hour between this class and my next one. If I can't knock off one of my assignments in that time, I will be up until two tonight."

His smile fades.

"I'm sorry," I say. "You're probably a legitimately decent person. But I don't have time for your apology."

"Two-second version, then. I'm sorry I was clueless. I'll try to do better."

He looks at me, his eyes serious, and that damned *something,* that coiling awareness in my stomach, starts up again. It almost makes me mad that he won't let me walk off steeping in my anger. No; he has to take that away from me, too.

"I'm sorry I lost my temper," I say, and I start to leave.

"Tina."

I turn back reluctantly.

"You were right about almost everything you said," he says. "But there was one thing you were really wrong about."

"Oh?"

He gives me another one of his smiles, and this one seems to curl around me, catching me up in a wave of warmth. "You said that I didn't notice people like you." His voice lowers. His eyes are relentlessly blue, and they cut into me. "That's completely false. You've never been invisible to me. I saw you the first day we crossed paths, and I've been seeing you ever since."

I don't know what to say. I don't know what to think. Against my better judgment, that little spark of something ignites in my stomach. A flame dances, ready to catch fire.

But I have to be vigilant.

"On the contrary," I hear myself say. "This morning, you cut in front of me in the parking lot. You were three inches from me. And…" I hold up my sleeve, showing the damage.

He winces.

"So when I said you didn't see me, I meant it. Literally."

His eyes shut. "Shit."

"It's okay," I tell him. "I'm used to it."

2.

BLAKE

*T*he kitchen window of my house high up in the Berkeley Hills overlooks fog-shrouded waters, interrupted by the bulk of San Francisco to the south and the illuminated towers of the Golden Gate Bridge farther north.

Twilight is coming and I haven't turned on any lights. I'm surrounded by granite and stainless steel, and I'm considering the benefits of an apple that I've rinsed, when my phone rings.

To be precise, it's not actually my phone. It's the highly experimental video chat app on my even more experimental watch.

My pulse picks up a few beats. I love my dad. But there is, after all, a reason why his ring tone is the ominous-sounding "Imperial March" from *Star Wars*. He's difficult, demanding…and I'm not about to make him wait. I tap my watch, accepting the call.

He appears on the tiny watch screen. Reduced to thumbnail size, he looks exactly like his publicity photos. His eyebrows are thick and bushy; his hair is turning to salt and pepper. Other than the hair, though, he looks a lot like me. Same wiry build. Same blue eyes; same Roman centurion nose.

"Blake." He must be at one of his standing desks, because he paces back and forth, his head shifting. In the back of my mind, I notice that the video is finally following his movements with nary a glitch. He frowns at me. "You're backlit."

"Julio," I say. "Lights."

My kitchen lights come on in a dazzle of brilliance—all of them, from the bright, recessed LEDs overhead to the warm under-cabinet lights that catch the gold flecks in the granite counter.

At the exact same time, the lights in my dad's office shut off.

"Goddammit," Dad says. "There's an unintended consequence. Julio, lights."

Obligingly, his experimental computerized environmental system turns his lights back on—and just as obligingly, mine plunges my kitchen back into darkness.

Dad lets out a sharp bark of laughter. I cross the room and flip the lights on, old school, with my elbow. "Okay, I'll file the bug report. What's going on?"

I'm holding the apple in my hand opposite the watch. I got it from the fridge a minute before and it's still cold against my skin. In a few minutes, my hands will warm it up until it's body temperature. I pass it to my watch hand. *One.*

"We have to talk about the Fernanda launch in March." Dad growls when he talks, an effect so powerful that unless he makes an effort to sound friendly, he comes off as perpetually angry.

I know him well enough to know that's just the way he talks, but still, a hint of anxious anticipation gathers in me at his tone. "It's only a few months away." His eyes spear me. "I think you should run it."

I swallow, feeling a pit open up in my stomach. This is far from the first time he's pushed me to take on a larger role in the company, and it won't be the last. And this particular role?

"Come on, Dad. Nobody wants *me* to do the whole launch. That's not how these things work."

One of his eyebrows rises. "Bullshit. These things work the way I say they work."

I don't think there is anyone in the world who could argue that my dad is not a great man—or, at the very least, a powerful one. Over the course of the last three decades, he built a Fortune 500 company from almost nothing. He's right; the world bends to him, not the other way around.

I used to think that was cool.

"I know you want me to take on a larger public role, but I'm busy with school."

He could point out that we scheduled the product launch to coincide with my spring break. Instead…

"Fuck school," Dad says succinctly. "College serves only two purposes. It teaches people to bleat on command, like sheep, and it lets assholes think they're 'finding themselves'"—he illustrates this with air quotes—"by getting degrees in Russian literature before they head into the real world and land jobs as insurance adjusters. You're not a sheep, and you're not going to be an insurance adjuster. Why do you give a shit?"

When my dad was my age, he'd already dropped out of Yale, started Cyclone, and made his first ten million dollars. Having avoided what he calls "stupid bullshit" all his life, he can't figure out why I'm interested in it.

"I'm just as much a sheep if I follow in your footsteps," I tell him. "Maybe I *do* want to find myself."

"Hippy crap."

"Maybe I have secret dreams of being an insurance adjuster," I deadpan. "The forbidden is always tempting." I switch my apple to the other hand. It's the second time I've moved it.

He snorts. Other parents tell their kids they have to go to college if they expect to amount to anything. My dad has been telling me the opposite all my life, threatening me with a career as an insurance adjuster as if nothing worse could ever happen.

He regards me skeptically now. He's forty miles away and his face is just an icon on an inch-sized screen, but I can still feel the force of his gaze. When he coughs, stocks plummet around the globe. It's hardly surprising that he can make me feel uneasy with just a look. He's that kind of man.

I'm not.

"It's been six months since you left," he finally mutters. "This is a really inefficient method of finding yourself, and I'm pretty sure it's bullshit. You're not trying to find yourself. You're trying to lose yourself. You're afraid that you can't fucking do this." He gestures widely to the office around him. "Well, I know you, and I say you can. Hurry the fuck up, Blake. I'm not going to be on top of my game forever. I need you. Run the goddamned launch."

For the last year, he's been offering opportunities like this to me. For the last year, I've had dreams where I say yes. Nightmares, really, ones that wake me in a cold sweat. During the last year, he's pushed and prodded me. Every time we've had some version of this conversation, I've imagined telling him the truth.

I can't do this, Dad. I have a problem.

But I haven't told anyone that. Most days, I try not to admit it even to myself. And I already know what he will do if I tell him. He'll look at me, frown, and toss out one of his foul-mouthed aphorisms. Something like *problems are for pussies.*

Right now, at least I'm standing up to him, and he respects that. If he knew the truth? I don't want to see him disappointed in me. Not now. Not ever.

"Not on top of your game?" I joke instead. "Shit. What do you need? A vacation?"

He doesn't laugh at this. He folds his arms. "Maybe. Maybe something like that."

I roll my eyes. I know exactly what it's like when Dad takes a vacation: He doesn't. For the last thirty years, he's worked and worked and worked without stopping, waking up in the middle of the night to leave messages for his chief engineer about every last improvement he's dreamed up. Going to some beach somewhere doesn't change his habits; it just means that his key staff have to change time zones to match his schedule.

When I was a kid, the prospect of inheriting Cyclone felt like it would be the winning move in a worldwide game. Today, I know it takes strength. Determination. A will stronger than steel.

In other words, it's going to take someone other than me.

"I get it," he says. "You're scared. You're using school as an excuse. You think you can't do this. You've bought into this bullshit that just because you're twenty-three and barely an adult, blah blah blah, you can't do this. Well, that's fucked-up. Stare your fear down. Come on, Blake. Cyclone needs you." He frowns. "*I* need you."

It's a paradox. If I'm not strong enough to say no to my dad, I'm surely not strong enough to run the company. If he manages to break me down, I'll know I can't do it.

I also know that in a long-term battle of wills between my father and me, I will never, ever win. Nobody does. The only solution I can see is to *get* strong enough to take over before he breaks me down.

"Dad. I can't." The rest of the sentence is on the tip of my tongue. *I have a problem.*

But he's already rejecting this with a dismissive chop of his hand. "Can't is for assholes."

Can't is the only word I have. Going away to college was a stopgap measure, the best I could come up with to buy time to fix this thing. It's not working. If this keeps up, he'll break me before I'm ready. I switch my apple back to the other hand. *Three.*

I know my dad *sounds* like a mean fucker, but that's just the way he talks. He doesn't play games. He loves me; he wants me to be happy. Cyclone made him happy, and so now he wants to give it to me. He expects me to continue his conquest of the world.

"Look," he says. "We have a vanishing window here. The board of directors will let you take over in the name of continuity and public trust at this point. The longer you stay away, the less weight that argument carries."

"You own twelve percent of Cyclone stock," I point out, "and everyone fucking worships you. The board of directors will do whatever you damned well say."

"Hmmm." He frowns, but doesn't disagree.

My dad may be something of a mean fucker, but he's a mean fucker with prescient vision, brilliant business sense, and an almost preternatural ability to know precisely what needs to be done at any given moment. Hundreds of people depend on his decisions.

I switch the apple yet again to my other hand. *Four*.

And the truth is… I know why he wants me to run the launch. It's not about wanting a vacation or needing to slow down. It's not even a manipulative attempt to yank me out of school and pull me back into his orbit.

It's because a little over a year ago, Peter Georgiacodis—Cyclone's chief financial officer, my father's best friend, the only person who could face my dad down and remain standing, and, incidentally, the closest thing I've ever had to a second parent—had a massive heart attack two nights before the launch of our third-generation tablet.

My father would never admit that preparing for our upcoming launch has afflicted him with anything so weak as lingering grief. He would never tell me that the memories are getting to him. He'd certainly never talk about fears of his own fleeting mortality. But when he says that he needs me, I suspect that's what he means.

If he *were* just a mean fucker, if all he had to offer was cash, I could tell him to piss off. But it's not about the money. Imagine that Darth Vader had the chance to raise Luke as his son. Imagine that he spent every day with him, loved him, and taught him everything he knew. Imagine that he put Luke first every day of his son's young life, even though he had an empire to run and galactic rebellions to squash.

It's easy to shout "I'll never join you!" when some random asshole makes ridiculous claims about your parentage. It's harder when that asshole loves you with a world-bending ferocity. And it's downright impossible when you love him back.

Dad and I stare at each other for a moment, both of us desperately wishing the other will change.

"Compromise," I finally say. "I'll draft the launch script. I can do that and stay in school. But you're still the public face of Cyclone. You stay in charge. You run it. Not me."

His eyes bore into mine.

I want to do everything for him. I want to be everything he thinks I can be.

But... *Dad, I have a problem.*

He doesn't need to hear about my problem. I'm going to take care of it on my own, and when I do, I'll come back. At that point, I'll be the person he believes I can be, not just the illusion of a son he can rely on.

He lets out a long breath. "Fine. I can work with that. I'll have George set everything up. Thanks, asshole."

"You got it, you bastard."

He ends the conversation.

And in that moment, I realize what I've agreed to. It's not the work that convinced me I needed to get away from Cyclone. I don't mind work. But Dad's not the only one with lingering grief issues. He's just the one who is managing his issues in a reasonably healthy manner.

Agreeing to script the launch will put me back in the heart of memories I can't suppress. And unlike my dad, *I* have a problem.

I remember staring at Peter's casket, seeing Cyclone employees, industry contacts—a crowd, really—surrounding him. And that's when I started to feel trapped. There were hundreds of people there, and he knew all of them—every single one—from work.

I switch the apple back to my left hand. *Five*. That's the rule. I have to switch the fruit from hand to hand five times, slowly, before I eat it. By the time I've done that, the apple will have reached body temperature and I can decide if I want to eat it and make it a part of me.

But my hands are flushed and hot. The apple's too warm now, as if it's absorbed all the heat of my emotions. If I eat it, that conversation will become a part of me, and I'll never escape it.

So I do the same thing I did after Peter's funeral: I go for a run instead.

I eschew sweatpants in favor of running shorts and a T-shirt. The weather monitor on my watch informs me that it's fifty-two and raining, but I feel hot. I feel the illusory weight of a hundred stares on me as I jaunt outside and fall into a warm-up jog. At first, my muscles are sluggish and the rain is frigid against my bare thighs.

I run harder. I'm a little hungry; maybe I should have eaten that apple after all. But here's a trick of physiology, one that I learned in high school even though the teachers didn't put it this way. The fight-or-flight response shuts down the parasympathetic nervous system. It's complicated, and physiology is not my bag of tricks, but it all comes down to the same thing: Your body can't digest food while you're running. If I could run all the time, I'd never get hungry.

I can't run all the time, but I can try. I run until the ache slips from my quads, until all sense of hunger dissipates. With every step, I imagine my body searching for energy, needing to find it somewhere. There is nowhere it can draw that energy from, nowhere except my body itself. I run, and with every step I get smaller. If I run hard enough, I tell myself, maybe one day I can run myself into someone else altogether.

Deep down, I know it doesn't matter how fast I run. I'm fucked-up at any speed. Deep down, I know I have to get out. But I don't know which direction is out any longer. I wish I could outrun myself. I wish I could trade this stupid problem for anything else.

Running is a double-edged sword. It's a huge part of the problem that has me so badly tangled. But it also rewinds my day, leaving the worst of it on the trail behind me. It takes me back through my conversation with my dad, leaching the emotion away. It takes me back through a lunch I barely ate, back through this morning.

God, this morning.

Sometimes, you build someone up in your mind. Yes, I noticed Tina's legs first. And her hair second—I'm a sucker for long hair, and hers, when she lets it down, falls halfway down her back, thick and straight and dark, catching light and releasing it in little glints. But she's also smart, focused, and determined. Tina seemed exactly the kind of girl I'd go for if I had my shit together. There's something that's sexy as fuck about a woman who knows what she wants. She seemed like the kind of girl who would see through my bullshit in a hot minute.

Look at that. I was right.

I go over her words, again and again, letting the truth in them hurt me as much as the ache in my lungs.

You do *know what it's like to get something in exchange for nothing. You're an expert at it.*

Nobody here would care about a word you said if your family was on food stamps. Try trading lives with me. You couldn't manage it, not for two weeks.

She has no idea how right she is. Hell, I can't even manage being myself.

Try trading lives with me. You couldn't manage it, not for two weeks.

Try trading lives with me.

It starts as a stupid, wistful idea, based only on the fact that I want to get out and I can't. *Try trading lives with me.*

Fuck. I totally would. I want what she has. I want that certainty. That determination. Me? I'm just a pair of legs and lungs, moving, moving, moving, for fear that if I stop, I'll vanish. But this idea doesn't go away.

Don't get me wrong; it's not a solution. I don't have solutions, not anymore. But some of my best ideas, my most brilliant answers, have come to me when I mixed things up and got out of my head. Maybe all I need is a different perspective. A radically different one.

Try trading lives with me.

I want, I want, I want. And maybe what I want, most of all, is someone who will finally see through my bullshit. Someone who will kick me in the ass and tell me to stop fucking around like this. I have a problem and I don't want it.

Try trading lives with me.

I would in three seconds. Any way I could.

3.

$\mathcal{B}$y the time I get home at seven, the rest of the day has eroded the worst of my morning memories. Another hour of classes, five hours at the library...my mind only has so much emotional space. The events of the morning are impossibly far away when I open my laptop. The hinge catches; I adjust it and idly check my email.

From: Maria Lopez

Subject: Something you're not telling me?

For a second, I have no idea what she could mean. Maria is my best friend and roommate. She knows everything about me—or at least, as much as any one person can know. Then the events of the morning come rushing back: me opening my big mouth, the class, *Blake Reynolds*.

I thought I was safe from the prospect of Facebook blowing up—but then, Blake *did* know my name. I open a new tab, check my notifications...

Mabel beat my score in an online game. Jen from high school tagged me in a three-year-old photo. There are a half-dozen likes on my post this morning about wearing my lucky sweater. Other than that? Nothing.

I let out a breath of relief, switch tabs, and click on Maria's email. *You left your phone at home*, the body of the message reads, *and your mom called seven times that I could see. Everything okay with them?*

Oh, thank God. Just that.

No worries, I reply. *That's just Mom. I'll talk to her.* After a moment, I add: *I had kind of a shitty day though. Someone got mud on my sweater.*

Her response comes a few minutes later. *Noooo!! Will it wash out?*

Don't think so. It's okay. See you soon.

I pick up my phone. Sure enough, there are twenty-three missed calls and no messages. My mother is not the most patient person in the world. It's a good thing she and Dad are happily married, because if she were in the dating pool, she'd be the sort of person who would call the guy she liked a dozen times in a half hour.

But instead of calling her back immediately, or even starting on my second project like I should, I pull up a third browser tab. A multicolored search logo greets me.

I'm going to regret this, but...

Blake Reynolds, I type. The search result pulls up a brief entry to the right, which features a fairly recent shot of Blake, alongside several of his younger photos. This includes a baby picture that is unfairly cute. Blake is the vice president of interfaces at Cyclone Systems, currently on leave. His birthday is February 14th. Of course. Even the universe thinks everyone should love him.

Beneath that, there are links to a smattering of news articles, his official page at Cyclone, a book review, and a YouTube playlist titled "The Best of Blake," maintained by BlakeFan1283. With some trepidation, I click on the last one.

It's a collection of ads, product launch clips, and interviews.

The first item in the playlist, of course, is the famous and now well-aged Cyclone ad, the one that broke them out of the server business when they started in on consumer electronics. The computer depicted reflects its age—this is obviously a high-end machine for the time, with a bulky CD-ROM drive and dual floppy disks. The camera focuses not on the tower itself, but on the user: an adorable, pudgy, blond toddler.

On screen, baby Blake grasps the mouse and starts a program. As it opens, he claps his hands in clumsy baby glee, laughing out loud.

"Cyclone Systems," the announcer intones. "Computers so easy, even a baby can use them."

There are a slew of adorable commercials of Blake, all of which have been named and labeled by his fans. I click on "Sorry," which has two million views.

Blake, maybe five years old and still sun-blond, stands in what looks like his room. He's filling a backpack with a sweater, a candy bar, a roughed-up teddy bear. By his sniffles, and the note the camera pans over, he's obviously running away from home. Child Blake squares his shoulders and hefts his bag.

The next shot is of him jogging down a residential sidewalk, swiping away a single tear. The camera comes close, focusing on his waist. There's a beep, a green light.

Little Blake stops and takes out the very-first-ever Cyclone multiuse pager.

Sorry, Blake. The message reads. *I love you.*

Blake turns to look over his shoulder. His expression clears. There's one last sniffle. Then he turns and runs home.

"Cyclone Systems," the announcer intones as Blake runs up a tree-shaded lawn and launches himself into his father's arms. "Still bringing families together."

It has never occurred to me before, but using your adorable son to sell your company's products is a special kind of fucked-up. I almost feel sorry for Blake until I remember that in compensation, he now has more money than God.

The next clip starts automatically. This one is an interview between nine-year-old Blake and David Letterman. Blake is wearing a suit and a bow tie; he shifts from side to side in his seat, restless and yet smiling.

Before the interview progresses beyond introductions, though, my phone rings. I jump, like I've been caught doing something I shouldn't, and pause the video.

"Tina!" My mother sounds happy when I answer. She doesn't say anything about the twenty-three missed calls. "You're so busy these days. Sorry to call and bother you."

I shift my phone closer to my ear. "You're not bothering me."

I turn away from the grinning child Blake, frozen on YouTube, to contemplate my room.

Technically, it's not just my room; there are two twin beds crammed in here. Also technically, it's not a room. It's a converted garage, for very relaxed definitions of the word *converted*. Large carpet remnants mostly cover the concrete floor; there's a rough bathroom and shower in the back. It's a lot cheaper than the dorms. It's also a lot farther from campus.

"How is everything?" I say. "Did you get my check?" Thirty dollars. I know there are some students who can drop thirty dollars on a single night in a bar, but I find that kind of extravagance bewildering. Thirty dollars is more than I spend on food in a week. It hurts to write that check, but that thirty dollars means gas to the pharmacy and the Medicare copay for Mabel's ADHD medication. My little sister just started high school, and now everything she does will be part of her record for college. She does well when she's on her meds. But my mom doesn't always believe what doctors tell her.

There's a little bit of a pause. "Yes, yes," my mother says. "We got it. This is why I had to call you."

My heart sinks. "What happened?" I try to sound calm. "Is Dad okay? Did something happen to him?" I can remember the last time Dad's leg acted up. It's a painful, visceral memory—of Mom working two jobs while trying to keep her other projects afloat, of my father refusing to go to the doctor because he couldn't afford the visit. Of the infection that followed and a late-night trip to the emergency room when his fever wouldn't break. They're still paying down that debt.

"No, not your father," my mother says. "It's Jack Sheng. You know Jack, right?"

I smile involuntarily. "I don't know Jack."

The idiom sails over Mom's head. "That's right. You never practice anymore."

I make a noise in the back of my throat.

"No, no," my mother says, "this is not a guilt trip. I promised you, no more guilt trips."

I pull back from my phone slightly and look at it askance. She *did* promise me there would be no more guilt trips, but let's face it, if it were possible to make a living running a guilt travel agency, Mom would be rich. She can send me on a round-the-world guilt cruise on two minutes' notice. If I complain, she'll tell me that it isn't a guilt trip; it's a guilt *journey*. I should know the difference; I'm in college now.

"About Jack Sheng," she says. "His petition was denied. The IJ said his testimony was not credible. Why is Jack Sheng not credible?"

Listening to my mother talk always used to confuse my childhood friends. She speaks English with a thick accent. After my parents' petition for asylum was granted, allowing us to stay in the U.S., she devoted all her spare time to helping friends navigate the immigration system. And Mom has many, many friends. Those friends also have friends, and both Mom and her many friends are on the internet, which raises the enterprise to a whole new level of acquaintanceship.

After years of helping others, her vocabulary is larger than most people would expect. It's also peculiarly specialized.

Long experience allows me to translate my mother's immigration shorthand. One of my mother's many, many friends/distant acquaintances/internet message board buddies from her Falun Gong practice also tried to get asylum in the United States. The immigration judge— that's the *IJ* my mother refers to; she's picked up all the immigration lingo—didn't believe that her friend had actually been persecuted by the Chinese government for practicing Falun Gong, and so denied his request for asylum. So Jack Sheng is going back to China.

"I don't know why Jack Sheng is not credible," I say, which is the simple truth. I stand up, pushing away from the frozen video of smiling child Blake, and cross the room to lean against the wall.

"Of course you don't know. I don't know, either. There is no legitimate answer." I can imagine my mother waving her arms, tucking the phone between her chin and face. "This is the question we must ask. Why is Jack Sheng not credible? We have to raise money for an appeal."

I pull my arms around myself. "Mom…" It's not so much a protest. I have forty-three dollars and twenty cents in my checking account right now, and that has to last until my next paycheck, nine days away.

"I know, I know," Ma says. "You're a student. You don't have so much. I'm not asking for your help."

I nod, even though she can't hear that.

"But I gave your check to Jack Sheng. So don't be surprised if you see his name on the back."

I swallow hard, leaning against the wall. Even with that support, my legs have all the strength of a rapidly falling soufflé. I slowly sink to the floor. I can't breathe. I can't think. And—I remind myself—I can't scream at my own mother.

"This month," my mom says, "Mabel can just try harder."

God, it hurt so much to send that thirty dollars. That thirty bucks I sent means I can never take the easy way out and order pizza when I'm too exhausted to cook. It means that on Saturday nights, when my friends are taking time off to recharge, I'm the one frantically trying to get a head start on my homework for the coming week, because God knows I won't have the time on weekdays. That thirty bucks means I never, ever get to take a break.

It was also supposed to mean that Mabel would get the meds she needs.

"Mom." My voice is thick. "I didn't give you that money for Jack Sheng. I gave it to you for Mabel."

"But Jack Sheng practices Falun Gong," my mother says, as if that's the end of the conversation. And for her, it is.

"Yes, but I don't," I snap out.

I can hear the silence on the other end of the phone.

"Oh?" my mother asks.

I don't say anything.

"It's true," she concedes. "When your father was in prison in China, you were not practicing Falun Gong."

There is no response I can give to that.

"When our neighbors hid us so that I would not be taken away and tortured, too, you were not practicing Falun Gong."

I shake my head. I was *six*. I remember almost nothing—nothing except a thick blanket of guilt, a dark wave of feeling that this was all somehow my fault.

"Falun Gong practitioners raised the money to bribe the authorities, smuggle us out of China, and fly us to America. You don't practice Falun Gong. You don't need to; they just saved your life, that's all. But it's okay if it's not so convenient for you to remember that anymore."

"You said you wouldn't guilt-trip me," I manage to choke out.

"That," my mother says quietly, "was only the truth. Any guilt comes from you, not me."

I don't know how to answer. So far, I've managed to get everything right, even working as much as I do. This year, though, my classes have reached a new level of hard. I thought organic was hard, but physical chemistry is that much worse. And if I thought introductory programming classes were difficult, now I'm drowning. Instead of turning in assignments that search and sort lists of numbers, we're designing our own programming languages. There aren't enough minutes in the day, and I'm not sure I can maintain the grades I need to make everything come together.

I can feel my entire future slipping from my fingers.

I don't know Jack Sheng, but right now, I hate him. I hate him so much for needing my money. I hate him because I've heard his story a hundred times before—tortured because he practiced Falun Gong in China, escaped to the U.S., and is now being sent back home.

This is what Blake Reynolds will never understand: When he and his father give money to charities, it never hurts. To them, it's just a check. It makes them feel good. It's a pat on the back. He will never understand what it means to hate someone over thirty dollars. He probably spends more than thirty dollars on his jeans. Fuck. I don't know what rich people spend on jeans. He would probably scoff at the idea that you could *get* a pair of jeans for thirty bucks.

"Mom," I say. "You have to get Mabel her medication."

"Next month, maybe."

"No." I swallow. "It's not fair to her to skip around like that." When you have as little as I do, you know it to the last dollar. I had thought about splurging, about getting my sweater dry-cleaned. But this is it; I can't afford my superstition any longer.

"I can send you a little more," I say. "But you have to promise you'll get her meds. Okay?"

I can manage twenty dollars. That should be enough. It'll leave me with twenty-three bucks for nine days. That's not that bad. I still have most of a twenty-five-pound bag of rice. I'm practically rich, as long as nothing comes up.

There's a long pause. From that, I gather that Mom didn't just sign over my check to Jack Sheng's appeal account. She's given more than my parents can really afford. I'm not going to be the only one figuring out how to eat on dollars a day.

"Please," I say. "It's really important."

People say that money doesn't buy love, and maybe they're right. I don't need money to love my parents or my sister. I love them so fiercely and so much that it hurts sometimes. I love them so much that I think of them every time I want to give up, which is practically every day. If I play my cards right, if I don't mess everything up, by the time Mabel is in college I can make sure that she never has to feel like this. I won't have to worry about my parents' nonexistent savings. I won't lie awake at night wondering if they accidentally forgot to pay their health insurance premiums this month. I'll just be able to take care of it all.

Money may not buy love, but it buys something like it. Not having any money makes love complicated. No matter how much I love Mabel, I can't quash the part of me that resents her existence. Part of me remembers that in China, she wouldn't even have been born. And while I would never want that—while I would take on anyone who tried to hurt my little sister—sometimes I think of a world without anyone who needs me. I imagine being able to breathe, being able to rest. I imagine being able to get pizza with my friends after class instead of making polite excuses. I imagine getting coffee with Blake Reynolds.

I don't want a lot out of life. I just want enough money to love without being tangled up about it.

"Okay," my mom finally says. "I promise."

"Thank you."

"And you… You are taking care of yourself? You are eating enough? Getting enough sleep? I hear about college students, and the…" She pauses. "The all-nighters. You aren't having all-nighters, are you?"

"No," I lie. "I sleep well, Ma. I have to take care of myself, right?"

"Good," Mom says. "And maybe you'll meet a rich boyfriend."

I let out a snort. "Right."

But as I speak, my gaze strays back to my laptop. I can see the little rectangle where I paused Blake's video. *I saw you the first day we crossed paths, and I've been seeing you ever since.* That little burn in my stomach comes back.

Stupid. He doesn't know me.

At that moment, my laptop dings—the two-tone note of a Facebook notification.

It has nothing to do with him, I'm sure. Still, my heart jumps. I stand up and move over to the computer.

"Right," I say more slowly, and I hope, very sarcastically.

I switch to the Facebook tab. I have a new friend request. My heart thumps as I click on it. It's from Blake Reynolds. I let out a little gasp.

Confirm. Ignore.

"Right," I repeat a third time, this time to remind my stupidly accelerating pulse. "Don't hope too hard, Ma. I don't have time for any boyfriends at all, let alone a rich one." I shake my head and push away from the computer. "Is Mabel there? Can I talk to her?"

My mind races as I talk to my sister, though. What does this mean? Why did he send me a friend request?

I sigh. Better question is: Why am I being so dramatic? I don't let myself think about Facebook for ten minutes. When I finally hang up, I tell myself I should start on homework. I should definitely not think about Blake Reynolds. And I *do* close the other tab without watching the interview.

But that brings the Facebook tab to the forefront. The request is still pending.

Confirm. Ignore.

Those are my choices. My heart is still beating at an accelerated rate, and I'd like to pretend I don't know why. The truth is, there's a part of me that's following my mother's wishful thoughts. A rich boyfriend would make things a lot easier for me. If I were the kind of person who could let someone take care of me, that is.

But if there had ever been any chance of that—and there never was—I bashed that over the head for good today.

Confirm. Ignore.

I should just ignore him. Ignore this. He's nothing but a distraction, and I don't need more distractions.

But instead of clicking ignore, before I let myself think what I'm doing, I click "send a message" and type out a short sentence.

Does your dad know the meaning of the words "age appropriate?"

He responds a few moments later. He doesn't ask why I want to know. He knows his life; it's obvious why I'm asking.

Of course he does, Blake writes. *He just didn't believe it applied to me.* And then there's a box with a question mark—undoubtedly some emoji that my computer is too old to decipher. It could be a smile. It could be an eye roll. It could be anything, and I'm not going to find out what it is. Because I don't have the money. And—I tell myself—because I don't care.

It's not very convincing. I turn away from the computer instead and go make dinner.

The request is still waiting when I come back.

Confirm. Ignore.

I close the tab.

C̸onfirm. Ignore.

Two days later, I still haven't responded to Blake's friend request. I don't know what it means and I don't have the time or the energy to think about it. Truth is, I'm a little too attracted to him to allow myself any closer. And yes, I understand that Facebook friendship is to real friendship as cigarette lighters are to intercontinental ballistic missiles. But somehow, this seems to represent a line. If I cross it, it will lead to…

Admittedly, whenever I try to map out the progression, it never seems terrible. Step one is Facebook friendship. Step two is unreadable emoji. Step three is probably going to be occasional nods in each other's direction, not the destruction of the world as we know it.

But my feelings aren't logical. Every time I tell myself to accept the request, I cycle back to that memory of Blake looking in my eyes and telling me that I've never been invisible to him.

And yes, my attraction makes a little too much sense. Blake has symmetrical features and meets generally accepted standards for masculine appeal. In addition, he's rich, smart, and powerful. I can tell myself that it's ridiculous as often as I like, but I'm fighting years of social programming. Even a hint of interest on his part is enough to spark my subconscious desire.

That's precisely why—logically—I want nothing to do with him. Television and books have all led me to hope, to believe that magic happens. Experience tells me that fiction is fiction and that hope leads to disappointment. Even assuming that he liked me, we've already proven that we're too different to get along in reality. Nobody will ever take care of me but myself, and I can't let myself believe anything else.

Friendship with Blake is not safe. It's not even Facebook safe.

I slip into a seat in the hall for the class we share a minute before the lecture is scheduled to start. Blake always sits in the third row. Not that I've looked for him before; it's just that he's the kind of guy that I can't help but notice.

I'm taking out my notebook when there's a rustle beside me.

"Hey."

I swallow at the sound of that voice and turn my head. Blake is tall—so tall I have to tilt my head back to look at him. He's standing beside my chair. I have nowhere to run, as I'm locked in place by the little desk arm in the theater seat. And it's just as well, because running away right now would be ridiculous.

"Mind if I sit next to you?"

I do mind, actually. Next comes duck emoji and, according to my mental progression, the zombie holocaust. I wrestle with myself for a few moments before I decide that it's better not to admit that I care.

I shrug. "Go ahead."

He sits.

There aren't many students in the very back row. Blake sits immediately next to me, not leaving an empty seat between us, and that feels weird. It's a violation of the rules of personal space. When there's only one other person on the bus, you don't sit right next to her. Not unless you know her.

And it feels like Blake takes up a lot of room. Even though I can't point to a single physical point of contact, I can sense him next to me. He doesn't touch me. He doesn't look at me. I can't even smell him. He's just…there, being Blake Reynolds, taking up a lecture hall's worth of personal space in one single seat.

When the professor begins, I have every excuse to ignore Blake. I try to do so. But he's not ignoring me, and I can't help but notice him noticing me.

He takes desultory notes on a tablet, but mostly he listens. His head tilts in my direction occasionally.

Nope. I'm not going to care. I ignore him harder, concentrating on the professor at the lectern below.

I'm trying so hard *not* to pay attention to him that I jump when he slips a folded piece of bright yellow paper under my arm.

It's a flyer for some meeting. On the back, he's scrawled a single sentence.

After considerable thought, I have decided to take back my apology from the other day.

My heart begins to beat a little more quickly. I'm not sure what he means by that. By the way he glances at me, he wants me to ask for an explanation.

Still a nope. Not going to let Blake distract me. Especially if he's decided to be a jerk. As soon as class is over, I'm going to click "ignore" on that damned friend request. And I'm not going to be distracted by him ever, *ever* again.

I stare at the professor for five more minutes, not hearing a word of the lecture, until finally I give up.

Are we nine, I scrawl in return, *and passing notes in class?* Apparently we are.

Instead of frowning when I hand this to him, the corner of his mouth lifts in appreciation.

Don't blame me, he writes back. *If I had your number, I would have just texted you.*

He catches my eye as I look up from the paper. He holds my gaze, and a hint of electricity arcs between us.

I swallow and scribble out a response. *I can't tell if that's a hint that you want it or a statement of fact.*

He ducks his head. *Cut me some slack. My media training didn't cover the old-fashioned art of paper-based flirtation.*

That last word hits me first—*flirtation*. I feel a wave of heat. Is that what he's doing?

Maybe. I look over at him, look back at the paper, and feel that stupid, illogical flutter.

Okay, definitely.

And that's when the first part hits me. Media training?

If I needed proof that we are totally different animals, this is it. I'm not sure what *media training* entails. Thousands of dollars, I suspect. At least. And I can't even afford a smartphone.

I remind myself of all of this, and still I find myself responding—not just to his words, but his tone. *Poor Blake*, I write back, a little more slowly. *Was that not age-inappropriate enough for your dad?*

He presses the back of his fist into his mouth as if biting back a laugh. But he writes back immediately.

See? If I weren't me, we would totally be friends.

I glance over at him. This, *this*, is exactly why I haven't accepted that damned friend request. Because he *is* him. He's the same guy who opines about the social safety net when he's never, ever needed it. His father owns a company that has an annual revenue larger than the GDP of most countries. We've barely spoken. We're not friends. I'm just fighting my stupid social programming, and he's…

I tilt my head and glance at him. He's smiling at me. Making my social programming act up. It's hitting me on the head and saying, *See? I told you so.*

I shake my head. *If I weren't* me, I write back, *we would be. I'll accept your apology, but that's all that's happening.*

He frowns when he reads this. *Too bad,* he writes in response. *Apology already withdrawn; it's too late to accept it now. I, on the other hand, have magnanimously decided to accept the offer you made on Monday.*

I consider this.

1. You spelled magnanimously *correctly without autocorrect. That paper-based media training must be good for something.*

2. WTF? What offer?

He looks over at me and raises an eyebrow. When he passes the paper back, I get: *You said that I wouldn't make it two weeks if I had to live your life. I don't want two weeks. I want the rest of the semester.*

I look over at him. He's watching me intently, his eyes narrowing on mine. I look down at the paper. I don't want to be intrigued. I don't want to be interested. I don't want to wonder what he means, what this entails. I don't want to know about him.

My pen moves up the page and slowly, very slowly, circles the WTF I wrote earlier. I draw a few arrows pointing to it and add a smattering of exclamation marks around it, just in case he misses it. In case he's not watching over my shoulder. I pass this over to him.

Come to lunch with me, he writes back. *I'll explain everything.*

4.

*B*lake stops by his car on the way to lunch. "I have to put on my disguise," he explains.

"Your disguise?"

He doesn't answer. Instead, he walks to the car. He doesn't take out a key. He doesn't need to. As he approaches, the silver handles—which used to lie flush against the door—extend toward him. He opens the back door, revealing a surprising jumble of stuff: bright red running shoes, a crumpled towel, a handful of books, and myriad old receipts.

"Apparently," I say dryly, "your media training also failed to include the old-fashioned art of cleaning up after yourself."

He just laughs. "You sound like my dad. He's a neat freak. I drive him crazy." He pulls off his coat and then, as I'm watching, takes off his tie and unbuttons his blue-collared shirt. He removes this all in front of me. I catch a glimpse of a silver watch at his wrist.

Now that he's stripped to nothing but a white undershirt, I can see his upper body. Blake is all lean muscles. That tattoo I glimpsed before is a complicated computer circuit board. The artist who did it has imbued the tat with a sense of a subtle glow, making it seem like those are real circuits embedded just below his skin. Despite myself, my fingers itch to touch it, to make sure that's all real muscle and not actual metal. The art climbs from his wrist all the way to his shoulder; from this angle, it makes him look like he's a cyborg in some science fiction film.

It's freaking brilliant.

He rescues a dark-blue Cal sweatshirt from the pile of crap and pulls it on. The shirt is overlarge; it completely swallows his wrists.

He kicks off his dark dress shoes, pulls out a case, and removes his contacts. Then he puts on the running shoes, dons thick-rimmed glasses, and as a finishing touch, rubs a pump of hair gel between his palms and rumples his hair. Like this, his khaki dress slacks could pass for cargo pants.

He turns to me. "What do you think?"

I think a lot of things.

I'm not sure what game he's playing, but I'm already berating myself for coming along. I can't afford to go to lunch with him. I can't afford the meal. And—I do have my pride I won't let him pay. I definitely can't afford to remember his biceps.

But despite my better judgment, that part of me that is swayed by classical standards of masculine appeal thinks he's pretty freaking hot. I think I looked more than I should have when he took off his shirt, and I think he knows that.

I give him a critical once-over. "Good disguise," I tell him. "But it needs a fake mustache."

He cracks up.

"True story," he says. "The only time I ever wore dress shirts before I started here was for events—

interviews or products launches. Shit like that. Now I wear them all the time. People see the outfit and they think it's me." He shrugs. "This way, I get a little privacy."

It would be so easy to let myself pretend I'm friends with Blake. He's funny, and more down-to-earth than I expected. But it's bad enough being attracted to him because of basic social programming. I can only imagine how much worse this would be if I legitimately liked him as an individual.

"That is awesome," I say. "I can sell that story to some enterprising reporter for at least a hundred bucks."

He gives me a patient smile. "Yes, but you won't."

"Because I'm going to be so blown away by your amazing charisma that I forget how much I need the money?" I wrinkle my nose to signify how likely this is.

"No. Because by the time lunch is over, you and I are going to be on the same page. Business-wise."

"Oh, yes." I frown at him. "That. What is this all about?"

He smiles enigmatically, but doesn't say anything more until we're settled into the half-empty top floor of a Vietnamese restaurant. We place our order and the waiter leaves us in peace.

Blake takes a paper napkin from the holder and unfolds it into a wisp of translucent whiteness, before rolling it up and setting it on the table between us. When he looks up, though, his eyes seem like flint—hard and impossible.

"So," he says. "Are you going to trade me?"

I look over into his clear, blue eyes. I think he may actually be serious. There's not a hint of a smile on his face. He picks up the napkin again and starts methodically ripping it to shreds.

"You're going to have to be a lot more specific," I tell him. "Because that could mean anything."

"You were right the other day," he says smoothly. "I'm clueless. I don't know what it's like to be you, or anyone like you, and I want to fix that. I offer a trade. I work your hours. I pay your rent. I live in your apartment."

"It's so cute that you think I live in an apartment," I interject.

"You get my house, my car, my allowance. You take over my duties at Cyclone, too—to the extent that's possible. We'll have to talk about that. There are details to work out. But that's the gist of it."

He shrugs, like what he has set forth is no big deal, and I'm left to boggle at him. There are so many things wrong with this that I don't even know where to start.

I pick apart the one thing that's simple. "An allowance? Please don't tell me you're getting an allowance from your dad on top of everything else."

"Ha. No." He has amassed an arsenal of napkin shreds in front of him. "I thought about offering you my salary instead, but…that's a dollar a year, so probably that wouldn't work for you. I asked my accountant to figure out how much I usually spend instead." He shoots me a look. "I'll give you that and we'll call it an allowance. It's probably not as much as you think."

I shake my head. "Is that how rich people think? 'I will impress everyone by taking an extremely tiny salary to show how meaningless money is.'"

"It's more like, 'Wow, who wants to pay taxes on ordinary income? Let's shift my compensation to capital gains tax at every possible opportunity.'"

Oh, thank God he said that. I had just been thinking we might have something in common. I wave my hand with more airiness than I feel. "Ah, tax evasion. As one does."

He gives me a self-deprecating shrug. "Legal tax evasion. It's the best kind."

"You asked me to trade," I say. "I'm just trying to understand your perspective. After all, you can't be blowing all your billions on something as gauche as a functioning government."

The tips of his ears turn slightly pink. "Billion." He coughs. "Really. It's just one billion. Not multiple billions."

I choke. I'd been trying for over-the-top hyperbole. What comes out, though, is, "And here I thought you were actually wealthy."

"A billion point four, depending on how you count stock options that haven't completely vested," he mutters. "It's not that much, not compared to my father."

That number is so vast, it takes me a minute to get my mind around it. He's worth ten figures. I'm worth...well, after I pay for this meal? One.

The balance of my checking account is less than a millionth of his *rounding* errors. We're not even in the same solar system. I feel like this conversation is careening off a cliff into a universe where gravity and ordinary income tax do not apply.

"That's good." I feel almost light-headed. "As long as you're only a billion-point-four-aire, this isn't awkward at all. How much does a billion-point-four-aire spend anyway?"

"Probably not as much as you're imagining. Fifteen thousand."

"A *semester?*"

"A month." He shrugs. "I told you. I'm not a huge spender."

My mind goes totally blank, trying to imagine how someone who thinks he's not a huge spender manages to spend fifteen thousand dollars a month. What does he *do* with all of that? Put gold nuggets on his cereal? Fund a small army? *Oh, no,* I imagine him saying. *I'm not a huge spender. We only go through a kilo or two of weapons-grade plutonium every year—scarcely enough to destroy the city of San Francisco. You should see what the other megalomaniacal billionaires can do when they're feeling tetchy!*

"You could buy four thousand pounds of oatmeal every month," I say instead. "Probably more if you buy in bulk."

He gives me a puzzled look. "Why would I do that?"

"I'm just saying. That's a lot of oatmeal."

The waiter brings steaming bowls of pho and plates of greens and sprouts. I take the opportunity to strip basil leaves methodically into my soup. I can't imagine what a billion dollars looks like. It's too big a number. It's like showing someone a teaspoon of sand and asking her to envision the Sahara.

But fifteen thousand? That is within my capacity to understand. Fifteen thousand times three months left in the semester means I could quit my job. For good. I wouldn't have to work at all through graduation. It would mean being able to pay my way if friends invited me out.

I can stop deleting those emails advertising prestigious but unpaid summer internships.

Forty-five thousand dollars means no more bitterness when my mom asks for money. I can just give it to her and feel good about it. I could pay off Dad's medical debt instead of watching it bleed my parents dry, month after month. Hope flutters inside me on breathless anticipation.

I squash it dead.

Because forty-five thousand dollars is just too much money.

"I have a question," I say. "Just a little one."

He desultorily throws a bean sprout in his broth. "Go for it."

"Most people don't need to pay forty-five thousand dollars in order to work at a crappy job. Or to live in a crappy apartment. Most people do it for free."

He stops in the midst of fishing out his sprout and puts down his chopsticks. "Yes," he says, a little more quietly. "I could do that. But I don't want to explain what I'm doing to my dad. That means I need to keep up with my duties at Cyclone. And that means I need someone smart enough to handle them. Someone who can think independently. Someone I can work with. That's you."

I know I'm smart. But Blake? We've exchanged a tiny handful of sentences. Out of all the people in the world, he picks me? I don't believe that.

I consider him. "That fifteen thousand a month is post-tax for you," I say. "I have to pay taxes on it. I want it adjusted up accordingly."

He doesn't blink. "Fair enough."

"And you'll earn stock options on the work I do, right? I should get them."

This has him wrinkling his nose in contemplation. "That's…a little harder to do as a straight transfer, but I can sign over an equivalent number of shares that I already own outright. But that isn't all that much right now, not with me on partial hiatus. It's worth maybe another ten or fifteen grand."

Yep. That just about proves my point. I stand up, take out my wallet, and carefully, painfully, count out nine dollars. I set this next to my bowl.

"This is too much," I say. "You're too eager to agree. There's something else going on here. It's like those emails where some government official offers an obscene amount of money in exchange for transferring funds from their accounts in Burkina Faso to the United States. I don't know what your scam is or how you're running it, but when something sounds too good to be true, it probably is. I'm out."

I set the money down and start toward the stairs.

"Tina." I hear his chair scrape the floor behind me. "Wait. Tina."

He takes hold of my wrist as I'm leaving, turning me to him.

I snatch my hand away. "Don't touch me."

"I'm sorry. I'm sorry." He looks at me; I look at him. For a second, the casual, smiling façade he usually wears is wiped away. There's something wild about him, something that scares me more than the offer he just made. "I'm sorry," he says again, swiping a hand across his face. This time, I feel like he's apologizing for something else entirely.

The stairs are directly behind me; all I have to do to escape is turn my back on him. But somehow, I'm rooted in place.

"What's really going on here?" I ask.

He runs one hand through his hair. "I'm sorry," he says for a fourth time. "It's just… Look. I don't know how to explain this to you. Maybe that sounded like a lot of money to you. But over the course of this conversation, random stock market fluctuations have changed my net worth by a lot more than sixty thousand dollars. We're talking about a heartbeat's amount of money for me. I don't need money. I gave up—easily—several million dollars in compensation when I went to school. That's how much I've already paid to get away."

He almost shivers as he speaks, like he's being blown by a wind I can't feel.

It's strange. For the first time since we sat down to lunch together, I believe him. I don't know *why* he's so desperate to get away—but I believe that he is. And that scares me, seduces me, and pisses me off, all at once.

"I understand where you're coming from," he says. "This is a little unusual. But my father always says that the person who can walk away from a deal is the one who is in control. That's where you are. You're in control. You tell me the terms you need to make this work."

"All right," I say slowly. "But that only answers half my question. Why can't you let me walk away? Why me?"

"I need someone to come up with a script for our newest product launch," he says. "And—I don't know if you've ever watched Cyclone product launches?"

I shake my head. It's not like I could afford their products anyway.

"You'll see, then. They're…personal. The launches. Whoever it is that I ask to help me will have access to our old scripts, complete with the change logs, and those will let you know a lot about me and my father."

I think of that commercial—of Blake running away from his home, of his father sending him a *sorry*. I wonder if his entire life has been turned into publicity for products.

"There aren't that many people I'm willing to let that close," he says, "and most of them work at Cyclone and would tell my father. My options are limited."

But you don't even know me.

He takes a deep breath. "Also, if you're going to write the launch script, you'll need to get Cyclone prototypes. It's not like you can write a launch for a product you've never held. And there's only one way for a non-Cyclone employee to get a prototype. You'll have to meet my dad. Which is bad enough in and of itself. But. Um. He's pretty protective of our new tech, and that's a huge understatement. It's not like he just hands out prototypes at my request." He glances down. "When you meet him, you'll have to pretend to be my girlfriend."

A wash of heat goes through me. For a second, I imagine what that would be like. And even that second's imagination—of Blake touching me, holding me, *kissing* me—is too much.

"Whatever you're imagining," Blake says, "it won't be like that. Just one afternoon. And Dad thinks PDA is gross, so no kissing even. Just holding hands. Nothing else; I promise."

I swallow. "You still haven't answered my question," I say. "Why me? I doubt I'm the only person in the world who could pretend to be your girlfriend."

Blake looks me over. It's the kind of look that makes me think of lottery tickets and unicorns, of things that don't happen in my world. I can feel his gaze like a caress.

"I'm shit at lying to my dad," he says. "I can only pretend so far. It needs to be someone I have reasonable chemistry with."

Reasonable chemistry. That's what this is for him?

"As for the rest…Tina, when do you think we first ran into each other?"

I swallow. "In class? A few weeks ago?"

"Last September. In the library. You helped me find a book." He looks over at me. "Like I said. I've been seeing you for longer than you've been seeing me."

I don't know if I believe him because I *want* to believe him, or because he's so genuinely sincere that I can't help myself. All I know is that if there is a chance in hell that this is legitimate, I can't say no. I can't afford to.

"If I do this," I say slowly, "I'll have to quit my job. I need a written guarantee that I'll get the money you've promised me for the entire semester, even if you can't hack it and quit after the first week."

"Done. Anything else?"

This still feels incomplete. Dangerous. I bite my lip and consider.

"You offered me a trade," I say next. "Not a purchase. You're not hiring me. You just told me that the thing you want is worth millions to you." I still don't understand how that can be true, but I know that if I don't insist on it now, it will never be recognized. "That means that what I put in has value."

He nods.

"So we come into this thing equally. I'm not going to spend three months listening to you bitch about how pitiful my life is. The things I care about, the things I have to worry about—for the rest of this…thing, whatever it is, they're as important as anything you have going on. I'm important, too."

"Agreed," he says. "You're important."

He's standing close to me, his gaze so intent on mine that it almost feels like the next step is for him to lean down and brush his lips against mine. He hasn't touched me since I told him not to, but I'm so physically aware of him right now that my skin prickles. It itches for what could come next.

I don't buy lottery tickets. I can do math, and I know the only thing you're purchasing is the right to scrape false hopes off a card with a nickel. You fool yourself into believing that the universe is on your side, that even though everything else is going down in flames, help will come like magic.

Spending time with Blake is dangerous. It's irresponsible. And I know that the more time I spend with him, the more I'll want to believe in the impossible.

But this time, the irresponsible choice has a hell of a lot of dollar signs attached to it.

I let out a breath. If you're ever forced to buy a lottery ticket, you have to set rules. You can only purchase one. You can't tell yourself that you'll spend anything you win on more. If you lose, you can't say you'll get one more, just one more. It's the *one more* that will do you in every time—never the single ticket itself. So before this starts, I know I need to make sure that I never let myself believe in *one more.*

"One last thing." I swallow. "When this is over, it's over. No strings. No entanglements. We're not friends. We're not Facebook friends. We're not anything."

I watch his eyes as I speak. They don't flicker, not one bit. Not with disappointment, not with hope.

"Subject to reevaluation," he says finally, "if—"

I can't let myself leave that door open. Through it will come hope, fear, and worry. But there is no hope. None. "Subject to nothing." I stare up at him and set my hands on my hips.

"What if—"

"I can't afford ifs." I look at him. "It's that or I walk."

For a while, he watches me. Then he rubs his forehead.

"Fine," he says quietly. "You have your conditions. When this is done, it's done."

5.

BLAKE

*T*he light next to my dad's icon in the video chat app on my watch is green. This means he's not on the phone or in another chat. It doesn't mean he's not busy. He's always busy.

I tap to call him anyway.

And here's the thing about my dad: If he can conceivably answer when I call, he will. Every time, no matter what time it is. Seven months ago, when I was trying to prove I was a badass, I entered a fifty-two-mile long race in Spain. I ended up dropping halfway through with a stress fracture. When I called my dad, he heard the word "fracture" and was on a jet as soon as he could get FAA clearance to take off.

So it's not a surprise when he picks up as soon as I ring. There's a flurry of gray and green pixels on my watch, resolving themselves swiftly into my dad's face. His eyebrows, thick and bushy, draw down.

"Blake," he says.

"Hey."

"Everything okay?"

"Great," I say. It's not a lie for once. Even though the rest of this conversation will be nothing but a string of falsehoods, that at least is not a lie. It's weird, but he's not just my father. He's also one of my best friends. I don't like lying to him, and I hate feeling like I have no other option.

We look at each other, our last conversation still separating us. I don't think that grim line will leave his forehead until I tell him I'm leaving school and coming back for good.

I'm going to make it all better. I just have to get outside my head, get a rest from Cyclone, and put myself back together again. *I'm going to fix everything,* I promise him silently.

I almost believe it this time.

"Do you have time for lunch this weekend?" I ask.

He tilts his head to the side. "Late. Two thirty at Sakshi's work for you?"

"Sure."

He looks away, tapping, no doubt putting this into his calendar.

"Is it okay if I bring my girlfriend?"

He blinks. His eyebrows rise and he turns his head back to me. "Really?"

He's not surprised that I'm seeing someone. I've told him about women before. I just haven't been cruel enough to introduce any of them to Dad since I took Sheila to the prom in high school.

"Really." I cross the fingers of my other hand behind my back.

"Sure," he says after a pause that's far too long to be natural.

"Her name's Tina."

I hear him tapping a keyboard on his end.

"Tina Chen," I tell him.

"Fine. Bring her." He doesn't say he's looking forward to meeting her.

"Dad, don't be a dick to Tina."

He looks up and gives me a little smile. "Give me credit, Blake. I'm not always a dick."

This is not a promise, and we both know it. There's a reason I've never introduced anyone to him since Sheila, and it wasn't because he was too *nice*.

I shake my head. "Fine," I tell him. "Be that way. But don't say I didn't warn you. You're actually going to like her."

Dad snorts in disbelief. "Really." It's not a question.

That is the one thing I am sure about. "Really."

TINA

*M*y shift in the library after my lunch with Blake is something of a disaster. I'm shaky—so shaky that I don't hear my boss talking to me, so shaky that I run a cart of books into a pillar. It's so bad that my boss finally asks me what's wrong.

I can't tell her. After a moment of fumbling, the best I can come up with is this: "I got an offer for an internship."

"That's great!" She smiles at me.

It isn't. "If I do it," I tell her, "I have to start immediately. And that means…"

We both know what it means. She looks at me with a much less friendly expression on her face.

I've been working in the library since I was a freshman. It's familiar. It's *safe*. My boss likes me, and if I leave her in the lurch mid-semester it will mean not only that I have no job, but that I have no *references*.

"I see," she says with a sigh of surrender. "That's less great for me. Good for you." She doesn't quite sound like she means it.

When I get the books back in place, I text Maria. *Will you still be on campus when I'm done or back home? I need to talk.*

Her response comes moments later. *I'll meet you here.*

She comes and finds me at five.

Maria and I don't look anything alike. I'm short, and I only ever wear sneakers. She's a hair over six feet tall and she wears heels all the time, except when she goes to the gym. She has glistening hair, cinnamon with frosted highlights and a wave. She always looks put together. She never gets carded.

My *mom* still gets carded, and she's in her forties.

"Hey," she says as she approaches my desk at work. "Is everything okay?"

"Everything is weird," I tell her. "Really, really weird."

"Let's blow this joint."

My boss gives me the okay to go, and I grab my bag. There's a bit of wind blowing inland when we step out into the last remaining sun. I pull my coat around me.

"So," I finally say. "How would you feel about moving?"

She looks over at me and her face falls. "No," she says in a flat voice. "No, Tina. I don't know what happened. I don't know how bad things are back home. But we can't go much further down, you know?"

My hands are shaking. She takes hold of my fingers and rubs warmth into them, and we start walking aimlessly.

This is the first year that Maria and I have roomed together. Her sophomore roommates were a disaster: the kind of disaster that involved yelling matches, a multitude of undone dishes left in unsanitary places, and an illicit mealworm farm. She agreed to move in with me, because—in her words—a shitty apartment was better than a shitty roommate. Maria has enough screwed-up drama with her family. She doesn't need it anywhere else in her life.

She's never said anything about moving out—yet—but it was my budget that determined where we lived, not hers. I've always suspected that deep down, she regrets living with me. Now I'm sure of it.

"I know how you feel about taking help," she says, "but you are *not* going home and you are *not* getting evicted mid-semester. We can make this happen."

Before I can explain, she turns to me. "Here," she says. "I got you a present."

She rummages around in her shoulder bag and takes something out. White flashes at me; thin plastic glints in the dying sunlight. I take it from her.

It's my favorite sweater. Wrapped up in plastic printed with the name of some local dry cleaner. I turn it over, examining it. The sleeve is pristine, clean and white. Just like new.

It probably cost her five times as much to clean the sweater as it did for me to buy it in the first place.

"I knew it would come out," she says. "You just needed to bring it to the right place."

For some reason, that makes what I have to say seem so much worse. She knew what my sweater meant to me, how much hope I let myself invest in it. And... And the gesture is so sweet, but it's just not the same. It has never been about having a clean sweater. It was about believing that when I wore it, I couldn't get dirty.

I'm better off without that illusion anyway.

But she doesn't need to hear that, not when she went to all that trouble. "Thank you," I tell her, and I give her a hug.

"See?" she says. "Whatever's happening, whatever is going on—it can't be that bad. We can make it work. So tell me, Tina. Why do you think we have to move?"

"I didn't mean that we need to go somewhere worse," I tell her. "I was thinking somewhere better."

She wrinkles her nose. "Better in what way?"

I don't actually know. I have no idea where Blake lives. Even thinking about this, even taking as tiny a step as telling Maria, scares me.

"Somewhere the heat works?" I venture.

She turns to me. And then, very slowly, she smiles. "Oh my God," she says. "This is not a my-world-is-ending kind of thing, is it? This is an I'm-so-happy-I-can't-express-myself kind of thing."

I don't answer.

"You're the only person I know where I can't tell the difference. What happened? Did your dad find a full-time job?"

"Not that."

"Sudden inheritance from an unknown relative?"

"Weirdly," I tell her, "some random stranger mistook me for one of the other many Tina Chens in the world."

"*Really?*"

"No, not really." I let out a breath. "In a way, it's like I got…an internship. An internship that pays really well."

"That's awesome! I swear to God, I will break our lease in one hot minute."

Yep. Definitely not happy with our digs.

"Luckily," I say, "we don't even have to do that. This internship comes with a built-in subletter."

She pauses. "Okay, what kind of internship does *that?*"

"The most fucked-up internship in the history of all internships." I let out a breath and I tell her everything.

In a lot of ways, Maria and I are nothing alike. But we've been friends ever since our freshman floor arranged a girls' night out.

I'd made my excuses because I didn't have the money or the clothes to come along. No fake ID, no cash for the cover charge, nothing for drinks or a cab after. My roommate used the word *broke* as a synonym for *I have to stop shopping or my dad will get mad at me*. My version of broke meant I hadn't been able to buy cough syrup two weeks before. I'd used the lingering sniffle as my excuse to stay behind.

I'd waved everyone off, told them to have fun, and expected to be the only girl around that night. But after the floor had grown quiet, I'd run into Maria in the bathroom.

She was dressed in a gold-sequined shift dress that ended halfway up her long, toned thighs. Her eyes were smoky-dark, a triumph of makeup artistry that belonged in an ad in some magazine redolent of perfume samples. A black alligator clutch sat on the counter.

She looked ready to take the world by storm. Instead, she was standing in front of the mirror, yanking off false eyelashes.

She froze when I came in, her eyes meeting mine briefly in the mirror.

"Are you okay?" I asked.

She looked away. "Fine."

"Are you sure? You're not with everyone else for girls' night out. Are you sick?"

Her lips thinned. "According to Tammy, I can't come because I'm not a girl."

She yanked off the other eyelash. She didn't meet my eyes again, but I could see her shoulder blades tense. The silence lengthened, and finally, I said the first thing that came to mind. Which, thankfully, was: "Fuck that."

Maria paused. Our reflections locked eyes. Slowly, she smiled. "I know, right? What's your deal?"

Maybe it was because I wanted to like her. But for the first time that night, I told someone the truth. By the end of the evening, we'd bonded over the fact that we were the only ones around, over the fact that we were part of the vast sisterhood of women who can't be googled because we have names so common that even the most dogged searcher would have to sift through hundreds, if not thousands, of results before finding us. We'd made a hundred little connections.

She's the only person in the world I can imagine walking with, telling this tale to. She listens. She believes me. She doesn't say that I'm full of shit when I say that Blake says he met me in September, even though I don't remember him.

"What do you think is going on with him?" she asks when I've finished my explanation.

"I don't know. Honestly, though, have you heard anything about Adam Reynolds that makes you think he'd be a *good* father? Maybe this is Blake's way of chewing his leg off to escape."

Maria bites her lip. "I don't know. Have you seen them together?"

The sun is almost gone and I rub my hands together for warmth. And that's when I finally admit the truth.

"Can we not talk about that? I don't want to care."

"About his reasons?"

"About him." I swallow. "There's an attraction." I don't look at her. "I can't ignore that. But no matter what he says, we can't really trade lives. He can work my hours, pay my rent, and live in our garage. But when my parents need money, he won't be the one who bleeds. He won't understand, not ever, and he thinks he can just pay money and make it happen. So I can't let myself care about him."

"Oh, honey," Maria says.

"That's what I have to remember. No matter how it looks, there's a wall between us. He won't remember; he doesn't even know it's there. Please. I don't want to speculate about what makes him tick. I don't want to find out."

6.

TINA

I refuse to be nervous as I enter the restaurant with Blake on Saturday.

It doesn't help that he primed me on the way down with some less-than-reassuring conversation.

"How good an actor are you?" he asked as we crossed the bridge.

"Not very?" I frown. "I mostly just shut up or say what I'm thinking. I'm not really good at anything else."

"All righty then," he says. "Then I won't tell you what's coming. Just go with the flow, okay?"

My dose of nerves is certainly not helped by the fact that Maria made her own contributions last night. "Oh, watch this," she told me, and I vanished down the rabbit hole of Adam Reynolds YouTube videos. He may be worth sixty-six billion dollars, according to *Forbes*, but apparently he is not what one would call a kind, courteous man. Quite the opposite.

And it certainly doesn't help that Blake takes my hand as he opens the restaurant door. He does it so casually that I can pretend that it doesn't mean anything, that he's just a friend who has locked palms with me. I can pretend that I'm not aware of his warmth, that when his fingers intertwine with mine, I don't feel a rush of heat.

But I do.

The restaurant he's taken me to seems surprisingly low-key for a man as powerful as Adam Reynolds. It's a hole-in-the-wall Indian place, with little plastic jars of tamarind sauce and mint chutney sitting on white faux-tablecloths. I was expecting something more upscale, but I guess even billionaires like good food. It smells amazing in here.

Blake guides me to the back table, where a man sits facing away from us. I recognize his father's profile, that messy salt-and-pepper hair, from last night's festival of YouTube fear. Adam Reynolds is holding one hand to his ear and murmuring into a Bluetooth headset.

"Then move the manufacturing to Shenzhen," he growls. "If Liansu can't guarantee the secrecy we need at the production speed we require, it's off. No more leaks." There's a pause. "I want solutions, not excuses. Whine to your shrink. I don't want to hear it."

He slides his hand angrily across his phone and then looks up. His eyes land on Blake and then— astonishingly he smiles, a brilliant grin that seems completely unforced. It shifts his face from *angry bastard* to something far more charming.

"Hi, Dad," Blake says easily.

Adam Reynolds takes out his earpiece and stands up, offering his hand to his son. Blake drops my hand; his dad gives him a fist bump that converts into a complicated handshake, a high five, and then a hug.

"Hey, asshole," Adam Reynolds says. "It's good to see you."

My eyebrows rise on *asshole*.

"Hey, jerkwad," Blake says smoothly. "This is Tina. Tina, this is my dad."

"Hello." Now that Blake's let go of me, I don't know what to do with my hands. I settle for bringing one up in a little wave. "It's nice to meet you."

Adam Reynolds, one of the most powerful men in the world, sizes me up in one glance. For some reason, he makes me think of a jungle panther. He gives me a single, dismissive look—as if he's determined in one second that I'm not only prey, but I'm not even important enough to consider eating. I feel suddenly aware that my jeans are fraying from age, that the soft sweater I'm wearing is just a little too short at the wrists.

"Huh," he says. Then he looks back at his son, discarding me.

"I need to use the facilities," Blake says. "You guys get acquainted."

"Blake…" My voice almost squeaks as he leaves. He doesn't hear me. Or at least, he doesn't turn around.

It's a good thing that Blake and I are only pretend-dating, because if this were remotely real, he would be so completely dead for abandoning me.

I slide onto the bench opposite Adam Reynolds and manage a polite smile. He glances longingly at his phone, no doubt imagining all the work he could do if he weren't stuck with his son's girlfriend. I can almost feel the disdain wafting off him. Then he sighs, pushes his phone away, and looks over at me.

The internet does not agree about many things, but one thing all sources acknowledge is this: Adam Reynolds is a first-class, grade-A asshole. There's a covert video that someone uploaded three years ago. The quality is grainy, but the words are clear. There are five minutes of Adam Reynolds berating his CFO in a restaurant far fancier than this one. Adam used every insult in the book, and some that have never been printed in any book. After a little public uproar, Cyclone issued a formal semi-apology: They were very sorry that the scene had caused distress to others, but the video had been taken "out of context." Like there's ever a context in which it's okay to call someone a pig-fucking cocksucker.

His dismissal shouldn't hurt. I'm only pretend-dating his son. I don't even want to like Blake, and I will never meet this man again. Still, to be judged unworthy in so short a space of time really pisses me off. I at least deserve a shot.

Blake vanishes into the bathroom.

As I'm marshaling the nerve to start a polite conversation, Mr. Reynolds looks off into the distance, hoists his water glass, and lets out a sigh. "Fifty thousand dollars."

My first thought is that Blake must have told him about our deal after all. I sit in place, waiting for him to give some explanation, to make some sort of demand. But he takes a long swallow of water and doesn't say anything more.

I fold my hands in my lap.

"Well?" he asks after a few interminable seconds. "I can't wait forever."

He's not even going to pretend to be polite, and I suspect that everything he says from here on out will only get worse. Fine. If he wants to play that way, I can come along for the ride.

"No," I say with my most charming smile. "*You* probably can't. Five minutes of your time is worth a fortune. But my time is worth basically nothing. So if we want to keep staring at each other, I'll win. Eventually."

He leans against the booth, letting his arm trail along the back. He has Blake's wiry build, but there's an edginess to him that Blake lacks, as if he has a low-voltage current running through him at all times. He drums his fingers against the table as if to dispel a constant case of jitters. His glare intensifies.

"Cut the innocent act. If you're smart enough to hold Blake's interest, you're smart enough to know what I'm talking about. My son is obviously emotionally invested in you, and I'd rather he not be hurt any more than necessary. If all you want is money, I'll give you fifty thousand dollars to walk away right now."

I pause, considering this. On the one hand, fifty thousand dollars to walk away from a nonexistent relationship is a lot of money. On the other hand, technically, at this point, Blake has offered me more. Besides, I doubt Mr. Reynolds would ever actually pay me. He'd just spill everything to Blake, assuming that revealing my money-grubbing status would end this relationship.

In other words, true to form, he's being a dick. *Surprise, surprise.*

"I see you're thinking about it," he says. "Chances are this thing, whatever it is, won't last. We've established that you don't really care about Blake. The only thing left to do is haggle over the price."

"That's not what I'm thinking." I pick up my own water glass and take a sip. "I think we need to make the stakes even. I'll accept sixty-six billion dollars. I take cash, check, and nonliquid assets."

His knowing smirk fades. "Now you're just being ridiculous."

I set my glass down. "No. I'm simply establishing that you don't love your son, either."

He almost growls. "What the fuck kind of logic is that? Sixty-six billion dollars is materially different than fifty thousand."

The bathroom door opens behind us, and Blake starts toward us. Mr. Reynolds looks away from me in annoyance. Blake approaches the table and slides in next to me. He sits so close I can feel the warm pressure of his thigh against mine.

He looks from me to his father and back. "What's going on?"

The fact that I'm not actually dating Blake, and don't care about the state of his relationship with his terrible father, makes this extremely easy.

"Your father and I," I tell him sweetly, "are arguing over how much he'll pay me to dump you. Stay out of this; we're not finished yet."

"Oh." A curiously amused look crosses Blake's face.

"He offered fifty thousand bucks," I say. "I countered with sixty-six billion."

Blake's smile widens.

"She's not negotiating in good faith," Mr. Reynolds growls. "What the fuck kind of girlfriend did you bring?"

"Don't mind me." Blake crosses his arms and leans back. "Pretend I'm not here. Carry on."

Son of a bitch. Blake probably *knew* something like this would happen. He set me up. He did it on purpose.

"I don't have to negotiate in good faith," I tell his father. "You brought money into this in the first place. That was a dick move. Why should I play fair?"

"You've admitted that you'd sell him out," he snaps. "That at some point, money is more important than he is."

"*You've* admitted the same thing. If I'm a faithless whore because I'll take a check to break up with Blake, you're the asshole who values your company and lifestyle more than your son."

"That's not just my company. That's my life. It's his life. It's—"

"Oh, and you think it's just money for me?" I glare at him. "You think that you'd give me fifty thousand dollars and I'd spend it all on shoes and diamond-studded cat collars? Fifty thousand dollars would pay for the rest of my college tuition. It would buy my dad a lawyer so that the next time his knee acted up, he could finally get disability instead of scrambling to find some job he can manage. It would make it so I didn't have to work for the next year and could concentrate on my schoolwork. That's a really ugly double standard, Mr. Reynolds. When money exists to make *your* life more pleasant, it's not just money. But when it's *my* family and *my* dreams at stake, it's just pieces of green paper."

Blake smiles softly.

His father reaches across the table and flicks Blake's forehead. "Stop grinning."

"No way." Blake is smiling harder. "She's kicking your ass. This is the best day ever."

His father grunts.

"The day I first went to lunch with Blake, I had less than twenty dollars in my possession. Total," I tell his father. "I would completely sell Blake out for fifty thousand dollars. Some days I'd do it for ten. Dollars. Not thousands. None of this makes me a gold digger. It just means that I'm poor. When times get desperate, I'll pawn anything of value to survive. I might cry when I do it, but I'm going to be realistic about it. So take your stupid does-she-love-Blake test and shove it."

Mr. Reynolds looks at me. He looks at Blake. And then, very slowly, he holds out his hands, palms up. "Well. Fuck me twice on Sundays," he says. From the expression on his face, I take it that this is intended to be a good thing.

"First time I talked to her," Blake says with a nod that could only be described as prideful. "Before I asked her out. I knew I had to introduce her to you."

"Shit," Mr. Reynolds says. He holds up a fist, and Blake fist bumps him in return.

Now they're *both* being dicks.

"Smile," Blake's dad says to me. "You pass the test."

"Oh, thank goodness." I put on a brilliant smile. "Do you really mean it? Do you mean that you, the one, the only, the incomparable Adam Reynolds, has deigned to recognize me as a human being? My life is changed forever."

Mr. Reynolds's expression goes completely blank. "Why is she being sarcastic, Blake?"

"Why is he talking to you like I'm not here, Blake?"

Mr. Reynolds turns to me. "Fine. Why are you being sarcastic?"

"You don't get to test me," I tell him. "You're not my teacher. You don't get to act like you're the only one with a choice, and I have to be grateful if you accept me. I don't have any illusions about me and Blake. Fitting our lives together is like trying to finish a thousand-piece puzzle with Lego bricks. But you know what? Bullshit like this is what's going to break us up. You had a test, too. You could have treated me like a human being. You failed."

Blake reaches out and twines his fingers with mine.

For a moment, I feel all the emotion that I've just expressed. I feel that we're hopeless, that there is an unbridgeable gulf between us. I look at our hands, laced together on my lap. I look over at his wide blue eyes, and I ask myself how our relationship can possibly survive.

Then I remember that we don't actually have a relationship. He held my hand for the first time this afternoon. *This* doesn't exist. It's just a reminder of why I need to be careful.

"Dad?" Blake says in a low voice. "What is the *one* thing I asked you to do at this lunch?"

There's a long pause. "You told me not to be a dick to Tina."

"I told you not to be a dick to Tina." His hand squeezes mine. "For one, she'll hand you your ass, and she won't be nice about it. But there's something more important than that."

He's talking to his father, but his fingers play with mine, whispering that there is something there. That he cares. I know it's an illusion, but still…

"I don't like it when people hurt Tina," he says. "I keep trying to convince her that she's wrong, that nothing will break us up." His hand exerts a subtle pressure on mine. "But you know what? I let you hurt her. If this was a test for any of us, it was a test for me, and I fucked it up. It won't happen again."

There is a long moment. I don't even understand why he's standing up for me in front of his father. In another handful of months, the truth will come out. I'm not his girlfriend. I'm not someone he cares about. I *am* only after his money.

But for a second, the lie seems real. Blake's eyes blaze. His hand holds mine. I can actually believe that he cares about me, that he's willing to stand up to his father for me. It's like Romeo and Juliet.

The version of Romeo and Juliet where the Capulets have nothing and the Montagues can crush them all without thinking, that is. The version where Juliet dies alone in the tomb from a drug overdose and Romeo says, "Oh, shit, I knew I was forgetting something, but I was trying to figure out how to get out of paying ordinary income tax."

His father's face becomes solemn. He looks between us. "This is serious." He reaches for his water glass and frowns at it. "Fuck. Is it too early to drink?" As if in answer to his own question, he grimaces and takes a swallow of water.

"It's very serious," Blake assures him. "This is how serious it is: I want her on the Fernanda prototype list."

His father chokes and spatters water all over the table. For a second, he coughs heavily.

Then—"Hands," Mr. Reynolds snarls, which makes no sense to me.

Blake brings our intertwined hands up, and sets them on the table.

"No dice," his father says. "You know the rule. Your girl gets on the prototype list when your ring is on her finger. I don't see a ring."

What the fuck? That, *that* was not something Blake mentioned to me.

"We're not in the same place yet," Blake says calmly. "But if it's up to me, you will. One day."

I know he's lying, but even so, he could convince me if I was stupid enough to let him do it. I yank my hand from his. He reaches over and takes it back calmly, as if he's making a statement.

"You know what?" I tell him. "Same holds true for you as for your dad. You don't get to announce that you're…you're…" I choke on the words. *Marrying me.* The concept is completely ridiculous. We don't even know each other. And even though he's acting, even though I know this isn't real, I don't even know why he's doing this. "You don't get to announce that without talking to me about it."

He looks me square in the eyes. "It's a statement of intent."

Fuck. I can feel a tension winding in me, curling tighter and tighter.

"I got her out to meet you under false pretenses," Blake says. "She doesn't know how serious I am. In fact, I bet she doesn't believe me now. She's coming up with a reason why I'd say this to you."

True. I have to keep reminding myself of that reason. He wants to do the swap; he thinks I should have the prototypes. Ergo, he must pretend to be serious about me.

"One of these days, though," Blake tells his father, "she's going to realize that I think the sun rises on her smile."

I inhale slowly. It's almost cruel of him to be such a good actor. If we were in any kind of relationship—if we'd so much as kissed before—I would have been completely snowed.

Mr. Reynolds simply nods, as if Blake makes announcements like this about girls all the time. "Fine," he says. "I'll start over. I can be polite. Hi, Tina. It's nice to meet you. What are you studying?"

"Chemistry and computer science."

He doesn't look impressed by this, which is unusual. He snorts instead. "And what are you planning on doing with that mouthful of letters?"

This, apparently, is his version of polite. He managed about two seconds.

"I want to be a doctor."

He blows out his breath. "Golly gee fucking willikers. At least that's one of the few things that you actually need a university education to do. It's a shit-stupid thing, of course. Being a doctor is like being a fast-food worker, except with less sleep and more money. But at least it's a thing." He looks at me dubiously. "You want to help people and save lives?"

"On my med school applications? Yes. That's all I care about. In reality? I just want to make enough money that my parents don't have to worry ever again."

He considers this. "The computer science degree seems superfluous to that goal."

"Yeah, well. If it were just chemistry, my application wouldn't stand out. I'm not going to be able to go volunteer with Doctors Without Borders in Ghana for a semester like half the other med school applicants. I wanted to do something different."

"Different means playing the fucking flute or raising show llamas," he says. "Computer science is just masochism. You're lying. Nobody would get a CS degree without wanting to use it. What's your deal?"

It's kind of scary that he's right. "Nothing that's going to happen." I don't drop his gaze. "Maybe I just want a fallback plan in case med school doesn't pan out."

He considers me. "Nah. You told *me* to go to hell. I don't think you're the kind of person who worries about Plan B. You're the kind of person who would make Plan A happen. What do you really want to do?"

I swallow. I can see how he came to be one of the most powerful men in the country. He's an asshole—but he's looking right through me, his gaze like a knife.

And so I tell him something I've never told anyone else before. "Maybe there's part of me that plays with the idea of going into medical research."

"What kind of medical research?"

I inhale. "Making tiny medical robots."

"Pipe dream." He waves a hand dismissively. "That will never happen."

"It has to happen," I reply. "Every year, more bacterial strains become resistant to more antibiotics, and we find fewer and fewer effective ones. Think what will happen when we can't perform open heart surgery or biopsies without risking serious infection."

He taps his fingers together. "So you're going to make tiny medical robots to do heart surgeries without risking infection. Huh."

I let out a breath. "No." The timeline is all wrong. I need to be making money by the time Mabel starts college, even if it's just the bare-bones salary of a medical resident. "I'm going to be a doctor. Someone *else* is going to make tiny medical robots."

But he's already looking off into the distance. "Actually, it's kind of an interesting project. What kind of venture funding will you need to get off the ground?"

"None, since I'm not going to do it." I take a deep breath. "That sounds horrifying. Running a company is the last thing I want to do. That just means worrying about new and larger amounts of money all the time. I'm not going to go through fifteen years of higher education just so I can worry about money more."

Adam Reynolds leans in. "In this world, you're either playing the game or you're a pawn on the board."

I shrug. "Okay. Then I'm a pawn. Pick me up and move me any time you want to wave your checkbook in my direction. But there's one thing I can do that you can't."

"What is that?"

"I imagine that running a massive corporation is like getting on a merry-go-round. It may not be going fast when you first start, but the harder you push, the faster it spins. At some point, you can't just get off the way you got on. Stay on long enough, and you get the impression the world goes in circles. I can get off, Mr. Reynolds. You can't. I want to keep it that way."

His face doesn't change, not one iota. But for a second, his fingers tighten on his water glass. "Touché," he says quietly. "Two-fucking-shay." He blows out his breath.

For a moment, none of us say anything. Then Mr. Reynolds shakes his head. "You want Fernanda," he says. "Do you even know what Fernanda is?"

"I didn't even know there *was* a project named Fernanda."

"Hey," Blake says at his father's raised eyebrow. "You know I don't talk about this shit. Not even with her."

"Fernanda," Adam Reynolds says, "is your ticket onto the merry-go-round. Welcome aboard."

7.

BLAKE

I follow my dad to the Cyclone campus. The ride is short—not even fifteen minutes. Just long enough for Tina and me to stew in uncomfortable silence. She's no doubt replaying every word I said in the restaurant.

I'm doing the same thing.

Funny. I knew I was into her. My body responds to hers, and sitting so close to her in the restaurant, sitting a mere eighteen inches from her now, has given my body some really interesting ideas. Now, in the car, she's twirling a strand of hair around one finger, playing with it.

I should tell her that I lied to my father, that everything's cool. Instead, I feel like I just tipped my hand. To myself. Not that I'm hoping for anything as specific as what I told him. It's just... I *want*. Watching her go toe-to-toe with my dad was a thing of beauty. I haven't seen anyone take him down so effectively since Peter passed away. I want someone as directed as her to want me back.

But that's straight-up fantasyland, right up there with the stupid idea my body has right now. Which, no, that wouldn't work, because there is no room for me between her knees in this car, not unless we folded the seats down. But then, male hormones have never really cared about the limits of physics.

"You know," she says, "it's a good thing we aren't actually dating, because if we were, I would break up with you right now."

That's right. There's fantasy, and then there's reality. The reality is that we're not dating. The reality is that in three months, we won't even be friends.

"Understandable," I say. "I threw you to the wolves. In my defense, I know the wolf pretty well and my money was on you. My dad can come off as a little bit of a dick at first, but you just need to stand up to him and he backs down."

"Oh." There's a dubious quality to her voice. "He's just a little bit of a dick. Sure."

"Really. He's not that bad. Unless he wants to be."

She gives me a sidelong look of deep suspicion. But I'm coming up to the Cyclone security gate, and that brings up a whole host of other memories. The sun is out today; it shines brilliantly in my eyes as the guard hands me a visitor's badge for Tina. The gate arm rises and I drive in.

She lets out a sigh. "A little warning would have been nice. You're a frighteningly good liar. Media training again?"

"Media training," I agree, even though that's a lie. "You'd be astonished how well I can lie. The only question is if you can keep up with me for another hour."

I turn into the garage and find my spot.

She sighs. "So what's the story? Did we argue in the car on the ride over? We would totally have argued, if this were real. Your dad has probably realized I'm not the 'shut up and simper' type by now."

"Sure." I glance over at her. "We argued. But I brought you around. I always bring you around. I'm good at that."

The half-height garage walls don't quite shield a wide green sun-drenched lawn on the other side.

She still seems a little out of sorts. "So we're going to play it like we're still good?"

"We kind of have to. If you fake-breakup with me, there will be no prototypes, and then this whole thing will be wasted effort. Do you think you can manage a little flirting?"

"I suppose." She shrugs. "But I've never had any media training. I can't guarantee the results."

"That's okay. I can lie well enough for both of us."

She casts me another look—this one a little darker—as if I've said something wrong.

But she doesn't understand the truth. I open the car door and step out into the cool air of the garage. She doesn't understand how much I'm going to have to lie.

My dad built this campus when I was twelve, and in some ways, it feels more like home than the house where I grew up. The sun is out, spilling over a lush green lawn where a handful of engineers are out playing a game of Ultimate. The buildings gleam, pristine white stone contrasting with smoke-dark windows. I could join the Frisbee game. I could walk into any building, any room, and find something I've worked on. This place is a part of me. It almost feels like my bones and veins extend into the surroundings. I'm rooted here.

It feels like a trap built of sunshine and nostalgia. Every muscle in my body itches. I want to move, to run. But no matter how fast I go, I'll always take it with me.

Tina, I could say, *I have a problem.* That would be the truth.

Instead, my smile is a falsehood, denying those roots that run deep here. "If you think I was bad in the restaurant, you haven't really seen me lie at all."

It's weird having her here, almost like I'm afraid that my memories will infect her. I straighten beside my car, and I make myself find that smile I need to wear. I try to erase every unfortunate memory I have. Watching Dad and Peter tromp over this land when it was nothing but weeds and aging strip malls. Pointing, sketching out the place it would be when their joint imagination gave rise to concrete and glass.

I push away the time when Dad told me that Asiv in interfaces was fucking with my design. I rushed over to that building, there, on the other side of the lawn, heart in my mouth, to find half the Cyclone campus lying in wait with Peter and a massive cake for my eighteenth birthday. I delete my memories of Peter altogether, one by one, until these are just buildings and I'm just here on an errand.

No matter how I try, he's present, lodged under my skin like unshed tears.

I inhale and smile harder. "Come on," I say. "Let's go in and I'll show you Fernanda."

She takes my hand in hers. Here's one thing that's not a lie: Touching her makes me feel better. My smile comes a little more easily.

"Hey, Blake!" someone calls from the field as we pass.

I wave, smiling. "Looks like you're getting creamed again, Steve."

"What? We're only down by two."

"For now," I call back with fake cheer.

Any further reply is lost in indistinct trash talk. We walk to the main building side by side, and I can pretend that this is nothing more than a nice, sunny afternoon.

On my way to my dad's office, I stop at every occupied cubicle. I smile. I greet. It's been weeks since I last stopped by.

"When are you coming back?" everyone asks. Half of them add, with conspicuous glances down the hall in my dad's direction, "It's not the same without you."

I don't answer. Instead, I introduce Tina.

The door to my dad's office is open by the time I get there.

"Hey." He glances up at me and slides a stack of papers as thick as his thumb across the table. "Legal sent these over. Walk her through this, will you?"

"Sure thing." I give him a cocky smile.

Maybe too cocky. Dad raises an eyebrow. "Don't get frisky, kids," he growls.

I'm not sure what he imagines we will get up to signing NDAs. But Tina smiles at him. "That's what disinfectant spray is for," she says.

Dad chokes. My imagination jumps instantly to all the many ways that might work out. Dad stares at her for a moment in disbelief, and then realizes that she's joking. He bursts into laughter. "Get out of here. And no, Blake, don't you *dare*. There are interior windows. I can see into your office. There are some things I don't ever want to know. *Ever.*"

We go three doors down to my office. Someone must come in here to clean regularly. There's no dust on the glassed picture on my desk. The plants are lush and green, newly watered. There are fresh pens in the holder. It's almost like I've never left.

I don't close the door. I can see my father across the way, and even though his attention has wandered elsewhere, I still feel like I'm on display.

Look, Dad. I'm okay. I like this girl. Everything's normal.

"Only my father," I say to Tina, "would imagine that anyone could find paperwork arousing."

"What?" Her smile is a touch too wide, a little too faked. "Don't tell me your media training didn't cover this, either."

I set the stack of papers on the flat surface of my desk and gesture Tina to sit in the leather-bound executive chair.

"What am I supposed to say, then? Come on, baby. It's a nondisclosure agreement. You'll like it. I promise."

She gives me an unimpressed look. "God," she says. "And I thought you were supposed to be a *good* liar. That's not how you do it." She bites her lip and then she leans toward me. Her eyelashes sweep down, and when she talks, she lowers her voice toward sultry.

"I don't know, Blake." She bites her lip and reaches gingerly for the papers, stroking her thumb along the edge. "It's so…big. I'm not sure it will fit."

I almost choke. She looks up with a touch of a smile.

Fuck. I started this.

"We'll go nice and slow." I pull a chair beside her and sit down, and very slowly take a pen from the holder. "Tell me if it hurts and I can stop anytime. I promise."

"Be gentle."

I know we're just joking. I know this doesn't mean anything. Still, my body doesn't know this is a show when

I lean toward her. I don't feel like I'm lying when I inhale the scent of her hair. It goes straight to my groin, a stab of lust. "Trust me," I murmur.

She's sitting in my chair. She's smaller than me and all that dark leather surrounds her, blending in with her hair. But when she looks up, tilting her head toward me, she doesn't seem tiny. She pulls the first paper-clipped section of pages to her, glances at the first paragraph, and wrinkles her nose.

"Ouch," she says in a much less sensual tone of voice. "It hurts already."

"It basically says that if you tell anyone anything about Cyclone business, we get one of your kidneys," I translate helpfully.

"How sweet." She hasn't looked up from the document. "Do your lawyers know you summarize their forms like that?"

"Disclose two things," I say, "and we get two kidneys."

"Mmm. Playing rough. What happens if I disclose three? You shut down my dialysis machine?"

"You get a commemorative Cyclone pen," I say mock-seriously. "Come on. We're not monsters."

She cracks a smile at that. She's not one of those girls who always smiles, and that means that when she *does* smile, it means something. Her whole face lights up and my breath catches at the sight. I lean in, as if I could breathe in her amusement. But then she drops her head and goes back to reading. When she finishes, she signs with a flourish.

"What's next?" she says. "Bring it on."

I hand over the next few pages.

WARNING, the cover sheet states in big, red block letters. YOUR CONDUCT IS GOVERNED BY THE SECURITIES EXCHANGE ACT AND REGULATIONS OF THE SECURITIES EXCHANGE COMMISSION. FAILURE TO COMPLY MAY RESULT IN CRIMINAL SANCTIONS AND SENTENCES OF UP TO TWENTY YEARS IN PRISON.

She holds it up and looks at me. "Don't lie to me, baby. I bet you make all the girls you bring in here sign this."

I have never before found SEC regulations this sexy. I lean close to her.

"No way," I murmur. "This is just for you."

"Really?" She manages that look of hurt skepticism so well. I reach out, almost touching her cheek—until I remember that this isn't real.

"No," I whisper back. "Not really. Everyone does sign it; it's company policy."

"Oh, too bad." She's still reading the page. "I was hoping you had a selective disclosure just for me."

Selective, I realize, is a sexy word when drawn out the way she does it, her tongue touching her lips on the *l* sound. So is *disclosure*.

"I can disclose," I hear myself saying. "Selectively."

"Maybe you can give it to me in a material and nonpublic place."

I lean toward her. "You know me. I put the *inside* in insider trading."

She's still holding the pen poised above the paper. I touch my finger to the cap and then slowly slide it down the barrel until my hand meets hers. A shock of electricity hits me, followed by a jolt of lust.

She's looking into my eyes. If I hooked my hand under the arm of her chair, I could slide her toward me.

She drops the pen and pulls away.

"No, but seriously." Her voice returns to normal. "I have no idea what any of this stuff actually means."

I let out a breath. Damn. It's a good thing this is only going to last an afternoon. More than that, and I'd forget we were pretending.

I clear my throat and straighten. "Basically it comes down to this: Don't trade Cyclone stock without talking to your lawyer. Don't tell anyone shit about Cyclone's business without talking to your lawyer."

"I don't have a lawyer."

"Well. Get one before you do either of those things."

She makes a face.

It takes us half an hour to get through the rest of the forms. I leave her to get them checked off with legal, and then to get Dad's sign-off on the prototype. Dad had someone stack everything else I need in a bag. Everything but Fernanda. That he hands to me.

"Have fun showing off your baby," he says.

And you know what? I actually feel nervous at this moment. Nervous, excited—like I'm about to tell her something important to me. Like I want her to approve.

Five minutes later, I heft the bag onto the table in front of her. "Here. Have these."

"What are they?"

"Enh." I wave my hand dismissively. "A phone. A tablet. Shit like that. Nothing big."

"Nothing big?" Her eyes widen.

"I mean, they're just the next generation versions. No big deal. Early prototypes just mean there are more bugs to work through." I'm cradling Fernanda in my hands. "And you can play with them all you want. Later."

"But *I* have never owned a Cyclone tablet—"

"It's called a Squall."

"Whatever. Or any tablet all. Maybe I want to..."

"No," I say. "You don't."

She trails off as I open my hand. Her eyes widen, and she leans in. "Oooh," she says in a much quieter voice. "The wild rumors are true."

Fernanda fits in the palm of my hand, the round watch face set in gleaming steel.

"Tina," I say, "meet Fernanda. Fernanda, this is Tina."

She waits a beat. "Is it supposed to answer?"

"Of course not," I say. "She's a watch, not a portable artificial intelligence. We're not that advanced. Hold out your arm."

She does.

I roll up the sleeve of her sweater.

Her wrist is tiny; the bones in her hand seem so delicate. And suddenly in this moment, I'm hit by another wave of want. I want this to be real. I want to be that smiling man who has no plans but to give her a present— the world's coolest present—and have her agree that it's awesome.

I knew I was into her. I knew I was attracted to her. But right now, looking into her face, I want her. All of her. Her smiles, rare though they are. Her approval. I can feel her pulse in her wrist. Given everything going on between us right now, wanting what I do is incredibly fucked-up.

Her eyes are on my hands. "Everyone thinks you aren't making one because you didn't announce when your competitors put out their first-generation smartwatches."

I slide the band around her wrist. This band is preproduction steel, not one of the stylish bands that will be available for the coming launch. Her skin is soft, and her breath catches as I latch the watch in place.

"We never announce products before they're ready," I say. "And she wasn't ready."

"Why is the project called Fernanda?"

"Happenstance. All Cyclone products are given production codenames. We draw them in order from the NOAA tropical cyclone lists the year they enter active development."

"Do you anthropomorphize them all, then?"

"Of course," I say. "I practically grew up at Cyclone. New products are as close as I ever came to having a dog."

She laughs.

"But Fernanda is my favorite," I whisper to her. "She's special. I was completely in charge of her, from her inception until a year ago."

"What makes her so cool?"

"Everything. Here, turn her on."

She touches the face of her watch and it sparks to life. It asks her to register her fingerprints and she does.

"The real challenge for a smartwatch is the input," I tell her. "Of course, there's a touch-sensitive screen. But my team and I also came up with this—the entire circumference of the watch is a biometric ring, one that only responds to the user's fingers so it won't be triggered by a cuff or a stray brush. You can use it to dial volume or scroll music, just by running your finger back and forth on the rim of the watch."

I demonstrate. Doing that requires me to guide her fingers. To hold her wrists in mine and stand close. To inhale the sweet scent of her hair. And she smiles again as she gets the hang of it.

"Okay," she says, looking up at me. "That's officially cool."

My smile is quick in response.

"It gets cooler," I say. "Here's the contact tap." I roll up my sleeve, revealing my watch. I set my thumb to mine, gesture to her to do likewise, and then tap my watch against hers.

Her contact information appears on my watch face.

"That's also cool."

"Isn't it?" I can't stop smiling. "The only uncool thing about Fernanda is that I have to keep her under wraps for now. And now you know the real reason I've been wearing suits on campus. If you wear a sweatshirt when it's ninety-five out, everyone thinks you're crazy. Nobody blinks about a button-down shirt, though, and I have to keep her covered somehow. But I haven't shown you the best part yet."

Her eyebrows rise. "There's a better part?"

"Yeah. So imagine that we want a true smartwatch—something that is a stand-alone device, and not just a satellite tethered to a smart phone. Without a proper input mechanism, it's just a niche product. You can't text on this small a screen. You can't do much more than scroll and click, which makes it worth…very little, actually. We realized that if we wanted a real smartwatch, we needed to make Fernanda do one thing, and do it well."

Tina leans forward.

"Video."

She looks taken aback. "You're kidding."

"I know. We did a ton of usability studies. Video on a computer is bad enough. Video on a watch is incredibly awkward. So I want to see what you think of our solution."

She looks up at me. "You know, Blake, I think you're more turned on by this than you were by dirty talk about SEC regulations. I am beginning to suspect that you are a dork. What will your many fans say?"

"My many fans, as you call them, probably figured out I was a dork when I voluntarily spent all my time immersed in interface design from the age of fourteen," I say dryly. "I'm about to get even more dorkily excited. Beware."

I walk outside the room and cross the hall. She can still see me, but we're farther away.

Dad sees me tapping my watch and gives his head a wry shake. I press call.

A few seconds later, her face takes up my watch screen.

"Nobody wants a video app on a goddamned watch." I hold my wrist in front of my face. "You have to use your wrist to center the camera, and who wants to talk to someone with your arm held awkwardly like this?"

She nods. "Exactly."

"That's why," I say, "Fernanda has six independent cameras in her face, her band, and even the clasp. And they're not stationary. They swivel, and they sync with the internal gyroscopes to track the user's movements. On-the-fly interpolation and facial-recognition software means that I can move my arm like this—or like this—" I demonstrate "—and the video on your screen…"

"Tracks your face," she finishes breathlessly. "That is freaking awesome."

"Ha," I say smugly. "I could show you more if we had more people around. We can manage up to five-way video calling—more than that looks terrible on the screen. You're going to love Fernanda. And if there's anything you *don't* love about her, tell us and we'll see if we can fix it."

She nods.

"The video angle can sometimes still be awkward, depending on how you're waving your hand, but you get used to the reasonable range of motion really quickly."

Our eyes meet. We're twenty feet away. Still, my chest feels tight. I'm not pretending. If my father is watching the way I'm looking at her now, he will never guess the truth.

Hell. I'm standing in the hall in front of the office that used to belong to Peter, and I'm still smiling.

I'm not sure *I* can tell that we're not together, and I'm in on the secret.

TINA

---

*T*he bridge over the Bay crosses dull, gray water. The sun is low in the sky; Blake's car is freakishly silent, gliding along with only the whisper of tires against road. I can't get used to how quiet his car is.

I'm trying to sort myself back into place. No more pretending. No more touching. No more acting. We got what we wanted, right?

I can't make out anything about him. I had assumed he didn't get along with his father; instead, they seemed to be genuinely friendly. He said he wanted to get away from Cyclone, but when he put Fernanda on my wrist, his eyes sparkled with real pride.

He told his dad he was planning on marrying me, but we spoke for the first time five days ago. I don't know who he is or what he's doing. I do know that today—that flirtation, those tiny touches we exchanged—came a little too easily to me.

"You said you wanted to get away from Cyclone," I finally say. "It doesn't look like it to me."

"I didn't quite say that." He speaks so calmly, as if this afternoon—an afternoon during which his father offered me a massive sum of money and we flirted over legal paperwork—makes sense. "I said I needed to get away."

"What would you do if you left for good?"

"Run, apparently." There's a dry quality to his tone. "When I don't feel like running anymore, I'll go back."

I shake my head. "I swear to God. I am never going to understand people with money."

His fingers trace the steering wheel up and down. "That's not money," he finally says. "Money has nothing to do with it. Haven't you ever loved something you hated? Or hated something you loved?"

My mind goes instantly to my mother. I love her; I do. She's a fierce ball of need—always looking after everyone but herself and her own.

"Maybe." I don't want to look at him. I don't want to feel *more* of a connection.

"Then you understand how I feel about Cyclone. I love interface design. If I do it well, a million people will never know how happy I've made them, not until they try a competitor's product. I have to pay attention to things people don't even know they want. I have a real gift for that."

He's stating this as a fact—and having his brainchild on my wrist now, I can't disagree.

"It's the other bullshit I can't handle."

I think I had a taste of *that other bullshit* this afternoon.

The rest of the bridge goes by in silence. He turns north, and the last of the sun spills over the windshield.

"I don't understand what I'm doing here," I finally say. "Are you really *that* good a liar, that you can tell your dad that…that *thing* you did without even blinking?" I still can't make myself repeat what he said aloud.

"I said what I had to in order to get you Fernanda." His jaw sets. "You *can't* plan the launch without her. It was necessary. I'm sorry I didn't tell you it was coming, but I didn't trust your acting skills, and I thought your honest reaction would be more convincing."

"It's fine. It's just that your acting skills are ridiculous."

"You've seen the commercials?" It's not quite a question, the way he asks it.

I don't want to admit that I've watched the entire YouTube playlist at this point. "Some of them," I lie.

"Then you know I've been acting since I was two. I *should* be good at it."

"So that's all fake? That buddy-buddy thing you have going on with your dad? He really is as big an asshole as he appears?"

"He's actually not an asshole," Blake says calmly. "And that buddy-buddy thing, as you call it, is real. My dad is my best friend. The trick to acting is to believe what you're saying."

I flinch away from him. "Bullshit. You said—about me—you *said*—"

"I used to see you in the library last semester," he says. "You came in at eleven in the morning on Wednesdays before your shift. You would sit at a table on the third floor and work biochemistry problems. What can I say? I have a thing for women who carry heavy books and know how to use them."

I blink. I did use to do that. But I don't have any memory of seeing him. None at all. I only have a vague sense of being aware that there were other people around when I worked.

He smiles. "It's not hard to act when you have good source material to draw on."

I feel that tug of attraction pulling me in.

"But I don't know that I'm today's stand-out performer," he continues. "You seemed pretty convincing yourself for a while."

It's not hard to act when you have good source material to draw on.

Maybe it was a little too easy to let myself get into the spirit of things. That's the thing about playing the lottery. It lies. When you think it's going well, it's just getting ready to slap you down. I glance in his direction. His gaze flicks toward me, and then slides away.

No. This is just an accident. A one-off thing. A little errant chemistry, nothing big.

I shrug. "Well. I can't let you take all the Oscars."

"Yeah?" He can't hold my gaze long; he's driving. Still, it feels like an eternity before he looks away. An eternity where my pulse picks up, where my hands grow hot.

"About that source material." His voice is low and it seems to lodge deep inside me, an insistent thrum of sensation running up and down my spine. "I think we should talk about the source material."

My gaze drops to my knees. I can't meet his eyes. I *can't*. He'll know.

I wait a little too long to answer. "There is no source material, Blake. We were faking." And once I'm sure I have myself under control, I look over at his profile. I make myself *not* want to reach out, to brush his hand that lies on the armrest next to mine. "We did what we had to do," I tell him. "Now we're done."

8.

*I*t takes us another six days to get everything in place: a contract to protect Tina (she insisted on it), a subleasing agreement (my lawyer insisted on that when she found out what we were doing), money transfers, bank accounts, a meeting with her current landlord.

We don't talk anything but business when we see each other, but the chemistry is still there, crackling between us. Our eyes meet a little too long; she refuses to look my way during the class we share. I know it's stupid to want her. I have shit to solve.

But hormones—damn, when they really engage, they don't let up. And mine have gone from interested to riveted.

It feels like the best of all possible worlds the day we switch places. The air is crisp and fresh when I hand Tina and her roommate, Maria, the keys to my place. On the one hand, I feel like I'm handing off all my worries.

Just the act of changing things up has made me feel hopeful. And now that we're really about to execute this trade, I don't think she can push me away with mundane details. I feel almost happy when I pack my things into my car and follow Tina's directions.

I kind of expected Tina to live in a dump, but the address she directs me to is in a tidy residential neighborhood, filled with tiny 1950s homes. I wouldn't live here willingly, but it could definitely be worse.

Tina directs me to stop by an empty lot, high with growing weeds, with a view onto the backend of a supermarket.

"Which one is it?" I ask.

She nods across the street. A peach-and-white trimmed house, with a clipped lawn, meets my eyes. Honestly, it doesn't seem so bad. I stayed in worse when I went backpacking through Eastern Europe.

"Cute."

Tina and Maria exchange amused glances, like I've said something hilarious.

"You're in the garage," Tina says.

My eyes travel behind the house to a detached structure in the backyard.

"Cool," I say again. "A converted garage."

That amused glance again. It makes me feel like I should watch my back. I sigh. "Let's go check it out."

Five minutes later, I'm convinced that my first impression based on Tina's reaction—"dump"—was more accurate. Calling the garage *converted* is like calling the empty lot across the street a rose garden. The garage door still works; the gaps that let in cold air have been duct-taped over, but there's still a persistent draft. The concrete floor has been covered with carpet remnants. At least those look clean, if a little haphazard.

The furniture is sparse—two beds with metal frames, a desk that wobbles when I toss my duffle on top, a dresser, and a bare clothing rod against one wall. The bathroom is a boxy installation of not-quite-straight wallboard.

There's something like a kitchen. Which is to say, there is a single sink, which I would have called *stainless steel* in another life, except it is most definitely stained, and a foot-long stretch of Formica countertop. A microwave and a hotplate round out the cooking gear. Cinderblocks and particleboard shelves make up the kitchen cabinets.

Okay, this is pretty crappy. It's also cold.

"Where's the thermostat?" I ask.

The women smile at each other again. "No heat," Maria says.

"What?" I stare at them. "Is that even legal?"

"No."

I blink. "What the hell? Why haven't you reported them? Do you just not—"

"Oh, I know," Maria says, waving a hand in my direction. "My grandmother is a lawyer for the City Attorney of San Francisco. I know how this works way better than you ever will. We'd report them. Then the city would decide that this does not pass inspection on about fifty different counts. And *then* we would have to find somewhere else to live, and nowhere that actually meets housing code will charge us only eight hundred bucks a month. The whole thing is totally illegal. But on the bright side, it makes breaking leases infinitely easier."

Fine. If they've put up with this, I can, too.

"Besides," Maria says, "it's the Bay Area, not Wisconsin. It's not like it ever really gets that cold."

"Outside," Tina says. "Sometimes, in the morning, it's kind of bad. Try and get out early; it's better that way."

"Yeah," Maria says. "But you don't need our advice. You're a big, macho man. You eat cold for breakfast."

I'm pretty sure she's making fun of me, so I refuse to rise to the bait. "Nope," I say. "What kind of idiot doesn't want advice?"

They exchange glances yet again.

Maria sighs. "Should we tell him about the space heater?"

"Honestly, he's better off not knowing."

"Come on," I say. "No holding out on me."

"Fine. But remember, you asked for it." Tina rummages around between one of the beds and the dresser and comes up with a black, plastic thing that looks like a fan. "But, um, maybe... There is something we should mention."

Maria elbows her, but Tina shakes her head.

While they're talking, I plug the heater into the power strip, turn the dial all the way up, and flip the power switch. The fan starts to whir; the elements inside turn orange. No heat, yet, but—

"You see, it's not that easy. If you—"

There's a loud click and the power shuts off. We're plunged into darkness.

"As I was saying," Tina says dryly into the darkness, "the wiring in the garage is ancient. So if you use the heater on anything but the lowest setting, you're kind of screwed."

"Yeah," Maria says. "Don't use it if you're running anything that draws power. Like a hair dryer."

"Or the microwave," Tina adds in.

"Or if the refrigerator turns on."

"Pretty much don't use it with anything on at all. And sometimes even then, it's too much."

Their voices are flat, but I can tell they're trying not to laugh at me.

Fine. Whatever. It's just a little inconvenience, right? I can take it.

I sigh. "So where's the fuse box again?"

A minute later, I've reset the fuse and we have light—crappy, overhead fluorescent light—again.

"Here's my computer." Tina gestures to a laptop on the desk. One hinge has been mended with the same blue duct tape that's been used to block the drafts.

She hands it over, and I take a look at it.

She must have gotten this used. As a freshman. It's an old-model laptop, boxy and heavy. I open it; the lid swings at an odd angle, so I have to stop and coax the poor thing into the semblance of an open position.

I turn it on.

It takes forever to boot.

Okay, the cold is one thing. The fuse box is another. Those things amount to roughing it. But when it comes to computer gadgetry, I am downright spoiled. I haven't gotten a logon screen after a full minute and a half. And it's been so long since I've used a non-Cyclone computer that I have no idea what to do with this beast.

"Also," Tina says, "about the bank account. As per our agreement, I've deposited a check with my entire net worth as of yesterday into your account." She hands me a deposit slip. "Congratulations. You have $15.22. There's also about nine pounds of rice left." She looks at me. "If you need recipes…"

"That's what Google is for," I tell her flatly.

This…sucks. I stand up and look around. No heat. No money. Objectively, it sucks. So why do I feel a sense of excitement, like I'm a kid at Christmas? This is exactly what I've wanted.

The laptop finally boots, and then, because that was apparently too much work for it, the fan turns on with a loud whir. Across the room, the fridge starts up with a hum. That thing must be decades old. I can practically smell the Freon leaking from it. And then—I should have known this was coming—the fuse pops with a loud snap and the lights go off again.

"Goddammit," I swear.

"I'm going to wait in the car," Maria says.

I don't blame her. I hear, rather than watch, Tina flip the fuse. Light returns.

"Probably not a good idea to run the fridge and the laptop at the same time," she tells me.

This is…fucked-up. On the other hand, even if I suspected shenanigans, I can't figure out how they could actually have arranged to make this happen.

"Because I'm nice," Tina says, "I'll tell you what it took us two months to figure out. Just don't use the fridge. Not for anything. You're a block from a grocery store. If you don't store perishables, you don't need the fridge." She takes a deep breath. "Also, save anything on the laptop before you use the microwave."

"Don't tell me." I eye the blue-hinged beast before me. "The battery doesn't work."

"Not really." She sighs. "It's like having all the detriments of a laptop with none of the portability."

I shake my head at her. "Why do I get the impression that you're enjoying this?"

Her smile is just a little shaky. "You seem to be under the impression that my life is some back-to-nature serenity camp. It's going to be amusing watching you realize that it's not simple. It's not a tourism home stay. You're going to crash and burn."

I let out a breath. She stands in place, her hands in fists.

And that's what it is. I *want*. For me, it's simple. For her...she hasn't had time for bullshit. I know she's attracted to me, at least a little bit. I also know she doesn't want to be.

I want her.

But you know what I want most? I don't want her to break down and quash her reluctance. I don't want her to surrender to me. I want her to want to want me, not to want me grudgingly against her will.

"You're right," I say. "I'm full of shit. I have no idea what I'm doing. This is going to be hard, and maybe I'm going to fail and fail and fail again."

Her eyes widen.

"But you know what? There's one thing I'm *not* going to do. I promised you when we started that you were important. So I'm not going to call your life a back-to-nature serenity camp or a tourism home stay. I may be clueless. I may be taken aback. It may be that I have no idea what to do with $15.22 because I have never even gone grocery shopping before. But this is your life. It matters."

She inhales sharply. "Fine." And then she turns to leave.

"One other thing."

She turns back to me slowly. She doesn't say anything.

"It's okay to like me," I tell her. "Eventually, just about everyone does."

TINA

*M*y hands are shaking by the time I go to his car.

It's okay to like me.

Too late; that seed was planted weeks ago. I'm a shitty enough liar that Blake's already seen everything I wanted to keep hidden. This isn't going to work.

A voice in the back of my mind stirs—my mother's voice, dimly remembered. *Xingjuan, you have to be careful.*

Ha. As if my mother was *ever* careful about anything. I yank the door handle—it still freaks me out that the handle comes out of the car for me as I approach—and, once I'm in, slam the door.

Maria is waiting for me in the passenger seat. She doesn't say anything. She doesn't point out that my hands are shaking. She knows I'll say something about it as soon as I'm ready.

This isn't some beat-up, decades-old Camry like my parents drive. Blake gave me a brief explanation on the way over. This is a completely electric vehicle, something so new and space-age shiny I wasn't even aware that it existed. It has a thousand features I didn't even know cars could have. This car, with its dark leather and sleek electronic displays, probably cost him more than four years of my college tuition.

It takes me two minutes to figure out how to adjust the seat and mirrors from their previous position—chosen to accommodate Blake's long legs. There are no levers, nothing manual. Everything slides whisper-smooth into place at the touch of a button.

That leads me to the second problem: I don't know how to turn the car on, and I'm not about to go back and ask him. There's no key, no ignition—it's an electric car; what would there be to ignite? There's not even a big button labeled "power."

I finally get out my phone in desperation and send a text.

Blake, how do you turn your car on?

The answer takes a few moments. *Are you sitting in the car? Do you have the electronic fob?*

Yes. And yes.

Then it's on. So long as the display behind the steering wheel is on, the car is on. It's just that the engine doesn't make any noise.

Maria casts me an inquisitive look as I start down the street. That's the way everything is for him. It happens automatically, without his even having to press a button. Hell, I'm feeling too much for him already, and all the encouragement he's ever given me is to...offer me paperwork.

"Everything okay?"

My hands are still shaking. "Fine," I say. "Awesome. Better than okay. Couldn't be any better."

"That bad, huh?"

"He knows I like him," I say, gripping the wheel as hard as I can.

"Oh," Maria says. For a moment, neither of us says anything. I pull onto the main road, but the traffic just heightens my unease.

I can't get over this car. It's everything I would have expected Blake to have. It's so silent that the only noise I hear is tires against asphalt. I scarcely have to press the—it can't be called the gas, can it, if the car is electric?—accelerator and it responds, as silent and as forceful as a ninja. The speedometer jumps.

Forty-five thousand dollars seemed like an impossible amount two weeks ago. Now, I'm realizing that it's nothing. One sideswipe from a passing car could do that much in damage.

Suddenly this whole thing freaks me out. I'm afraid to look up the value of his house, but I suspect the number is firmly in the millions. This car. The electronics he handed me. A prototype, which, if stolen, could cost his dad's company millions in falling stock prices. Billions even.

Adam Reynolds was right. Fernanda *was* my ticket onto the merry-go-round. I'm in a position where I can do real damage.

I feel like I've been outfitted with boxing gloves and ordered to juggle three Fabergé eggs across the Golden Gate Bridge. I'm going to break something. Everything.

A passing car honks.

"Tina," Maria says. "You're going fifteen in a thirty-five zone."

"I know," I choke out. "But—if I crash…"

She looks over at me. "A car like this is not made to go fifteen. Are you sure you're okay? Did he do something to you? Because I don't care who he is or what he's paying you, if—"

"No, it's nothing like that." I pull into a parking lot and stop. "It's just..."

My heart is beating hard. I don't know what to say.

"This isn't safe," I finally manage. "Not him. Not this car. Not the prototypes or the NDA or anything along those lines. It's not safe, and I'm afraid I'm going to fuck it all up."

She doesn't say anything. Instead, she reaches over and takes my hand. My fingers feel cold in hers. But she holds on anyway, sending me warmth.

"Honey," Maria says finally, "there's only one thing to do when you find yourself behind the wheel of a car like this."

"What?"

I know we're not just talking about the car. My voice shakes, but Maria doesn't say anything about that. She just squeezes my hand.

"You floor it. Because you know what? Blake has good insurance. We're both on it, remember? We signed the forms."

I laugh uneasily. But I don't move.

"Do you want me to drive?"

"Yes." I let out a breath. "Could you?"

We trade places. She adjusts the seat smoothly, and when she pulls out of the parking lot, she floors it.

7:09 PM
Hey Blake. I'm sorry I snapped at you earlier.
I don't think you're going to crash and burn.

> *7:11 PM*
> *no?*

7:11 PM
No.
I'm actually more worried that I will.
I have no experience with any of this.
How do you do anything?
The stakes are so high.
It's paralyzing.
What if I completely fuck everything up?

> *7:12 PM*
> *You won't.*

7:13 PM
You can't know that.

> *7:14 PM*
> *Yes I can*
> *b/c if you get stuck, you'll ask me*
> *and we'll figure it out like reasonable people.*

7:15 PM
Still no good.
That way I'll spend more time around you.
I'm trying not to like you.

7:15 PM
Honest question
Does it suck to know failure is inevitable?

7:16 PM
God. You're so conceited.

7:17 PM
I guess that's not surprising.
Or entirely unwarranted.
I'm going through the Fernanda materials.
You're right. You do work hard. And she's brilliant.

7:17 PM
Why yes
I was something of a genius with her
Thank you for noticing

7:18 PM
Argh. That just made it worse, didn't it?
I knew I shouldn't have said anything.
Stupid sense of fairness.

7:19 PM
Wrong.
We just traded
so now it's your turn to be a genius.

7:20 PM
Here's a hint
I knew you could be one the day
you told me I was full of shit.
Not many people notice that

7:21 PM
Stop it. I'm trying not to like you
Remember?

7:22 PM
Not working out so well for you, is it?

7:22 PM
Jerk.

7:23 PM
That's English for yes?

7:23 PM
Pretty much.

7:25 PM
Thought so.

9.

TINA

*T*he work I'm doing for Blake doesn't take me less time than my job in the library; it takes more. Blake's time estimates were based on his own abilities. But he drew from a storehouse of knowledge that I will never have. If I want to do a creditable job—and I won't give him the satisfaction of doing anything less—I need to get my feet under me, and do it quickly.

I watch Cyclone launches while I'm brushing my teeth, walking to school, even taking a five-minute break from homework.

The launches are lavish affairs, scripted to the hilt, practiced as much as possible. Alternates are chosen in case of accidents. Blake had his assistant pull out the last twenty launch scripts for me, and it turns out the scripts are a source of far more than just a description of what is supposed to happen. They're all stored in a proprietary Cyclone format, one that contains prior versions, comments, stage directions—just about everything you can imagine.

Online, there are Cyclone launch groupies, and they've made my work easy by breaking the launch into parts. There's the financials stage, where Adam talks through what Cyclone has accomplished in the last year or so. There's the refresh stage, where he—or a product engineer—introduces new versions of old products. And then—sometimes, not always—there's the new product stage.

At some point in this affair, there's what the groupies call "the Adam and Blake show." Internal Cyclone documents have adopted the same name. At some point, father and son both end up on the stage, interacting with whatever new toy they have, showing off its features. The more elaborate the gadget, the crazier the script.

During the launch of the Tempest smartphone, Adam was interrupted in the middle of his initial presentation. His phone rang loudly in the middle of a discussion of cloud storage. He looked around and slowly pulled out the as-yet-unannounced phone.

"Yes?" he said shortly, looking around the audience. "This isn't a good time. I'm kind of busy."

The audience laughed good-naturedly in response.

Adam's features changed as he listened. "Where's Blake? He has *detention?* This isn't a good time for that. He was supposed to be here an hour ago."

Louder laughter erupted.

"Well," Adam said, "yes, I can understand where you're coming from, Mr. Whitesend. I'm not trying to argue that my son should have special treatment. Wait. Yes. I *am* trying to argue that. Can't he do this next week? He'll stay twice as long."

A deeper frown.

"Oh, you already offered that as an option and he said no?" Adam rubbed his forehead. "I see." He hung up and slid the phone back into his pocket.

"Hey, Adam," someone yelled from the audience. "What was that?"

"You'll see," he responded.

But the best part was when he got to the Tempest reveal. As Adam started showing off the smartphone features, Blake started texting.

It was one of the funniest things in a launch ever—Blake sending pictures of his teacher, taken with perfect comic timing. He sent a video near the end of the teacher in charge of detention looking up, frowning, and starting down the aisle.

Finally, a single text appeared on Adam's screen.

This is Mr. Whitesend. What is this thing?

Everyone online initially assumed it *had* to be staged. But the other students at Blake's high school insisted that it had really happened—that he had gotten detention, that he'd argued. Two students had even been in detention with him as it all happened, and they swore it really went down that way. The internet is still arguing, eight years later, over whether it was real or not.

I have access to the scripts, and I get to find out the truth. Yes, it was scripted. All of it. Both the principal and Mr. Whitesend were in on it, with signed releases and everything. Mr. Whitesend apparently got paid a mountain of money in exchange for looking like the bad guy.

There are years of launches, hours of Adam and Blake shows. And once I start diving into the edited scripts, I only get more confused.

"We're selling family," Adam wrote in an earlier comment as he crossed off someone else's suggestion. "We make people want to be part of the Cyclone family. This doesn't do that."

But when someone else suggested a truly heartwarming scenario three years ago, Blake nixed it.

"Cute," he says, "but can you see Dad and me doing that? It has to be a true construction."

Those are the words I see over and over, in every launch script over the last ten years: True construction. The Adam and Blake show may be scripted, but it's also something real. It has to be something that could happen, something, perhaps, that even *did* happen. It's fake, but it's based on good source material. The launches chronicle their growing relationship from father and son to friends. They're sweet. They're endearing. They're authentic. And—I remind myself—they're putting all of this on display for the purpose of selling more products, which is completely fucked-up.

There's only one launch I can find in the entire twenty-year period that isn't entirely scripted. It happened a year ago, when one of the key presenters passed away two nights before. Without any explanation that I can find, Blake and Adam axed the entire goofy script they'd put together.

There was nothing written to fill the space, just a short interchange between Blake and his dad. Blake deleted the idea that had come before. He added two lines in its place.

Announce moment of silence.

Stage direction: Don't cry.

His father, in turn, deleted the second line with a comment of his own. *Irrelevant. I don't cry.*

Blake added the line back in. *That's for me, asshole.*

It takes me three days to understand what Blake has asked me to do. He was right; I can manage most of the launch. There's an entire team that is involved with the script. They've been doing this as long as Blake has, and they've already sent in suggestions that I will only have to modify.

Blake doesn't need me to write a product launch, not really. He needs a true construction. He wants me to write the next chapter in his relationship with his father, the man he loves so much that it hurts.

If he can't do it, how can I?

I don't like being taken by surprise. I especially don't like discovering that I've landed in the middle of a morass.

After a few moments' contemplation, I head south to meet Blake after work.

I had the responsibility of finding Blake a suitable job—and trust me, that wasn't as easy as it might seem. His name is recognizable enough that he'd draw notice almost everywhere. His resumé is glowing—so glowing that for an entry-level job, it's practically radioactive. Imagine applying for a job in fast food with *Vice President of Interfaces, Cyclone Systems* as your last position.

Luckily, I know someone who owes my mom a favor.

It's ten at night when I open the doors to the restaurant where he's working.

"Closed!" sings out Mr. Zhen from the back as I slip inside. The walls are paneled in faux-rosewood scenes that are supposed to give off an indeterminately Chinese vibe. At least they would if I didn't know that the chop in the corner translates to something like "Turgid Mutton."

"We're closed," Mr. Zhen insists, bustling through the kitchen door. But he stops when he sees me and a smile spreads over his face. He takes off his hairnet, revealing approximately three strands of hair.

"Tina!" He switches to Mandarin. "I'm glad you came. Nice boy you sent to me. I'm really happy."

"He's going to work out?" I have to admit I'm a little surprised. Not that I thought Blake would be unwilling to work; he's too competitive not to try his best. I just kind of assumed he would suck at manual labor.

Mr. Zhen waves a hand. "A little slow, but he'll speed up. We just have to break in his soft hands." He laughs. "But I see why you sent him my way. It's nice to have someone back there who speaks Mandarin for a change. My last dishwasher was Mexican and we could never talk about anything."

Blake speaks Mandarin? This is news to me. I smile tightly. "I thought you'd like that," I say instead.

The kitchen door opens and Blake comes out. He's wearing jeans and a white T-shirt. It must be humid back there, because the shirt clings. Just a little. He's not built like a wrestler—he's far too thin for that—but there's nothing on him but muscle. His tattoo is visible, rippling on the skin of his arm. I swallow.

"Thank you, Mr. Zhen," he says in passable Mandarin. Son of a bitch. "I…" He pauses, thinking. "Now bowls clean. Tomorrow I more fast."

His vocabulary sucks. His grammar is terrible. Blake Reynolds speaks white-boy Mandarin. But he actually speaks it.

At that point, Blake looks over and sees me. He blinks, and then, very slowly, he smiles.

He holds up his hands. "No bowls!" he says.

"I thought I'd give you a ride home," I say in English.

He switches naturally. "Ah. You're a goddess." He smiles at me. "I thought you were just here to taunt me."

"Why taunt you as you walk past when I can taunt you the entire way home?"

"Good point." But he grins at me and puts on his coat. Which is good. I didn't want to look at Blake's biceps anyway.

He follows me to the car parked just outside, starts to go to the driver's side, and shakes his head ruefully, circling back to the passenger side.

He slides in and leans back against the seat.

"Tired?" My tone is not entirely innocent.

In response, he groans. "Last year, I ran a fifty-mile race in the mountains of Spain. It was cold and raining. Someone died of hypothermia. I fractured my tibia." He shuts his eyes. "That was worse than this. Marginally."

It's a good thing he's shut his eyes. This way, he won't notice that I'm only going twenty-five miles an hour.

"So," I say. "You speak Mandarin."

"My dad took me to China for three months when we were working out some manufacturing details. I forced myself to do some crash-course learning, enough to be polite. It smoothes things over when my father—um." He stretches and rolls his neck. "Speaking of impressing people. You've been holding out on me."

I pull out—slowly—onto the main thoroughfare. "*I've* been holding out on *you?* You have to be kidding me."

"Yeah. You give that whole our-lives-are-equal-value speech, and then you don't tell me that your mother is some kind of badass."

"*My* mom?"

"Mr. Zhen told me all about her. What is she, some kind of super-lawyer?"

I don't want to get into this with him. I hate trying to explain Falun Gong to Westerners. Sometimes, I wish my parents had been caught up in something comprehensible, like tax reform or Tiananmen Square. I've tried telling people before, and it rarely goes well.

Falun Gong is a system of exercises, something like Tai Chi or Qi Gong. It's illegal to practice it in China, so illegal that the Chinese government runs reeducation camps to forcibly brainwash practitioners.

No, it's not a freedom-of-speech issue. No, it's not a religion, not like you understand it. It's never going to make sense to you, which is why immigration judges don't always get it. It's like free exercise of…exercise, and my mother spends all her spare time beating her head against that wall.

"Come on," Blake says. "You can tell me."

I sigh. "She's not a super-lawyer. She's not even a lawyer. She quit school when she was sixteen."

He frowns at this, sitting up straight. "Huh. From what Mr. Zhen told me, I imagined her sitting in a tiny law office in Southern California, striking fear into the hearts of xenophobes everywhere."

"No. She only strikes fear into the hearts of xenophobes buying cakes at Walmart."

At his puzzled look, I explain.

"She decorates cakes for a living. The immigration stuff is just…a hobby. She helped a friend figure out what she needed to do, made some connections. Then she helped her friend's friend. The next thing you know, she's the person who knows random things. She helped Mr.

Zhen find a decent lawyer. Then she helped him pay the bills."

Blake considers this, rubbing his chin.

"I'm pretty sure that makes her even cooler. By day, she frosts cakes."

"By early morning, really," I interrupt. "She goes in at five. She's off by two."

"By late afternoon," Blake continues, without missing a beat, "she's...uh..."

"Please don't give my mom a superhero name."

"Fine. What is it like having her for a parent? That must be totally cool."

I think. "Terrifying."

A silence descends on the car for a moment.

"And you know what?" I say. "I didn't pick you up because I wanted to talk to you about my mother. I need to talk to you about your dad. *You've been holding out on me.*"

He doesn't bother pretending that he doesn't know what I'm talking about. He puts one hand over his face. "Yep," he mutters. "The Adam and Blake show. Here we come."

"Were you going to mention that to me?"

"I hinted at it. Earlier. I told you the launch touched on personal topics. I was going to talk about it as soon as I knew what to say."

I wrinkle my nose. "Are you trying to make me fail? You could get away with that short thing six months ago because you only had a few product refreshes. But Fernanda is huge. She's new. You're going to need something epic, and I don't know you and your dad well enough to do this."

He sighs. "I know."

"I started making a list of possibilities, but they all sound stupid and fake. If I'm going to get this right, I need more information. What is it like, working with your father?"

He turns away from me and looks out the window. For a few long minutes, he doesn't say anything. And then finally… "Terrifying," he says shortly.

"Dammit, Blake."

"Why are you going twenty miles an hour?" he asks. "You could be going twice as fast. Faster."

"Because," I say through gritted teeth, "I *like* driving at this speed."

"Seriously? Are you a terrible driver or something?"

"I swear to God, if you give me that Asians are terrible drivers spiel at this moment, I am going to kick you out of this car so fast—"

"Tina, I'm asking if you're a terrible driver because you're driving twenty miles an hour and everyone is passing you. This is a thing that terrible drivers do."

I don't know if I can explain why I find this car so frightening. It's powerful. It's fast. I could go sixty and not even notice, and that's the problem. I feel like I should notice having power like this. Like if I ever *stop* noticing, I'll lose something important.

I grit my teeth and inch the speed up to twenty-four. "Satisfied?"

"Not really."

I don't look at him. "It's terrifying. It's all terrifying, okay? And you're one to talk—you're picking on my driving because you don't want to answer my question. What is the deal with you and your dad right now?"

He sighs again. His fingers drum against the door. But after a long moment, very quietly, he speaks. "I don't want to disappoint him."

I let that sink in, playing with it.

"Fernanda is your baby," I finally say. "You had control, up to a point. So this is about your presenting your hard work to your father. Laying it at his feet for approval, so to speak. I can make that work."

"Glad we got that figured out." He smiles at me. "Then I can go back to being me. Or, rather, you."

BLAKE

*B*y the time Saturday comes around, it's been a few days since I've openly signed on to the Cyclone intranet. I've been on, of course, and Tina has been using my logon, too, but we've both been setting our statuses to invisible. After all, if Dad started a chat with Tina-pretending-to-be-me, the entire setup would be revealed. I haven't really wanted to talk to my father.

But this has been a good week. All my life, I've had things appear for me without my having to think of where they come from. Fruit magically appeared in bowls. I've had a personal chef who would put my favorite foods in single-serve portions in the fridge, so I can reheat them and stare at them for a while before tossing half of it in the garbage.

Now, I've had to go to the store. I've had to look at price tags, something I've never even thought about before. I've been too busy to run, and too tired to play half my food games. I'm trying not to feel hopeful; I've had good weeks before. But maybe, just maybe, this thing will solve itself.

So I log on to the Cyclone intranet Saturday morning before Tina comes over. I set my status to available. And, just as I suspected, it takes about thirty seconds before the chat icon blinks.

What the fuck, asshole, my father writes with his usual bluntness. *Are you avoiding me?*

I pull a blanket around my shoulders, but the goose bumps that pop up on my arms have little to do with the morning cold. Yes, I admit it. I've been avoiding my dad. For one, I haven't exactly told him about the swap. That would lead to difficult questions, questions that I don't want to answer.

I've also put off his attempts at video chatting, simply because I don't want him to see my surroundings. It's been five days since we've spoken, longer than we've ever gone before. From his point of view, it must feel like I disappeared off the face of the planet.

Possibly. I have some stuff on my plate. I need to disconnect a little, so I've been conserving my time to take care of the script.

The light indicates that he's typing a response. It comes in piece by piece.

Disconnect?

What new fucking rancid bullshit is this? If you are blowing me off for some new-wave meditative retreat shit, I swear to God there will be a nuclear explosion down here.

People think that my dad is an asshole because he says shit like this all the time and they think he means it. He doesn't. He's not really an asshole. He's just fluent in the language of asshole and likes using it.

Jesus, Dad. Mushroom clouds are 60s-era scare tactics. They're not even frightening anymore. Get with the program. Dirty bombs are the new black.

He comes back with: *I'll compromise with weaponized anthrax, but that's as modern as I can manage. You can't teach an old dog new methods of mass destruction.*   •

Ha. With you, it's more like weaponized affection. There's a pause after I send this. After staring blankly at the screen, I get up and make another mug of coffee with the remaining hot water. It's tepid, and I only have instant—really terrible instant—but it's bitter, it's liquid, and it's caffeine. I'll take it.

When his reply comes, it's matter-of-fact, down-to-earth—and I can tell from what he's not saying—just a little hurt.

Fine. We can talk about that later. But since you're doing the script, I have a suggestion for the Adam & Blake show.

With a little trepidation, I type back: *What do you have in mind?*

I stare at the screen as the words appear. *Launch is in six weeks. We chose the date to coincide with that thing you have—that school thing right after midterm exams?*

Funny, that Dad knows almost nothing about college life. He did go—for one semester. He proudly flunked every single one of his classes and was given a stern round of warnings. He flipped them the bird on his way out. Since then, of course, Yale has done its best to kiss his ass, but it's not like he cares.

You mean spring break, I tell him. *It's pretty iconic. Beaches, booze, babes. Not really my style though, if that's what you're thinking.*

Yeah. That. I was thinking we could do a flip.

My heart gives an extra thud. I already have one trade going on in my life. Does he know? *What do you mean, a flip?*

If you're going to be a college student, we play to the expectation. Everyone's thinking you'll jet off somewhere wild for spring break. Instead, after I do the financials, I hand off to David Yu, grab a copter, and get somewhere that looks like it will work. Fuck, a painted background on a mock set will do. And then we use the vidcall feature to make the announcement. I'm going on spring break, and you're taking over for the next six months.

I look at this, frowning at the laptop screen. My heart starts to beat a little faster. *Yeah, and what do we tell them two days later when you're still in charge? That it's just a joke? The whole point of these little family interactions is that they're supposed to be a slice of Reynolds family life. True construct, asshole. We'll ruin the whole thing if we throw out something objectively false.*

He types one word in response. *Well.*

Just that single word, but it sends a chill down my spine. Nothing else comes for a few seconds that seem far longer than they should, and then the icon blinks, indicating that he's typing once again.

Maybe it doesn't have to be objectively false. We both know you're going to take over eventually. Why not then?

Because I'm not ready to be my dad for the rest of my life. Because six weeks is not enough.

I have to take a pass on that one.

His reply comes swiftly. *Fuck me, Blake. I'm not telling you to take over permanently. Just a few months. Something where people will know I'm waiting in the wings. Keeps investor confidence up, allows them to build faith in you as a person.*

I try again. *It's the middle of the semester, Dad.*

So what? You withdraw, or whatever the official term is. Or you don't and you flunk all your classes. Who the fuck cares what happens? I didn't spend the last twenty-nine years busting my ass building a legacy just to have you fuck it up because you're afraid that some pansy-ass tweed-wearing bespectacled professor might wring his hands in your direction.

Now he's making me legitimately angry. My hands shake as I type. *That is such bullshit. A legacy is like a $50K trust fund. You're talking about a company with a $413 billion market capitalization. And you want things to transition smoothly because you like beating the competition, not because you give a shit about me and my "legacy." You want me at the reins so you can fake step down but still be in control, because you can't bear to hand off to someone who doesn't get your vision. God forbid anyone ruin your fucking stock price record. This is all about you.*

So yes, I am avoiding you, and I will continue to do it until you stop this shit. You're the competitive one. You're the cutthroat one. You're the one who smells opportunity and sweeps in like a shark on a wounded beluga. I'm not you. I'm never going to be you. So stop trying to shove me into your box. Stop. Now. While we're still friends.

I'm shaking when I hit return.

For a long time, I don't get a response.

And then, finally…

Blake. Please. Come home. I need you.

And that shakes me more than anything. My dad doesn't beg. He doesn't ask. If he wants something, he demands, and if you intend to say no, you have to shout "No, fucker, get out of the way." I don't know what to do with this.

Truth is, it brings to mind memories that are a little too inconvenient. It's one thing to tell my dad that he's trying to make me over into himself. But he's also the man who would pause board meetings when I was three so that he could find the plastic dinosaur I lost. He's the one who made his executive team attend my baseball games so he wouldn't miss them.

I have never doubted that my father loved me. And now... I know, and he knows, even though he won't say it, that his appeal is about more than me taking over the company.

I know, I say. *I'm sorry. That was out of line.*

It's bad for me. For him? He didn't just lose his CFO. He didn't just lose his best friend, someone he spent every day with for seventeen years.

Peter had a violent heart attack when they were both working late—and Dad was there at the office with him. He watched him die while they waited for the paramedics.

Dad never flinched. He never let a hint of his distress show. He did the fucking product launch without shedding a single tear. The only outward sign of his grief that anyone saw was that he installed AEDs on every floor in every Cyclone building with a single-minded intensity. He gave over two million bucks to a local emergency room to make sure that they had exactly the equipment they needed if this ever happened again. And every day since then, he's become just a little harder, just a little more brittle. As if he knows now that his mortality is showing, as if he expects with every product we put out that he'll lose someone he cares about again.

The only time I've ever seen him break down was two months after the funeral. I had come downstairs late one night to get a glass of water. I saw him in the living room with a stack of papers. He wasn't looking at them. He just held them in his hands, crumpling them. And then, while I watched from the stairs, he broke down, curling over and sobbing quietly.

My dad doesn't break. He doesn't. I have never seen anything so terrifying in my life.

We've never talked about it, but it's always there.

Slowly, I type my next sentence. *I can't take Peter's place,* I tell him. *And you have to stop trying to put me there.*

A long wait. And then... *Fuck the whole idea. It was stupid anyway. Everyone will know it's a fake beach—there's nowhere in range that would work—and so that violates the true construct rule.*

I type the words: *Dad. I have a problem.* I don't hit enter. I watch the screen, watch the black letters against the cream background. They are everything I want to say to him, and nothing that I can admit. I don't hit send. I've typed the words, but I'm still completely silent. Finally, I delete them.

We'll figure it out, I write instead.

Fine. We have six weeks.

I'll figure it out, is what I mean. But when I shut the laptop, my entire body itches. I know I shouldn't. I know I can't. But between class and my new shifts washing dishes, I haven't had time to run this week. My body feels weird; a combination of restlessness and exhaustion compounded by the fact that I've had nothing this morning but two cups of coffee. I change into running gear and take off. Easier than trying to navigate my way through the unspoken morass of my emotions.

The road, at first, goes straight up the hills and so do I. My heart rate rises; my stride length falls. There's nothing but the hill, nothing to me but my quads pushing further, faster, my lungs burning for air.

Running takes everything away. My anger and confusion all dissipate in sweat, leaving nothing but a pool of inchoate sadness. I'm stuck, stuck because I love my dad and I can't tell him no forever. I'm stuck because I know that it's turning into a war of determination, and he's the one who can dismantle the fiercest business competitors. I pose no real threat to him. I can't fight him, not really, and I don't want to.

I can fight this hill.

Harder. Faster. When I run, I disappear. There's nothing but the pain, and the longer I run, the less I remember.

I hit the entrance to the park behind the hills an hour into the run. Concrete sidewalks give way to dirt paths covered by leaves and sloughed-off eucalyptus bark. I keep going. It takes two hours to find the summit. From here, I can see a wide green valley fringed by mansions. Beyond the hill to the west, there are the gray waters of the Bay, the Bridge, stretching in the distance against the sky. But the entirety of the East Bay has disappeared, hidden by the hill. It's almost like my worries have vanished.

My hair is plastered to my head with sweat, and now that I've stopped running, the wind is cold. I take a moment to have some water and a terrible-tasting energy gel. And then—because I can never run far enough—I go back.

It's another two hours before I turn onto the street where I'm staying, and by that point, I'm so low on blood sugar that I'm about to bonk.

And that's when I remember that I had an appointment—that Tina was coming over to go over the first week of our arrangement. I'm forty-five minutes late. She's sitting outside in the car.

Fuck. I slow to a walk. She looks up from whatever she's reading and sees me. My chest hurts—and this time, it's not just from the run.

God, I want this to be real. I want to be just a guy with a job, someone whose biggest problem is that he's late for a meeting. I want to just be able to flirt. To *want*. I inhale and pretend that I'm that person. That I'm not being erased from the world and turned into someone else.

She gets out of the car.

"Sorry," I say with a smooth smile. "I was out for a run and lost track of time."

I'm not sure if she believes me. But that's okay. I don't believe me either.

10.

*B*lake is messing with me. I'm convinced of it. He lets me in and disappears into the shower. I can hear the water running in bursts, can imagine him under the stream of the showerhead all too well. Glistening muscles come to mind: pecs, firm and rounded; water sliding down a well-formed chest to brush against abs…

I've got to get my mind off that before I go any lower. No—too late now. I can feel my body heat and I sigh, trying to imagine that the sound of water means anything other than Blake naked a scant few yards from me.

Like…baby elephants playing in a stream, splashing each other. Really *ugly* baby elephants. It works, kind of. At least I'm no longer flushing by the time the water cuts off.

He comes out wearing jeans and…and… Nope, that's it. Jeans.

I wad up an advertising circular that's sitting on his desk and throw it at him. "Put on a shirt."

"Am I distracting you?" He smiles, like he knows that he is.

"Yes. You're going to catch a cold, idiot, and then where will you be?"

He turns to me, which does not help. Transitioning from hot shower to cold room has made his skin tighten all over, pebbling his flesh with goose bumps that cry out to be smoothed away.

"Hey, science genius," he says, "germs don't work like that."

"Fine. Freeze. I don't care."

He turns away—alas, not to put on a shirt. Instead, he takes an apple from the kitchen counter and comes to lean against the desk near me. He doesn't say anything at first, just passes the apple from hand to hand.

My imagined reconstruction of his chest, it turns out, isn't as sexy as the real version. I forgot about his tattoo— that weirdly translucent circuitry tracing down his right arm. He's looking me over frankly, his eyes traveling slowly down my body. It should make me feel uneasy. Out of place.

It doesn't. I just feel warm.

"Here." Instead of looking at him, I open my laptop—a brand-new lightweight Cyclone model in black matte metal. "This is what I have for the script so far."

He picks it up and opens the file. He scrolls through the pages one by one. I hate feeling like I'm waiting for his approval. His face doesn't change as he reads. He just keeps going. When he's done, he looks up at me. And instead of telling me what he thinks, he asks his own question. "So, what do you think?"

"I think this part here—" I scroll through the file until I find it "—isn't funny enough. We're going from one serious part to another. We need to break that up."

"I agree."

"I think we need something way better to demonstrate the relatively smooth video tracking that Fernanda can manage. Something escalating—so at first, mild hand gestures. Then bigger ones." I demonstrate. "Then something completely over the top—juggling, maybe? It has to be something that looks super-cool on-screen but gives us stable video. We'll need to do some experiments."

"Sounds good."

"And then there's the Adam and Blake Show. It doesn't feel quite right to me."

He stiffens, not looking at me. "Yeah." That comes out a little lower.

"So," I say with a sigh, "I guess it's back to the drawing board."

"Hell, no." He raises an eyebrow. "This is the part where we upload it to the team, give them the direction you just gave me, and have them brainstorm. They'll do the testing. They'll generate ideas. That's what they're *there* for."

"So it's okay?"

"It will be more than okay by the time everyone's done with it." He makes a few tiny alterations and uploads the file.

"Congratulations," he tells me dryly. "Now you're going to start having to mediate arguments about whether *a* or *the* is the proper article to use."

"Fine." I reach for my purse. "That's it, then. Next week, same time?"

He simply raises an eyebrow. "You can't go yet. You're holding out on me."

"I am?"

"Yep. We spent this whole time talking about *my* life." He takes a bite of the apple he's holding. "Trade me: Why is your mom terrifying?"

I shake my head. "Trying to explain my parents is a futile endeavor."

"Too bad. Rule one: Your life is as important as mine. We just spent half an hour on the piddly details of my life. And here's the thing: I'm working hard. I'm exhausted. I've never had this little money in my life. But I'm not *terrified* by your life. So what am I doing wrong?"

I thought he would never notice that he's missing the bulk of my life. I hadn't planned to press the issue, because what good could come of it?

But he's looking at me now as if he expects some kind of explanation.

I let go of my purse and tilt my head back. "You're never going to be terrified." My voice is low. "Because if something goes seriously wrong—if you get sick, if the laptop stops working—you can always cheat. I can make you walk a tightrope, but yours is only a foot off the ground. If you work so hard you can't keep up with your classes, you get Cs...and then what? It makes no difference. I would lose my entire future plans."

"Okay." He runs his hands slowly over his bare arms. "I get that. But you said your *mom* was terrifying. Not just your life. How does that play out?"

For a moment, I don't know how to respond. My throat closes, trying to communicate everything. Instead, I open my laptop again and navigate to a familiar website. I motion him to sit down next to me.

It's a mistake. He does. His leg brushes mine; his shoulder is inches away. When I look down, I see the circuitry of his tattoo.

Here we are, sitting on the bed together.

I take a deep breath and try to push away my awareness of him. It doesn't work. He's still there, so close. So warm.

I give my head a little shake and log on to the website.

My parents' electricity bill comes up. I've been away from home for more than two years, and I'm still checking this website.

"See?" I say. "Terrifying." I point to the amount due—$83.26—and the due date—which is two days from now. "It gets worse," I tell him.

I get out my phone, find my mother's number, set the call to speakerphone, and dial.

It takes a few moments for her to answer.

"Hi, Tina!" she says excitedly. "I just got home. Guess what happened today?"

"I don't know."

"The big boss-lady showed me something cool at work. I'm on the blog again!" She sounds absolutely delighted.

Since I immediately know exactly what she's talking about, I put my head in my hands. "Oh, God. Mom. What did you do this time?"

"Just what the customer asked," she says, far too innocently. "Go look. You'll like it."

"I'm bringing it up now." I type in the URL for a blog that catalogs terrible professionally decorated cakes. I'm pretty sure that *most* cake decorators don't consider it an accomplishment to have made the "worst of" lists for three years running, but my mother has a twisted sense of humor. She decorates cakes in the classical style known colloquially as *OMG, what the hell happened here?* with an occasional dash of *WTF* just for seasoning.

I bring up the day's offerings and scroll down. I know—immediately—which one is hers.

"Mom. *No.* "

"Exactly what they asked for," she insists.

The cake pictured is a large, white sheet cake, fringed in iced purple flowers. "Welcome back, Bonzo!" proclaims the main lettering.

That's not the bad part. Little bits of encouragement have been added around the edge. Things like, "Way to go!" in the upper left, and "Here's to good behavior time!"

"They said they were putting on encouragement for a man just out of jail," my mother explains. "I just added the *best* advice."

Sure enough, she has. It's in the lower right. "Only talk to cops with a lawyer there."

Blake, who is reading over my shoulder, puts his hand over his mouth to keep from laughing.

"Don't know why the family was so mad," my mother continues. "I gave them what they asked for. Encouragement to keep him out of jail. It's better than 'You can do it.' You have to be careful what you say to the cops. Everyone knows that!" She tsks. "Even the blog comments agree with me. Read them."

"Well," I say dryly. "If the internet commenters agree with you, you couldn't possibly be wrong."

"Speaking of internet. I got an email from Zhen Liu. Why didn't you tell me you have a boyfriend?"

Crap. I know Mr. Zhen because he owes my mom a favor. I should have known he'd talk to her.

"Oh," I say as breezily as I can, not daring to look at Blake. "He's not a boyfriend. Just a friend who is a boy."

"Not according to Zhen Liu," my mother singsongs. "He says you came for him after work."

Shit.

"Zhen Liu says he's nice, for a white boy. He says he speaks Mandarin."

"Yeah." I frown at Blake. "Seriously, Mom. He's not a boyfriend."

"Is he rich?"

God. I blush fiercely and grab for the phone to take it off speaker, but Blake takes hold of my wrist and shakes his head.

"Do you think he'd be washing dishes for Mr. Zhen if he was rich?" I ask instead.

"Ah. Too bad." I can almost hear her shrug. "I thought—maybe, if you had a rich boyfriend giving you money—but no, never mind."

"Speaking of money." I swallow. "Mom, is there a reason you haven't paid the electric bill yet?"

"Why? The late fee is not so bad," Mom says blithely. "And they don't disconnect for three months. No point wasting money."

"Ma." I wince. "You know how this works. If you put it off another month, you'll have to pay more than twice as much then. You have to keep on top of these things."

"I meant to," she protests. "I just forgot about it earlier. You know. Jack Sheng's appeal. When I gave him the money, I didn't think about this."

"I gave you a checklist." I put my hand to my head. "You're supposed to go through it every month before you give away money you need to pay bills."

I can almost hear her indifferent shrug. "I don't remember where you put my checklist."

"*Mom.*" This is what it's always like. My mom just doesn't take care. She doesn't pay things; she brushes off late fees. I've tried letting her fail to teach her a lesson. She never learns her lesson. She just keeps on failing.

"Fine," I say. "I'm paying it."

"Tina, you're a student. You need to keep your money for your studies. You give us too much."

Those are just meaningless words. If she wanted me to give less, she would pay attention.

"It'll be worse if I'm worrying about you," I say shortly.

"But Tina," my mother says, "how are you going to take your boyfriend out on a hot date if you spend all your money on us?"

"He's not my—" I shake my head, biting off the words. "Stop distracting me. Mom, you have to take care of yourself first. Stop giving away everything."

There's a noise on the other end, one I can't decipher without the aid of a picture. "Of course," my mother says, her tone obstinately polite. "Just as you say. I'll stop as soon as I forget."

I feel a lump in my throat. I don't really remember China. We left when I was six. I remember flashes, sensations. Sometimes, though, a stray smell—a whiff of car exhaust or the scent of roasting duck—will bring back a profusion of poorly understood feelings, things that tap into parts of my brain I don't understand. I'll find myself besieged by emotions I can't quite place: fear, guilt, happiness, and something deeper, something that squeezes my heart like a vise. As if all my childhood memories are still there, waiting for me to rediscover them.

The only thing I really remember is my mother's hand squeezing mine as we walked onto an airplane with fake papers and fake smiles. I don't even know if that's a real memory, either, or something I've reconstructed after the fact from being told the story too many times. I don't remember facts at all. I just remember being afraid, so afraid that they'd find out and take Dad away. Again.

I don't remember, and even I can't walk away from my feeling of obligation.

"Mom," I say instead, my voice shaking, "you and Dad have to be careful."

Mom sighs. "No more cakes on the blog, huh? I told my boss it's good for us. It brings in business."

I try to laugh. I really try. It comes out kind of sickly. "No more cakes on the blog."

I hit the end button. But it's not over. I can feel Blake's eyes on me. I can almost feel his pity and it pisses me off.

I don't look at him. I curl my toes in my shoes and stare at the far wall.

"She's not stupid," I say in a low voice. "She remembers every immigration filing deadline for every friend she ever talks to. She doesn't remember the utility bill because she doesn't want to."

"Tina." Blake is still too close to me. I don't want to look at him. I don't want to look in his eyes. But I do anyway. "I was not going to suggest that a woman who makes cakes celebrating Miranda rights was stupid."

I let out a shaky laugh.

"How long have you been handling your mother's bills?"

"Since I can remember. At first it was because I was the only person in the house who wrote and spoke English well enough to understand them. Then I kept doing it because I was the one who did it." I shrug. "Now... Maria says I'm enabling my mother."

"Are you?"

"Maybe. But it's not like she has a drug habit. She's helping people. *Someone* should enable her." I don't look at him. "It's stupid, but all I want out of life is to be able to put my parents' bills on my autopay. I don't want to worry that she's skipping an insurance premium. But I'm afraid that if I do, my mom will just find new ways to give away money. At least a drug habit is finite—there's only so much coke you can do in a day. This? There's no end to it."

He doesn't say anything. He's so close to me, so close I could lean over an inch and set my head on his shoulder. So close that he could slide his arm around me in comfort. And part of me wants that. I want it so much.

"You have the wrong idea about me," I tell him. "You told me I'm focused. That I'm responsible. I'm not, really. I don't know what I'm doing any more than anyone else does. I'm just too terrified to do anything else."

He doesn't put his arm around me. He doesn't touch me. He just looks at me like he wants to.

"Out of curiosity," he says, "that money I transferred to your account. Have you spent any of it?"

I haven't wanted to touch any of it. I want to let it build up, a huge sum to ward off any possible danger.

Still, I slowly nod my head.

"On anything extravagant? Anything silly?"

I swallow. "I bought mangoes."

He smiles a touch sarcastically, and I reach out and give him a little shove. That's a mistake. It puts my hand in contact with his shoulder. His bare skin is cool to the touch, and I don't pull away.

"Hey," I say. "Mangoes are *expensive.*"

He doesn't laugh at me, even though I know that to someone like him—to someone who spends fifteen thousand dollars a *month,* something I can't even contemplate, mangoes are nothing. Even though I haven't moved my hand from the point where it rests on his shoulder, and my thumb itches to caress him.

"I'll make you a deal," he says. "I'll pay your parents' utility bill this month."

I have some idea how little money he must have. I know exactly how much that would cost him.

"But—"

"Hey," he says. "No arguments. We're trading lives. I'm taking that on. If you're terrified, I should be, too. But you have to do something for me in return."

I still haven't moved away, and I know I should. Sitting here this close to him, touching him—I'm giving him ideas. I'm giving myself ideas. Fuck, I don't know what to do with these ideas. I have a sudden urge to slide my hand down his chest, feeling the ridge of every muscle, the whisper of short, light hairs against my fingers. I could undo his jeans. Find out precisely how much of that bulge there is fabric, and how much is *him.*

"What?" My voice is hoarse.

"I don't care," he says. "Something you wouldn't normally do. Something risky. Something silly. Go skydiving. Buy a name-brand purse. Do something that terrifies you, something you can't get out of your mind, that you've been holding back on."

I look at my hand on his shoulder. I've never wanted to go skydiving. I've never lusted after purses. I'm just getting used to the luxury of the occasional mango. There's really only one thing I want right now that terrifies me.

"I'm thinking of something." My throat feels dry. "Something blindingly stupid. Risky. Idiotic."

"Do you want to do it?"

My mouth goes dry. "Yes."

"Then go for it," he says.

For a second, I'm frozen in indecision. It will change everything. It will start a snowball rolling down a mountain, and I'm not sure I'll escape the avalanche.

Still, I turn to him. I look into his eyes. My hands tremble.

"Okay," I say, and my voice trembles, too. "Here goes."

And before I can think better of it, I do the stupidest thing possible: I kiss him.

BLAKE

*F*or a second, I'm too shocked to react.

I don't know why; this thing has been lurking between us for weeks, never dormant, always present. But she's been wary, pushing me away, and I didn't expect this.

My surprise lasts almost no time at all. Just a second's worth of her lips against mine, her hands, warm against the cool, bare skin of my shoulders.

My last intelligent thought is that I'm not letting this go to waste, and then I'm kissing her back. Wrapping my arm around her, bringing her close so that her body lies flush against mine. My free hand tangles in her dark hair, wrapping it around my fingers, following it up to her scalp, the line of her ear.

She tastes so good—sweet, like an apple. Her hands slide down my chest, leaving a trail of heat, coming to rest on my hips. Tina shifts her weight and then straddles me. My nerves light up at that, sparking with desire.

Fuck, I want her. She's wearing jeans. I'm wearing jeans. Doesn't matter that there's layers of thick denim between us; my body still recognizes the feel of hips pressing against my pelvis. The friction of fabric is rough against my cock, but it's everything I could have asked for. Her hands rise again, sliding up my chest to rest against my shoulders.

She kisses me like she's been thinking of this as long as I have, like this kiss has been building from the first day we saw each other. She kisses me like there's no space between us.

And there isn't—not much.

I'm not trying to escalate things. I'm not even really *thinking* about it. But when she smoothes her palm down my chest, my hand creeps up by her side, sliding up until I find the fabric of her bra.

Under other circumstances, I might rip it off. But I don't want to freak her out. I cup her breast in the palm of my hand.

She gasps instantly. I was already hard; with that, I find myself turning to stone. Needing, wanting stone.

If I'm stone, she's fire. Her hips grind into me as my thumb finds her nipple. My lips graze her neck. My tongue darts out and traces down her collarbone. I can't even remember why I ever thought it was cold in here. It's a fucking furnace. I pull her close.

She's so fucking responsive. It's hot beyond belief to watch her go up in flames on top of me, to watch how the smallest touch, the slightest pressure in the right place, gets her going.

I don't have much of a thought process, but it goes something like *yes, yes, more now.*

And she must be thinking the same thing—thank God—because she takes her shirt off. She's wearing a simple white cotton bra, no padding, and her nipples poke through. I lean forward and catch one in my mouth.

She likes it. She grinds against me. Her fingers clench on my shoulders, gripping tight, so fucking tight. I find her other breast—small enough that I can palm it with one hand, so that my fingers can explore every last inch.

She's letting out little moans that seem to go straight to my dick.

"You," I growl out, "have awesome tits."

She freezes on top of me. And then, seconds later, she pulls away. "Don't." She reaches for her shirt. "Don't lie to me. I have nonexistent boobs."

I run my finger over her nipple. "Yeah? What's this, then?"

She shivers.

"You have awesome tits," I repeat. "I love touching them. Licking. Sucking. It makes me fucking wild to be able to drive you crazy like this. Tits are a fucking gift for sexual pleasure. So never tell me you have nonexistent boobs again. I think I just proved otherwise."

She draws in a deep breath. Her eyes meet mine. She looks almost shattered.

And then she turns away. Before I can say anything else, she's standing up and pulling her shirt back on.

"I'm sorry." She doesn't meet my eyes, won't even look in my direction. She grabs for her coat and checks her watch. "I have to go."

"Tina."

"I...I really have to go." She grabs her keys. Her hands shake as she opens the door. And that's the point when the blood rushing to my cock stops interfering with the functioning of my mind and I remember how this all started.

I want to do something stupid. Something risky. Something mind-numbingly idiotic.

That's what she said. And then she kissed me.

5:07 PM
Are we okay?

8:13 PM
Tina?

8:57 PM
Hey.
I'm sure I said something stupid.
I'm sorry.
Just yell at me and I'll make it right.
ok?

9:22 PM
What are you talking about?
I just remembered I had something to do.

9:25 PM
Bullshit.

10:33 PM
Fine. It's bullshit.
But I want it to stay *my* bullshit.
Can we do that?

10:34 PM
I don't know
can we?

10:34 PM
Argh. Be that way.
MAY we.

10:36 PM
I wasn't correcting your grammar
I just honestly don't know if that's possible

11:04 PM
I prefer it when things are simple.
You're not simple. I freaked out.

11:05 PM
You're getting to me.
I don't let people do that.
I'm sorry.

11:12 PM
I'll take that.

11.

BLAKE

When I walk out of the kitchen at Zhen's a few minutes after ten on Monday, Tina is sitting at a table waiting for me. Her hands are folded and she's sitting with perfect posture, like she's an advertisement for some kind of ergonomic chair.

I stop.

Her eyes dart up to mine, and then she looks away.

I come to stand by her. "Hi, you."

We haven't talked—or texted—since our brief exchange on Saturday night. And that's okay. I can be patient.

I don't pretend to understand her, but I understand this: Like me, she's caught. She wants to be responsible. She doesn't like losing control—even as little as we did together.

And I don't want her terrified. I want her naked. I want her beneath me. And when she's there, I want her to be sure.

She looks up at me. Our eyes meet. For a moment, they hold, and the memory of a few days ago, of Tina on top of me, flashes through me. A wave of want washes through me.

I tamp it down.

She stands. "Hi." She's trying for nonchalance. "I thought I'd give you a ride home."

There's nothing to say to that, but... "Thanks."

I follow her to the car, slide into the passenger seat. She doesn't say anything. At every light, she glances at me. When she catches me looking her way, she turns away swiftly. Every time. Finally, I make myself look out the window.

Liquor store. Cat food store. Group of college students, standing on the corner and smoking. The car is quiet; it's late enough that there's almost no other noise.

"My father always says," Tina finally says into that silence, "that if you owe someone an apology, you should do something nice for them. I'm pretty sure I owe you an apology."

I want to look at her, but somehow, I feel that's a bad idea—that doing so will prevent her from saying whatever she's going to say.

"There was a guy first semester of my sophomore year," she finally says. "We had two classes together. We used to study."

On the street to my right, I see three students stumble by.

"The day before our first finals, we were joking around. Playing. I liked him a lot. And we were touching, sitting close. He just put his arms around me, and then...things went on from there. We had sex, and I liked it." Her face is utterly straight. "For one day, I thought I could have everything. That I might be able to do all the things I have to do, and still have someone."

There's another long silence and I count businesses again. Chinese food, wine bar, locksmith.

"After our first final together," she says, "he asked if I wanted to grab a beer. He was already at the bar when I got there, sitting with some friends. I walk up; he turns to me and before I can say anything, he says, 'Hi, Tina. This is Elaine. She's my girlfriend.' That's how I found out."

I exhale sharply. "That's fucked-up."

"I'm not saying you would do that," she says. "But you have to understand—it hurt. It hurt a lot. I still had four finals left. I just wanted to curl up and disappear, and I couldn't. I didn't have time to care then, and I really don't have it now. I can't let myself get hurt."

My hands twitch on my lap, and for the first time, I look over at her. Even though the street is mostly deserted, she's going slowly, as if she's still afraid to do more. "I understand," I say. "I don't want to hurt you, either."

"Yeah?" She glances my way dubiously, and when she sees me watching her, quickly turns back to the street. "Tell me, Blake. What are the chances that you'll stay here? That we can kiss now and not break up later?"

The truth is, I'm only here until I get a grip on my problem. My dad needs me. The instant I'm capable of walking away, I will.

I shake my head.

"Exactly," she says. "That's what I would put our chances at. Approximately zero. I freaked out on you. But I had a good reason."

She turns onto the street where I'm staying. She doesn't say anything and I don't either. She pulls up in front of the house, and finally I turn to her. She's not looking at me; she's staring down. Her hands tangle on the black leather wrapping the wheel. Her hair is loose around her face, obscuring her from my sight.

I open the door and step out into the night. Her head is bowed; she doesn't look at me as I walk around to her side of the car and open her door. She turns, looking up at me.

She's told me why she *can't* kiss me; she hasn't said why she did it in the first place. She doesn't have to. I can see it in the way her eyes refuse to leave mine. I can see it in the way her lips press together, and then slowly, her tongue darts out, wetting them. I can see it in the darkness of her eyes.

Hell, I tasted it on her the other day.

"It's okay," I say. "I get it. Hell, I'm terrified for you."

I can hear her breath in the silence of the night. She looks down and then away. Her hand clenches, and then she undoes the seatbelt. She stands, even though that puts her right next to me. I can feel the heat of her, so close I could touch her.

I don't.

There's never anything like real stars around here. Just a few of the brightest constellations and the lights of planes overhead. Still, she tilts her head up, looking into the night sky.

"I don't know why anyone thinks that looking at the stars is so romantic," she says. "Have they ever read Greek mythology? It's all the same story—God sees mortal, God desires mortal, mortal suffers gruesome fate and is rewarded with an eternity of pain in the cosmos." She shrugs.

"You could always make up your own stories."

But she's already shaking her head. "No. Those stories are written in stardust millions of years old. I don't think I get to change them."

"Then I'm thankful for light pollution," I say.

She makes a little noise, something close to a laugh, and it sets off a cascade of desire in me.

You'd think I would be spoiled after a lifetime of getting anything I've ever wanted. Maybe I am. But I've spent a year wanting, a year yearning for something that deep down, I'm afraid I'm never going to get. This new, frustrating level of want is right up my alley.

And at least wanting Tina won't kill me.

"You're a lot more decent than I thought you would be," she says.

I want to hold her right now, to put my arms around her and tell her it will be all right. But I can't even tell myself that.

And so instead, I run my thumb down her cheek. I know I shouldn't touch her. I know I shouldn't think this. I know that I shouldn't let my hand rest on her lips.

But I do.

"Good night, Tina," I say. "Don't look at the stars."

"I won't," she says. "They don't mean anything anyway."

TINA

*B*lake looks tired when he slips into the seat next to me in the theater seating for our class. The little things bring me to that conclusion. After a few weeks of our trade, his usual attire—business slacks and a button-down shirt—no longer looks so crisp. The cuffs aren't perfectly ironed. His hair lies flatter against his head, and he doesn't smile at me in that same cocky way. Instead, he slouches in the seat next to me.

If this attraction were just a matter of social programming, those small changes would break down the desire that I feel. Now that he's not sending off those same power signals, I shouldn't want him so much.

Instead, the moment feels intimate, like I've caught him off his guard. Like we're both off guard, floundering, reaching for each other.

I glance over at him. "Hi, Blake."

His eyes meet mine. God, I can't stop thinking about kissing him. About his hands on my body, about the heat that sparked up between us. It's been two days since I kissed him, two days during which I've tried to draw the line back to where it was before I crossed it. Two days in which I've tried to pretend that *this*—whatever *this* is—is not happening.

"Tina." He takes out a pen, some paper.

No matter what I told him, no matter what I said, I know I'm in trouble.

I need to build a wall between us, a wall that shields me from hope. Right now, my fantasies are whispering. What if I just…let it happen? What if the stars are wrong? What if it doesn't end?

Every little girl dreams of a prince to take her away from the drudgery of life, someone who will sweep her off her feet and take care of her. It's something that comes from that first swell of Disney music that we hear as children. And the truth is, Blake would be such a prince.

He's sweet. He's caring. He looks at me like there's nobody else in the world. And he kisses like...

But, I remind myself, that's all it is: cultural programming. It's the effect of too many animated movies watched at too young an age. It isn't real.

In fiction, the story ends when Prince Charming whisks Cinderella away to his castle.

But there's a reason why the poor girl who wins herself a prince is usually an orphan. Because if she wasn't...

"Darling," Charming would say in the scene after the end, "you know I love you, doll. But we have to talk about your parents. I'm thinking I should buy them a cottage, maybe something high up in the mountains, yeah? Don't worry. You can always call. You can even visit them when I'm busy with my affairs of state."

Even with Cinderella's essentially family-less status, the story always ends before the painful, embarrassing scenes that come a few years in.

"Darling, I never meant to fall in love with Snow White. I swear it. But she was raised in a castle as a princess, you know? She gets me in a way you never will."

Blake interrupts my reverie with a note.

There's something you should know, he writes. *You do mean something to me.*

I crumple the paper and turn my attention back to my notebook. At least I try to. But no matter how much I stare at the professor, I can scarcely pay attention to what he's saying.

There's a reason the hero is always called Prince Charming in all the stories. It's not just an interchangeable name. It's the same damned knight on a white horse, looking for a girl who's grateful to be rescued. Once he's managed the deed—and once she's forgotten what she has to be grateful about, and started to realize that this is the rest of her life—there's nothing left but regret. Snow White will have decades to remember that at least the seven dwarves said "thank you," goddammit. And then there was that nice woodcutter boy who worshipped her. He never would have looked down on her, not once.

My life means something to me. I've been on this track for years. I'm not about to mess it all up just because a man is good at kissing.

Beside me, Blake lets out a sigh.

I don't look in his direction. I can't. I'm afraid he'll break me down. If I meet his eyes, I'll remember that I like him, and once I remember that…

God. If it's like this between us when we're *not* together, how much more will it hurt if I let it happen?

He starts to write again.

I'm trying to block out my awareness of him. Really. I'm trying. I'm trying not to wonder. I'm trying to ignore that tight coil of nervous anticipation that is building. I'm telling myself that whatever he says, whatever he thinks, it's not going to change my mind. There's nothing he can offer me in the long term—just a chance to feel ashamed of who I am and where I come from.

I have to hold on to that. I have to hold on to myself or I'll lose everything.

Still, I read the second note when he slides it over.

I've been Blake fucking Reynolds since I was two years old. I've never had a chance to be anyone else. I don't know if you understand why I find you so fucking hot. It's because you know who you are, where you're going. You have a plan and nobody will distract you from it.

I feel like I'm disappearing.

When you kissed me, I felt like I existed—me, not the kid who's been on this same path since birth.

Me.

I know it will never mean the same thing to you. I know you want to forget it. But I'm going to remember that long after you've forgotten that I exist.

My stomach tightens. There's a rawness, a nakedness to this, one that sweeps through my attempts to push him away.

I get out another piece of paper. Up in front, the professor talks. I can pretend that it doesn't matter. I *can*.

But I don't. Instead, I write back.

I'm scared I'll tell myself lies. I'm scared I'll—fall in love with you, I want to write. But that's too big, too scary to even put down in words, even in the hypothetical. Instead, I settle for *get attached to you. I'm scared I'll pin my hopes on you and I don't have so many hopes that I can afford to lose one.*

My hand is shaking as I pass this back. Truth is, it's too late already for that. And I already know what he's going to say: *Don't be scared, baby. I would never hurt you.*

But I don't want to be comforted. I'm shaking, trying to figure out how to explain that my fear makes me safe. That I don't want to get rid of it. Without fear, I am too comfortable. Without fear, I make mistakes. I have to be careful.

But he doesn't say what I expect.

Instead, he writes: *Is there anything I can do to make you feel safe?*

My throat closes. It matters that he doesn't tell me that my feelings are stupid, that they need to be shoved aside. My emotions are a tangling, irrational mess—but they're still mine, and my fear mixes with confusion, respect, and appreciation.

For a moment, I imagine it. I think of that future where I can kiss Blake and not fear. I imagine my heart unshielded, open and ready to be crushed. I imagine the kind of person who could put herself out there like that.

I imagine reaching over and taking his hand, saying to him, "There is something you can do, and you just did it." My fingers inch to the edge of the desk. My palm tingles. One motion, and…

Xingjuan, be careful.

The words are like a slap. I flatten my hand against the desk, quashing that impulse. I concentrate on my breath—each inhale crystal clear, filling my lungs and then spilling out once more—until I don't want anymore.

Then I finally let myself answer.

No, I write. *There's nothing you can do. It's just not safe.*

He reads this. He looks ahead. His chin squares, and for a moment, I think he really will protest. But a few minutes later, he sends back a note.

Okay. If that's what you need.

I let out a shaky breath, afraid to believe. *Adam Reynolds's son, showing restraint?* I write. *That's hard to believe.*

He turns his head and looks at me. His eyes are impenetrable. And then he bows his head and writes again. *On the contrary. Adam Reynolds's son knows what it's like to be pushed too far. He would never do it to anyone he cares about. Friends?*

Friends, I write slowly. *Until this is over.*

12.

"Friends" is supposed to be a bad word, and I suppose my body thinks it is. Spending time around Tina leaves me on edge, horny and restless in a way that no amount of running—or, let's be honest, masturbation—can cure.

Truth is, I want her and I want her bad. It's worse now that we've kissed. Now that I've touched her almost all over, now that I know how she responds to me. Those wants feel embedded permanently in me, a tattoo of lust that resides just beneath my skin.

But—and this is going to sound weird—I actually enjoy it. It fits with the life I've adopted for now. I wash dishes; I stumble through my classes in a haze. I spend time with Tina, going through details of the launch.

The want gives me something to do, something to focus on. Something so that sometimes, I forget myself and I can eat without choking on my own food. The desire distracts me; I almost don't even have to run to push everything else away.

Almost.

Want is always present, fierce and ferocious, a punch to the throat. *Here*, it says. *Here this is. Here you are. Here is one thing you want.*

I want, therefore I am.

Tina and I don't talk about how much I want her, not for weeks.

It hits me hard one day as we're doing homework together before my shift. I'm not sure when we started hanging out together—it's partially because I want to spend time with her, and she spends an inordinate amount of time doing work, and partially because as we come down to the last few weeks before the launch, there are a thousand tiny details that we have to discuss.

We're sitting in my kitchen. She's frowning at her computer, reading through a discussion on the Cyclone intranet. And then her phone rings.

She glances down and her face tightens. It's scary how well I know her. She shuts her eyes and pushes back in her seat.

"Your mom?" I ask.

She nods.

Her parents call regularly, and ever since that first time, she's let me listen silently on the calls. Her mom doesn't always need money, but when she does, Tina always sends it. And I always pay.

I can only imagine what it must have felt like for her to feel every spare dollar—and then some she couldn't spare—slip through her hands. I would resent it, but for me, it's temporary. For me, this is just another form of an ultra-marathon. It feels difficult. It seems interminable. But I'm doing it to myself, and that makes it bearable in a way it wouldn't be for her. Deep down, I know it's going to be over.

For her? There is no end. The marathon never stops. She can't get off. She can't rest. It just keeps going on.

This time, her mother is calling about another friend, an appeal that will be heard in a few weeks.

"Any way you can come down?" she asks Tina. "Maybe find someone you can carpool with. Then you can come to the hearing with me."

The other thing I've learned is that Tina's mother, in her own way, is as relentless and indefatigable as my father.

Tina winds her hair around her finger. "Mom. That's a Friday. I can't miss class."

But she's already pulled up her schedule and she's frowning at the date.

"You just have two classes on Friday. You have a test?"

"No." Tina bites her lip. "But…"

I reach over her shoulder and type on her laptop. *You should go.*

"You can't get notes from someone else?" her mother asks insistently.

"Yes, but—"

"Because this is Jimmy Ma. You used to babysit him, remember?" Tina's mom makes a distinct clucking noise through the phone. "I told his parents to file for citizenship as soon as he turned eighteen, but did they listen? 'Too expensive,' they said. 'He can do it later.' You should come. We can show the judges he is part of a community."

Tina types in response to me: *How?*

She hasn't told her mother about the trade— unsurprisingly, given her mom's propensity to spend other people's money—and so it's not like she could buy a plane ticket without occasioning questions. And driving my car down, I suspect, would lead to even larger questions. Questions like: *Where'd you get a car that costs six figures?*

Tina runs her hand through her hair and looks at the ceiling. "I don't think the judges will care."

This is met with silence. Then, her mother shifts tactics. "It could have been you. If the community hadn't come together when your father lost his job and paid the filing fee for your citizenship, it could have been you. That is why you should come. Because it's not just about Jimmy. It's about all of us."

This I did not know. Tina shuts her eyes and sets her fingers on her forehead. "Mom."

"Was that a guilt trip? Sorry. Didn't mean it." Her mother sounds singularly unapologetic.

I'll figure it out, I type. *I can get you down there. Without too many awkward questions. That's my job, right?*

"It couldn't have been me," Tina says sarcastically. "Because—this may surprise you, Mom—I would never be found with fifteen pounds of meth in my backseat."

"True," her mother says. "If you ever transported methamphetamines, you would hide it under the car. Harder to find, less likely the pigs will see it if they pull you over in a traffic stop."

Tina lets out a little snort. "Thanks for the vote of confidence."

"And don't use dryer sheets, either. They confuse drug dogs, but it's still a bad idea. All the judges say the smell gives the cops probable cause to search. Better to not raise suspicion."

"Great." Tina rolls her eyes. "No dryer sheets for me."

Her mother considers this for a moment. "Not that it will make a difference. Cops just need any reason to tell the judge. It's, 'She looked jittery, Your Honor. I thought she was on crack.' Or, 'she looked too calm. I thought she was on weed.' Or 'she had a cold; I thought she was snorting cocaine.' You always lose. Better remember that, in case you decide to quit school and turn to a life of crime."

Her mother actually sounds excited by the prospect, and based on what I've heard of her thus far, I suspect that she really is.

Tina rolls her eyes. "Great. When I become a drug mule, I promise that you'll be the first person I consult." But she's smiling ruefully.

"So you'll come," her mother says excitedly. "We'll plan your future as criminal mastermind."

"I'll see."

"You'll come."

Tina sighs. "*Fine.* I'll come."

"Bring your boyfriend."

"*Mom.* He's not my   "

"Ah, ah. Not what Zhen says. How many times have you gone to him after work now? And so late at night, too. I don't know what to think about you seeing your boyfriend so late."

"That's irrelevant. He's *not* my boyfriend."

"Oh," her mother says with a hint of overly saccharine politeness. "I see. Then bring your very good friend who is a boy but *not* your boyfriend who you see late at night."

Tina glances over at me. I give her a thumbs-up.

"Fine," she says. "I will. But only if you promise not to call him—"

"Oh, would you look at the time. Too bad. I gotta go. Bye, Tina. See you in a week."

The call ends. Tina looks up at the ceiling. "Oh, God." She doesn't say anything else.

I glance over at her. "It's *hilarious* that your mom calls the police pigs. Seriously, where did she pick that one up?"

"She's down with all the idioms for the police," Tina says. "If it's immigration or crime, my mom is all over it. But just watch what it's like when my dad and I try to explain Beyoncé to her."

"I like your mom," I say. "I wouldn't mind meeting her."

"That," she says succinctly, "is because you're not related to her."

"Probably."

She sighs, shakes her head at her laptop, and stands up. "Well. I'm going to start dinner." She looks over at me. "Are you sure you won't let me feed you?"

"That would be cheating," I say glibly.

"Because I think you're losing weight, and I didn't think that was possible."

I am saved from answering this by the sound of the "Imperial March" emanating from my watch. I swallow, check to make sure that Maria isn't in the room, and then very carefully, I hit accept.

"Blake." My dad is sitting at his desk, which is unusual. Usually he stands, paces even, like he can't bear to be still for even the duration of a video conversation. Today, he looks...tired. More than tired. I've seen him tired before, and usually, he can hide it. This? He has dark circles under his eyes.

"Dude." He lets out a sigh. "I've been trying to get ahold of you for days."

"I've been answering your emails."

"And I've been telling you we need to talk." He glares at me.

"Okay. So." I don't look at Tina. "Talk."

"So. We have to talk over the Adam and Blake scenarios for the Fernanda launch. I actually liked your number three."

I try not to glance at Tina. *Like* is not the word I would use to describe how I feel about her third scenario. It's the closest I can come to the truth at present. In her draft, Tina's written us with our usual banter, our typical friendliness—except with just a little added distance, a little formality. It's obvious from the script that I'm trying too hard.

"Blake," my father is supposed to say at some point. "What's going on with you?"

"This is the first project I've taken on by myself," I will confess. "I just want you to be proud of me."

"Always," Tina has my father saying. "I'm always proud of you."

I don't *like* this scenario. I want it. It makes me feel naked and exposed. It's not just a true construction; it's a whisper of my deepest desires.

"Yeah?" I'm carefully nonchalant. "You liked that?"

"It's heartwarming," Dad says. "It's sweet without being maudlin. It's exactly what I want—something that reinforces the fact that you're an adult now, entirely capable of anything that gets thrown at you. But I want to ramp up the ending. We need to add in that I'm stepping down temporarily. Effective as of the launch."

My whole body goes cold. "Dad. That's three weeks away."

He looks at me. He doesn't launch into an immediate argument, and maybe that's what sends a chill down my spine. Instead, he simply shakes his head gravely. "I know," he says quietly. "Can you take over for me?"

"I'm in school. I have classes."

He lets out a breath. "Blake. I know. I *know*. But— please. Do this for me."

My hands are cold.

I have always known that there would come a time when my will would get pitted directly against his. When all the misdirection, all the tricks I've employed, will not be enough to keep him at bay. I had just hoped I would have more time.

"Dad." I glance away from him, over to Tina. It doesn't last long; my gaze is drawn back to his. My hands are shaking. I want him to be proud of me, and I've finally come to the point where I either have to lose myself completely or disappoint him. "I don't want to take over."

He lets out a breath and rubs a palm against his forehead. "Yeah," he says. "I know. I kinda figured that one out when you thought it would be more fun to go waste time at a fucking university than stay here. But, Blake…" His hand drops and he looks at me. "If you really wanted to leave, you'd have gone more than forty miles. Right now, you fucking bastard, I really, really need you."

He doesn't explain why. I have no doubt that he'd probably choke before telling me the truth. But I've been watching him fossilize slowly in his office over the last year. I've worried about him. I don't want to fail him.

I can say no to his brashest commands. But this?

I can't, Dad. I have a problem. But now, both he and Tina are watching. It's been better, a little bit, these last few weeks. I know it has. I'm sure it has. I just need more time.

But Dad would only beg if he was on the verge of breaking down. *I have a problem,* I want to scream. But I swallow those words.

"Fine," I hear myself say. My voice sounds very, very far away. "Promise me it's only temporary. Because I can't do it for long."

I can make it a month, I tell myself. Six weeks.

I'm already running in my head. Even though I'm standing here, I want to get my shoes and get out the door. At least if I do, I'll disappear *my* way.

But Dad lets out a long breath. "I promise," he says. "I'll talk to the board. And Blake—thanks, asshole."

I'm still standing in place when the conversation ends. It's only in my head that I'm reduced to rubble. Tina is looking at me. I press my hands firmly together.

"Wow," she says. "That was harsh. Does your dad usually call you an asshole? And a fucking bastard?"

"Yeah." I turn away from her. "But he doesn't mean it like you think he means it."

"Oh, yes. The well-known *other* meaning of fucking bastard."

"It's a joke," I say. "An inside joke."

"Ha ha. So funny." She makes a face.

"It is. Kind of. Five years ago, Peter—um, that's Peter Georgiacodis, who used to be the CFO—told my dad that if he didn't learn to watch his mouth, he was going to get sued one day. So he forced my dad to take corporate sensitivity training."

"That worked well," she says sarcastically.

"Actually, it kind of did. He's…better, now. Really. With most people. But Dad said he wasn't going through that sensitivity bullcrap unless Peter and I did it with him. And he was a little belligerent about it, as only he can be. Halfway through, he tried to explain that he just didn't think that cursing was that insulting. Look, he said, *I* didn't mind, and I was barely eighteen. So how bad could it be? In any event, the instructor lost his temper and told him that he could call the people he loved 'you fucking bastard' as much as he wanted, but that he had to treat his employees like real people." I shrug. "Ever since then, that's been the way we say 'I love you.' We swear at each other."

She looks at me. "You know that is deeply fucked-up, right?"

I smile at her. "Aw, I love you, too."

She shakes her head. "I guess I'm hardly in a position to judge. My mom tells me she loves me by explaining the best way to transport meth."

For a moment, we smile at each other.

And then reality hits: I just agreed to take over for my dad. The launch is in three weeks. After that, there will be no more afternoons with Tina. I won't have time for a job washing dishes. This trade will be over—and I still don't have a solution to my stupid problem.

I pull out a chair and sit. "I'm going to have to end the trade early."

There are a thousand things she could say. I'm bailing early, just like she thought I would. I couldn't hack it. It wasn't real; it was never real. I couldn't put down my life, any more than she could let go of her own terror. We're still the same people we were before, scarred in the same ways we were scarred before. Everything I thought I could accomplish was fake. I can't look at her.

"I won't be in school anymore," I say, "so there's no question that you'll stay here. And the money is yours— we agreed on that up front. You were right. We can't trade. Not really. There's nothing I can do to get out of my life."

But it's more than that. Once the trade is over, *we're* over. We're nothing. And we've tried—hard, so hard— not to be anything. But... I glance over at her and... My body yearns to press against hers. My lungs long to breathe the air she releases. And deep down, somewhere inside of me, I just *want*. I want everything we haven't had.

Don't walk away, I imagine saying.

"I still want to meet your parents," I tell her. "And just think—three weeks from now, your mom will never tease you about me again."

She doesn't say anything. But even though I try to cover what I'm thinking with a smile, she knows what I'm saying. She reaches out and takes my hand.

There are a million things we could be to each other, if only we were different people. If I were a different person, I would have asked her out last September. If she were a different person, we'd have been in bed weeks ago. Instead, we're us. Close enough to hurt, but not close enough to do more than touch for an instant and let go.

"Until then," I say, "I don't want out of any of this."

She doesn't let go of my hand. "Until then."

But she's already turned her head away.

TINA

*T*t's nine at night, and Blake has gone to work, when my watch buzzes on my wrist. I glance down, expecting a calendar reminder. Instead, a little green notification appears.

Incoming call: Adam Reynolds.

I let those words fill my vision for a moment. Not because I intend to make him wait; it's simply that for a second I freeze. Blake's dad is a wolf, and I feel very much like the rabbit. The last time Adam and I talked, it didn't turn out particularly well. But right now, the CEO of Cyclone—and the man who, incidentally, still thinks I'm dating his son—is calling me.

What can I do? I hit *accept.*

He appears on the screen: messy pepper-gray hair and beard scruff in need of a shave. His gaze fixes on mine.

"Tina." His voice is just a little hoarse. He clears his throat and sniffs. "Is Blake there?"

"No."

"Good." He frowns. "Look. Blake's a little distant right now. Is something going on with him?"

Something is obviously going on between them, but even I can't tell what it is, and I suspect I know about as much as anyone on the planet except these two.

I shake my head. "I'm not talking to you about Blake."

"Yeah." He blows out a breath. "Probably just as well that you're loyal to him. I just…" He pauses, tapping his fingers against his cheek.

"It's not that," I interject. "It's just that you're an…" I choke back the word I'd been planning to put in that blank. Last time was bad enough. "You're a little intense," I finish.

For a moment, he stares at me. Then, ever so slowly, he smiles. "Don't start holding out on me now. I'm an asshole." My surprise must show, because he shrugs a shoulder. "I've never claimed otherwise."

I suspect this is as close as Adam Reynolds will ever come to apologizing for his behavior in that restaurant.

"*Blake* doesn't think you're an asshole."

"Blake," Mr. Reynolds says with a roll of his eyes, "is a ridiculously good kid. There's a reason I'm a little protective of him. I'm always afraid people will take advantage."

I don't say anything. A *little* protective is what he is?

Despite my silence, he sighs and waves his hand. "Good point," he mutters in response to the thing I didn't say. "It hasn't happened yet, and God knows if he were as naïve as I really feared, it would have by now. Of all the women he could have had, he *did* choose you."

I think this is intended as a compliment.

"Still," his dad continues. "I worry. Is everything okay with him?"

I have the distinct impression that even though Blake has never said so, most of his problems lie with this man. Somehow. Some way.

"This is a conversation you should have with Blake."

He puts his fingers to the bridge of his nose. "Fuck." He doesn't move for a few moments. And then—of all things—he sniffles. Unconvincingly.

"Mr. Reynolds, are you faking tears to try to get my sympathy?"

The hand lowers. He glowers at me—obviously dry-eyed. "Fuck me," he says. "First, call me Adam. *Mr. Reynolds* makes me sound like some bullshit old fart. Second, I don't fucking cry. I especially don't fake cry. Emotional manipulation is for morons who don't have the strength of will to get people on their side with reason. I have a cold."

"Aw. Poor baby. You should get some rest." I incline my head toward him, and then widen my eyes. "Oh, wait. I forgot. You can't."

He shakes his head, but he's smiling. "Yeah, yeah. My kid has good taste. I'm fucking things up for you. I hope it won't be too much of a disturbance."

"You know." I swallow. "I think Blake gave you the wrong impression about us."

"What, that he's into you more than you're into him? I got that from him."

I don't say anything in response.

"That you need to be convinced? That he's going to end up convincing you, no matter what you're telling yourself right now?

I let out a breath.

"Exactly." Adam points a finger at me. "That's what I thought. My money's on my boy. But hey, don't tell me what's going on. Who needs details? Surely not his own father. I'm not invasive."

"Right. Calling me in the middle of the night when Blake's not around isn't invasive at all."

He just snorts. "If I were really invasive, I would check the fucking logs. You and Blake are both wearing GPS-enabled devices equipped with 3-axis accelerometers and heart rate monitors. The whole fucking point is that we're supposed to be able to detect exactly what you're doing with every minute of your day. Every ounce of data you generate is getting dumped to Cyclone servers every midnight." He rubs his forehead. "Sometimes I fucking hate myself for believing in privacy."

"But you do," I say to reassure myself.

For a long moment, he looks at me. Then he sighs. "Yeah." He swallows. "Peter Georgiacodis—I don't know if Blake's told you about Peter. But Peter felt very strongly about it. And there was a point, when we first started data collection a few years ago, when Peter told me if I ever used any logs we collected to satisfy my own curiosity, he'd make Blake hack into the server and post my logs for the public, just so I could see how it felt. Peter's...not here anymore, but I think Blake would do it. Just on principle."

"And that's enough to scare you? What would your logs tell us about you?" I ask.

He fixes me with a steely stare. "They'd tell you I have a fucking cold," he says. And then he cuts the connection.

13.

"*I* need another word for devour." Maria is sitting on a stool at the kitchen island, chewing her lip and staring at her laptop.

"Eat?" I suggest.

She waves her hand. "Used it already."

"Bolt? Chew?"

"Something that suggests more carnage."

"Swallow whole?"

She looks up at me. "These are zombies," she says with a toss of her hair. "They don't swallow whole. They tear. They rend—oh, hey, that's it. Rending. Thanks!"

"You're welcome," I say in amusement. "But I thought you were trying to avoid zombies."

She adjusts the glasses that she only uses for reading. "I've given in. I couldn't resist. The math is strained, but at least it's funny. Asteroids next week."

My roommate—housemate, I suppose I should say now that we're no longer sharing rooms—has a secret blog. I have a secret life. Funny how that works out.

"Adam Reynolds called me last night," I say.

She looks up. "Seriously?"

"He thinks I'm dating his son."

"Whoop-te-doo." She rolls her eyes. "*I* think you're dating his son."

I point a finger at her. "Et tu, Maria?"

"I'm just saying. If you're trying not to get hurt, you're doing it wrong. You're still friends. You still care about him. You still do things for each other, and you're still going to hurt when you walk away. It's just that the way you're doing it, you have fewer orgasms."

She raises an eyebrow at me. I have to admit that she has something like a point. Blake isn't *less* under my skin right now because I've managed to keep from kissing him.

"He wanted to know what was going on with Blake."

"Did you tell him to join the club?"

I don't answer this. I keep trying *not* to wonder. The thing is, I know everything's not right. I mean, I'm *here*, in this house, and he is, at the present moment, washing dishes. He hasn't told me what he's looking for, and I suspect he hasn't found it.

But this is ending. At this point, I've written the script for how our relationship will come to an end—literally. I know that a little bit less than three weeks from now, there will no longer be early afternoons spent together going over launch details. There will be no hours where I talk to my mother and try not to worry, no time when he listens to me fret and takes care of things.

"I don't want to talk about Blake," I say. "And you're one to talk about orgasms anyway. You didn't give Hot Tattoo Guy your number."

"Irrelevant." Maria absently types in a sentence. "That has not made him any less instrumental a figure in my orgasms."

There is that. I could respond in kind. I could tell her that I've thought of Blake a little too often, a little too much. But my own fantasies are not ones I want to examine. I imagine myself touching him. Taking off his clothing. I imagine myself going down on him, feeling the hard length of him in my mouth.

It's easier to imagine myself giving than receiving. If I'm giving, I'm still in charge. I'm not vulnerable. If I'm giving, he won't have the chance to break me down the way I know he could. I can't let him in that much, not even in my fantasies.

I shake my head. "I'm going down to see my parents this weekend. I'm going to be leaving Thursday afternoon."

She looks over at me and raises an eyebrow. "Wow. You might not see Blake for three whole days. How will you manage?"

My cheeks flush. She lets out a guffaw.

"He's *coming?*"

"It's complicated."

"Well. *That* will convince everyone he's not your boyfriend."

"I… It's…" I shake my head. "It *will* help, actually. You know what my parents are like. They could drive anyone away. It's all complicated now. I just need to remember…"

Maria is watching me with a flat expression on her face. And that's when I realize what I said.

My parents could drive anyone away.

"No," Maria says quietly. "Not anyone."

I exhale and wish I could take my foot from my mouth. But those words are out there now, no matter what I say. My parents are difficult, embarrassing, impossible even. But they are also my parents, and they've never wanted me to be anything other than myself. By contrast, when Maria told her parents that she was a girl, they kicked her out of the house.

She was twelve.

If her grandmother hadn't taken her in…

If I had been trans instead of Maria, I can imagine how my come-out would have gone. My mother would have been confused as hell. She would have asked me to explain it three or four times, and I'm not sure she would have gotten it even then. But I am sure of one thing: she would still love me. There is one person in this room who knows what it's like to have parents who literally drive others away. It's not me.

"I'm sorry," I say. "That was dumb of me."

She shrugs, but her expression is flat. "It's just a figure of speech. I'm not going to break. I know what you meant."

But the fun has fled the room. We're not talking to each other about boys or making jokes about orgasms any longer. She bends over her laptop and once again applies herself to her blog.

And me?

I have a product launch to work on for a man I shouldn't care about, who isn't here, and who isn't ever going to be my boyfriend. I shake my head and look down at my screen myself.

*I*t turns out that getting to my parents' house is surprisingly easy.

Blake comes up with a great story—we're borrowing a friend's car for the drive. And because it would be completely unbelievable that a friend would let us borrow a brand-new fully tricked-out Tesla, Blake calls his lawyer and arranges for us to pick up a fifteen-year-old Toyota ten miles from my parents' house. This, I point out, is cheating on the trade—but at this point, with the end in sight, neither of us has the heart to care.

I tell my mother when we talk on the phone that he's coming, and no, he's *not* my boyfriend.

"Looking forward to meeting your boyfriend," she says as she hangs up. I can't tell if she doesn't believe me or if she's just teasing.

But all these things feel like details, and distant details at that, as we get in the car and start down.

It's true that Blake has come along to drive. This is necessary because I still can't make myself drive his car at anything other than a crawl.

"Music preferences?" Blake inclines his head to me as we coast out.

"Whatever."

He punches up something on the screen.

"Satellite radio?" I glance over at him. "In this car? Isn't that for peons?"

He smiles. "What am I supposed to listen to instead?"

"I don't know. I don't have that long left to put myself in your shoes. I'm trying to think like a billionaire. I guess I just imagined that you'd hire a team of musical experts to study your tastes, and they would create a never-ending stream of perfect music for you."

"Nah." He shifts his hand on the steering wheel. "That's not how a billionaire thinks. A billionaire hires a team of engineers to interface with a team of musical experts. We study everyone's taste and create a service that automatically creates a never-ending stream of music that automatically tailors itself in response to feedback. Then we sell that service to someone else for a few million bucks. Or we grow it ourselves and get a hundred million people to pay us five dollars a month."

"Oh."

He glances at me. "Hypothetically speaking, of course."

"Don't worry. I won't tell anyone about your secret music business. I signed an NDA, remember?"

"No point pursuing it. Someone else already did it." He grins. "But you know, hiring a team of musical experts to do my bidding… Trust me, it wouldn't work like that. People aren't robots, however much money you have. Whoever I hired would have their own favorite songs, which they would foist on me. When I complained that I hated Rush, or whatever it is that one of them adored, they would get mad. The anger would fester, and then one day, when I was stuck in a car for a six-hour drive, they would send in their resignation and put the Macarena on continuous repeat the entire time. Believe it or not, even billionaires find it easier to treat the people who inhabit their lives like they're actually people instead of machines."

It would be easier if he were an asshole like his dad. This would all be easier. Maybe that's one of the reasons why I asked him to come down with me: because I know that I like him too much. I know I don't want to let him go. And I need to remind myself of the many, many reasons this needs to end when he goes back to Cyclone.

I'm going to get what I need this weekend. I let a few miles slip by.

Finally, I speak again. "Look. I just want to make one thing clear. My parents can be…"

Embarrassing, I think. *Difficult.* But I refuse to be ashamed of them.

"They come from a different culture," I finally say. "There are things Chinese people think are private that Americans don't. And there are things that Americans think are taboo that Chinese people talk about freely. It can be a little jarring."

He's only listened to them on the phone. He has no real idea what's coming. He's driving—a smooth eighty miles an hour, I note with jealousy—but he still glances in my direction.

"Okay," he says. That's it.

"I mean it." I watch the road slip past. "My mom is going to say something that will strike you as off. Don't look at me. Don't act like I should join you in making fun of them later. I'm *not* going to be embarrassed by my parents. I'm proud of them."

"Of course you are," he says.

I try—very hard—not to think of the fact that my mom *still* refers to Bethany from high school as my fat friend. Even when Bethany is around. No matter what I say to her, I cannot convince her that this is not appropriate. My mom *is* embarrassing.

But she's my mom.

And I know that when Blake tells me afterward that she's a little *too* much… I will be able to hold on to that memory. I'll use it to remind myself.

See? We would never have worked.

"Just so we're clear on that." I give him a tight smile.

"Hey." He smiles. "I am one hundred percent onboard for a no-parent-shaming compact. Do you know how embarrassing my dad is?"

"Nice try. I'm sure your parent who features regularly on the news is completely comparable to my outspoken activist Chinese mother."

"Ha. You didn't see him when I was a kid. When I was twelve, my teacher asked my dad to come and talk about what it was like to run a major corporation."

"Just to set the stage, I'm guessing this wasn't a public school?"

"Nope. But my dad being my dad, it took him about thirty seconds to drop an F-bomb. The teacher, of course, interrupted him. And explained that she didn't allow *those words* in her classroom."

"I can imagine that went over really well."

"Your imagination is precisely on point. Dad said, 'Why the fuck not?' And when she tried to explain that the kids had to learn professionalism for their future careers, he came back with, 'Why are you lying to them? Businessmen swear all the fucking time.'"

I can't help but smile at this.

"Of course she got mad. And she told him that swearing was indicative of a lack of creativity. She said that anyone could swear, but it took real imagination to come up with a good insult."

I don't know Adam Reynolds well. But I understand him well enough to know that he's deeply competitive. I wince.

"Naturally," Blake continues, "Dad took this as a personal challenge. And so he asked her for a demonstration. So my poor hapless teacher said, quite primly, 'Well, you could call someone a spitting goat, or say they have a mouth filled with putrescent filth.' Dad nodded along like he was agreeing with her. And he said, 'You mean I could refer to someone who told me not to swear as a wizened fruit or as having the intellectual capacity of a desiccated rabbit corpse.' And of course everyone knew he was talking about her and she got even madder."

"What did she do?"

"Oh, nothing. Because then Dad turned to the class and said, 'Here's the thing. If *spitting goat* is a good insult, isn't *spitting goatfucker* better? And if you're going refer to putrescent filth, shouldn't you take the time to call it putrescent ass-filth?'"

I can just see Blake's dad doing that—looking over the class and growling profanities at twelve-year-old kids with no compunction. I bite back laughter.

Blake sighs. "So imagine how that went over with the other parents. Their kids came home calling each other 'wizened cock-fruit suckers' and 'bastard sons of a desiccated rabbit corpse.'"

I can't help myself. I'm laughing.

"And that is how you came to be looking at the only kid who ever got expelled from Middle Prep because of his dad."

"Seriously? He didn't just pay them off or something?"

"No! That was the worst part. He refused to even try." Blake drops his voice in a gravelly imitation of his dad. "'If those dipshits are so fucking moronic that they're afraid of a few short Anglo-Saxon words, why should I give them good fucking money to teach you?'"

"Okay," I admit. "That is pretty embarrassing."

"He used to do this thing, too, where if he got mad about something I was being taught in school, he'd just show up in class and argue with the teacher. In front of everyone. And they never knew what to do or how to get him to leave them alone, because he was *Adam Reynolds.*"

"Let me guess: Your dad got mad a lot?"

"The worst time was when I was eight and they made us make Mother's Day cards. When my dad found out, he flipped his lid. He went in and..." Blake trails off and looks over at me. "Well, let's just say that one was ugly. I think the teachers all fought just so they wouldn't have me in their classes."

I know the official story of Blake's mother, which is that there is officially no story. The only thing that either Blake or his father have ever said in public is that his mother has never been a part of Blake's life. There's been no explanation why. Blake's Wikipedia page is quite clear—someone went and looked up his birth certificate, and the only parent listed was his father. His mother was listed as *unknown.* How that happens, nobody quite knows. Money, I guess. Lots of it.

"Are you adopted?" I ask.

"Nope." His face doesn't flicker.

"Are you sure? Because I wouldn't put it past your dad not to tell you—"

"First, it wouldn't matter even if I were. But second, aside from the obvious physical resemblance between us, we tested a DNA app a year ago. I am one hundred percent certain that I am my father's biological child. And in case you're wondering, no, I have never wished I had a mother. My dad contributed about three parents' worth of child rearing."

"I know." And, strangely, I do. I'm not even being sarcastic.

"If you're thinking of asking," he says, "I don't even know her name. I'm pretty sure Dad would tell me if I asked. But I haven't." He doesn't look at me. "I don't want him to think that he hasn't been enough for me. So I don't ask."

His hands grip the steering wheel tightly as if he expects some kind of argument.

"Okay," I say to him.

After a long silence, he speaks again. "We all have our limits with our parents. You won't be embarrassed by yours. And I won't ever, *ever* hint, think, or in any other way countenance the implication that I need anyone other than my dad. Because it hurts him. Every single time someone asked in an interview if he'd been thinking of getting me a mother, as if he could just pick one out of a store, every time someone asked how he could possibly do it alone—I could just see him gritting his teeth." Blake lets out a breath. "I don't want to do that to him. That Mother's Day card...I started that one. My teacher told me I had to make a card for my mother, and I refused. She said I should be grateful to the woman who gave birth to me, and I—um—may have thrown a tantrum." He shrugs. "I regret nothing."

I look over at him. "You really love your dad."

"Yes. I'd do anything for him." There's a roughness in his voice. "Doesn't mean he's not embarrassing, though."

We drive for a while longer.

"There is one thing I know about my mother," he finally says. "One thing that is not a part of the public record. And I'll tell you if you promise never to tell anyone."

"Oh my God." I press my fingers against my temples. "You mean nobody except Maria, right? I can tell Maria."

"Not Maria. And you can't ask any questions afterward, either. It's a strict no-discussion item."

I shut my eyes. We don't need more secrets between us, but…I want to know. I want to know too much about Blake Reynolds, and it's not a good idea.

"I promise," I say against my better judgment. "But this better be a good secret, and not something stupid that anyone could infer from genetics."

He smiles. "My dad told me that my mother was the only woman he's ever kissed."

"What!? But—"

"Nope, no questions."

"But—"

"No discussion either."

"That," I say severely, "was rude. *Really* rude."

He glances in my direction. "Okay. Here's one you can tell people."

"About your mother?"

"Kind of. You know how most kids, one of their first words is some variant of mother? Mom. Momma. Something like that."

"I'm guessing that wasn't the case for you."

"Why would you think that?" His eyes are glinting. "Because I don't have a mother? Wrong. Think about my dad. One of my first words was…"

He pauses for dramatic effect, and I have to admit that it works. I lean toward him.

"It was motherfucker."

I laugh.

He sighs. "Dad was so proud."

"That's good, but it still doesn't make up for what you said before. That was a good secret," I admit. "A really good secret. I'm trying to figure out how to pay you back for that."

"I'm sure you'll think of something."

"Unlikely," I say with a sigh. "My mother tells everyone *everything*. There are no secrets."

---

*M*y parents live on the second floor of a concrete three-story apartment building in the middle of Rosemead. Despite my brave words to Blake earlier, I'm all too aware as we pull into the parking lot how my home must appear to him.

Browning weeds poke up through cracks in the asphalt; a crushed beer can decorates the gravel to the side. The sun is setting, giving color to an otherwise nondescript rusting car from decades past, propped up on cinder blocks in the parking lot. I've never seen Blake's childhood home, but I can imagine. It's nothing like this.

I shake my head. Screw this. I'm not dating him. We're just friends—temporary friends at that—and three years from now, when he's running Cyclone, he won't remember this trip.

He puts the loaner car we picked up twenty minutes ago into park and pops the trunk.

"Well?" He smiles at me.

I smile back, but my expression feels like a tense, coiled thing, ready to spring out of alignment at the slightest provocation.

Before I can say anything, the door to my parents' apartment bursts open. My little sister darts out, and she dashes down the concrete stairs.

"Tina, Tina!" She cannons into me; I grab hold of her. We squeeze each other hard. She's getting so big now—she's just an inch shorter than I am—and she hugs my breath out.

"Stop," I croak. "Mayday, mayday!"

"I'm so glad you're here. Can you tell Mom that I am *too* old enough to go to a coed sleepover?"

I give her a once-over. "Sure," I say, "as long as the parents kick it off by caponizing all the boys."

Beside me, Blake chokes.

"What's caponizing?"

"Removing the testicles," I say. "It improves the temperament of the male animal. Try it sometime."

Blake clears his throat.

"Oh," I say. "Mayday, this is Blake Rivers."

We've agreed—and by *we've agreed* I mean *I've insisted*—that we won't give his real name. No point opening that door. Mom is bad enough when she thinks he doesn't have any money. I can't imagine what it would be like if she knew the truth.

"Blake, this is my little sister. Her name is Mabel, but I call her anything that starts with an M. Mayday, Maple, and Muggle are my favorites."

She wrinkles her nose at Blake. "You can call me Mabel." Mabel purses her lips and looks at Blake. Blake looks right back at her. Some people say that Mabel and I look alike, and I guess we do, in the most superficial sense. We're both Chinese. But Mabel's hair is short and dyed blue, and she wears it pulled over her eyes. Her eyes are set more narrowly than mine. And—this is really unfair, but I swear I am not bitter about this—she is thirteen and she's already in B-cups. Which, ahem. Is more than I will ever manage.

Mabel shrugs. "Hi Blake. You're the guy who is definitely *not* Tina's boyfriend."

Blake shifts the shoulder strap of his bag. "One of many, I presume."

"Nope." Mabel twirls away. "You're the only one. The rest of the boys aren't dating her."

"Oh, well," Blake says vaguely. "That is an important distinction."

I try to jab my elbow into his side, but he sidles away.

"And you're the only one she talks about like this: 'Mom, he's *not* my boyfriend.'"

Oh, that imitation. It's just a little too spot-on. I raise a finger at her, but she twirls away before I can get her back.

"Come on. Mom is cooking. This is the first time you've brought a boyfriend home from college."

"He's not my—" I stop, because my sister's lips are twitching.

"Fine." I pick up my own bag.

"Lay on, Macduff," Blake says.

Mabel stops and turns to him. "Hey. Only Tina can call me M-words other than Mabel."

"Sorry."

"Tina and her boyfriend," she corrects. "So you're okay. I guess."

"*Mabel.*"

My sister grins and clambers up the stairs.

14.

*M*abel wasn't kidding when she said my mother was cooking. Most of the time, my dad cooks. He's actually pretty good, so that's not a problem. My mother only cooks on special occasions, and this, apparently, is a special occasion.

Her cooking style can best be described as eclectic. If I were being generous, I'd call her style "Asian fusion." But that usually evokes the marriage of delicate Asian-inspired flavors with classical French technique. Mom's food is more like…Asian Frankenstein: Chinese peasant food stitched together into a meal with boxes of random crap from the 99-cent store.

As an example, there's a dish of lion's head meatballs, huge round hunks of ground meat bigger than my fist. But instead of serving it in a traditional broth with thinly sliced vegetables, Mom has paired it with Hamburger Helper stroganoff and chopped-up celery. There's a casserole of canned green beans, oyster sauce, and crisped rice noodles. And there's a dish of stir-fried vegetables, toasted almonds, and tater tots.

"It only looks horrifying," I whisper to Blake. "It's actually really good."

My mom takes one look at Blake, shakes her head, and heaps food on his plate. "You," she tells him, before they've even been introduced, "need to eat more."

She doesn't—thank God—tease him about being my boyfriend. Yet.

"So, Blake," my father asks as we sit around the table on an eclectic mixture of chairs and stools. "What are you studying?"

Of my parents, my dad is better at small talk, at putting people at ease.

"Economics," Blake says.

"What do you plan to do after school? Go into business?"

Before Blake can answer, my mother interrupts. "Business school is a waste of money. Do you know how much it is now? Fifty thousand a year. At least. And not so many jobs anymore."

Blake's eyes dance. "Funny. My dad says the exact same thing."

"He must be a smart man. What does your dad do? Tina never told me."

Blake glances at me. "Computer repair."

Luckily, nobody asks further questions. "And your mom?"

Blake clears his throat. "She's not with us."

I remember the conversation Blake and I had on the way down and tense. I can only imagine what my mother will say.

But my mother just smiles brilliantly. "That's good! Too many boys your age get spoiled by their mothers. They don't know how to cook, how to do laundry. Tina is going to be a busy doctor. She'll need someone to do all that for her. Better if you're not used to having someone else take care of you."

I sink down in my seat. Blake is trying not to smile, but he's not quite successful. "That's probably true, Mrs. Chen, but Tina and I are just friends."

It is obvious from the glances my parents exchange that nobody at this table believes that. Not my dad, who smiles beatifically, the way he does whenever he traps someone into a corner. Not my mom, who's shaking her head. And definitely not Mabel, who snickers.

Possibly not even me.

"Eat more," my mom advises Blake. "You're too skinny."

"Mom."

"What?" She turns to me.

"Be polite. Please?"

"How is that rude? It's just the truth. He has eyes; he knows he's too skinny. And he's not eating anything at all." She tsks.

Blake, obligingly, takes a bite of Hamburger Helper. I'm not sure if he's ever had Hamburger Helper in his life. Well, tough. Too bad. He has now.

"Better," my mom says. "Good thing he's *not* your boyfriend, though, Tina. He's so skinny, I think a condom would pop right off."

Oh my God. She did not say that. My whole body flushes in a wave of heat.

"*Mom,*" I mutter in a low voice. "Please."

"Better make him wear two," she continues merrily. "Just in case."

I hide my face in my hands. "Gah." It's the only word I can manage.

I want to crawl under the table and take up permanent residence. If I did, at least it would distract my mom.

And that's when Blake starts laughing. Not just chuckling, but full-on belly laughing. He's laughing so hard he starts to choke; my dad thumps him on the back, and he coughs.

"I'm sorry," he finally gasps. "It's just—on the way down, Tina gave me this huge lecture about how she refused to be embarrassed by you guys. There was this whole spiel about how there were cultural differences and just because you said things that were unusual by American standards, that didn't make them wrong. She said that she refused to feel badly about it, so I was just going to have to adjust."

"Rub it in, why don't you?" I mutter.

"Sorry, Tina." Blake pats my shoulder. "But—this one is all you."

"That's not a cultural difference," my dad interjects. "Everyone thought Hongmei was inappropriate in China, too."

"Yeah," Mabel chimes in. "Dad embarrasses me in front of my friends at school. But Mom embarrasses me *everywhere*. It's not a Chinese thing."

"It is one of my many talents," my mother says with a modest smile. "I put sand in everyone's oysters."

"That's what Tina says," Blake says. "So tell me about Jimmy Ma. What's he up for?"

The appeal we've come down to see is the perfect topic of conversation. My mom loves talking about her...work? Her hobby? I don't know how to think of it. She jumps right in. Blake listens and nods.

And me? Once I get over that flushed, heated embarrassment, I realize that things are worse now, not better. Blake is kind of perfect—drawing my mother out into the most animated version of herself, bringing my father into the conversation, even getting Mabel to talk about music and how she wishes she had her own saxophone. This, I remind myself, is media training in action.

I have to stop lying to myself. It's more than media training. Blake's always been easygoing. Hell, I've seen his comments on scripts going back a full decade now. He was like this at eleven: complimentary, interested, kind without being weak. He's probably been serving as his father's foil his entire life. His father growls about manufacturing and secrecy; Blake learns Mandarin and compliments the factory owner on the side. His father says that an idea is shit; Blake comes back and points out the good in it. This is what he does: he smoothes things over. He's so good that Mom doesn't even notice that he's eating only a fraction of the food on his plate. I wonder if it's always like this for him, if he's always fixing things while nobody notices him.

He passes on the day-old Walmart cupcakes that Mom has brought home for dessert, and offers to do the dishes afterward.

I help him. We work in silence—mostly. But at the end, when he's drying glasses, when my parents are watching TV in the other room, he leans toward me.

"For the record," he says, "you should stop worrying. Your parents are awesome."

I didn't want to be embarrassed by my parents…but maybe I did. I wanted to watch him not fit in so that I could remember that he *doesn't* fit in. But it's becoming harder and harder to remember that.

There's just one reason to keep him at arm's length now: He's leaving. We're over before we ever started.

"Thanks," I say.

"Also for the record," he says, "no, I wouldn't need two condoms."

I flush all over again, but this time it's in heated memory. I've felt him, after all. I've been on top of him. I know precisely how thick he is, how long his erection is.

"I remember." My mouth is dry. I don't want to look at him.

But he brushes a strand of hair away from my face, and involuntarily, I look up. I don't know what I'm seeing in his eyes now. Something raw and hungry.

Or maybe I'm just seeing a reflection of my own want.

"Good," he says. "Keep on remembering."

BLAKE

The Chens' apartment is small: two bedrooms, a dining/living room, and a kitchen just off it. It's cozy, and it feels lived in. By the various decorations on the wall, lined deep, and the layered bric-a-brac covering the shelves, it feels like they've lived here at least a decade.

It's Friday morning. Tina has gone off with her mother to the hearing. Her father, pleading knee pain, has stayed behind. And because I suspect that Tina wants time to talk with her mother without me around, I claim that I have homework to finish.

After about an hour of playing around with a textbook, however, I stop pretending to work. And when Mr. Chen invites me to join him on the couch in front of the television, I do.

The windows are open, and light spills into the living room. It's as tidy as any cluttered room can be, filled with knickknacks ranging from the expected (some thick red vases adorned with white cherry blossoms, which I guess are Chinese in origin) to the inexplicable (a plastic, moving clock-slash-telephone featuring Felix the Cat, whose tail ticks the seconds away).

Mr. Chen grunts as I gingerly seat myself on the opposite side of the couch from him.

Some people—like my father, for instance—are loud news watchers. They yell out insults anytime they disagree with anyone, and growl anytime someone is wrong—which, according to my dad, is usually everyone all the time.

By contrast, Mr. Chen seems abnormally quiet. "Hmm," he says in response to a discussion on the volatility of oil prices. "Hmm" is also his only commentary on some ongoing protests in New York. When the news engages four pundits in a back-and-forth discussion on the prospects of a presidential hopeful, he listens quietly, shaking his head. At the end, he delivers his longest comment yet: "Hmmmm."

I wait until a commercial comes on before I try to engage him in conversation. "Do you enjoy watching the news?"

He looks over at me. For a second, I think he's going to say, "Hmm." Instead, he shrugs. "Yes. If they don't say anything stupid. Today, not so much."

"Is the news much like this in China?"

He mulls this over. "I don't think so," he says. "But if it was, I wouldn't know. We didn't have a television." He smiles. "I watch a lot of television now."

"Just news, or everything else?"

"Everything. I like MTV. Basketball. I really like football."

"Did you learn about football when you moved here, or were you a fan before?"

"I learned when we came over." He has less of an accent than Tina's mother—maybe because he watches so much television. There's a glint in his eye. "I had to learn. All my favorite TV shows would get... What's the word? Ah, preempted. Yes, preempted by football. So I learned."

"Who do you root for?"

He shrugs. "I always want the Rams to win."

I glance sideways, but he doesn't seem to be joking about this. Maybe he's just naturally stoic.

"And you?" he asks politely.

"I'm a 49ers fan."

"Of course." He smiles at this. "You spent your whole life in Palo Alto. That's natural."

"Yeah. Although that's not the only reason..." I stop suddenly. We talked about my major. We talked about my fake version of Dad's job last night. We didn't talk about where I lived, and most of what Tina has said about me to her parents is that I'm not her boyfriend.

The news starts again, and he leans forward, focusing on the screen. For the next few moments, he doesn't say anything. It shouldn't feel this awkward to sit and watch television in silence. I shift in my seat, trying to get comfortable, but there's nothing physical about my unease. For some reason, Mr. Chen makes me nervous. I look across the room, making eye contact with Felix the Cat. The plastic sculpture rolls its eyes at me and waves its tail. Maybe it's a cultural thing.

"So," Mr. Chen says at the next commercial break, "does Tina know your father is one of the richest men in the world, or are you only lying to us?" His tone is utterly calm.

My throat grows dry. I glance over at him and lick my lips.

He doesn't look angry or mean; he's watching me with his head cocked, as if my answer is about as interesting as our small talk about the news.

"Tina knows," I croak.

"That's okay, then." He leans back.

I still can't tell if he's serious or sarcastic. He's smiling just a little bit, but there's a sharpness to his eyes. "How did you know?"

He smiles. "I told you already. I watch a lot of TV." He doesn't say anything more, and after the silence stretches on and on, into the next commercial break, I realize that he's finished with the subject.

Tina told me once that people underestimate her father. I suspect I just did, too. He's quiet and soft-spoken. He watches MTV, for God's sake. I had kind of thought that Tina got her backbone from her mother.

Somehow, I'd missed the fact that her father had withstood three months of torture by the Chinese government.

"I'm sorry we didn't tell you," I try again. "This whole thing is complicated and my dad and I are...even more complicated at the moment. Tina and I decided it would be easier to not go into too many details."

"Lying to me is easy because you don't think you'll see me again," he says with a nod. "Don't worry. I don't mind."

I'm fumbling for an answer that doesn't sound completely awful, when he shakes his head.

"I can tell it was Tina's idea anyway."

I pull back. "Don't blame her. If I tell a lie, I'll take responsibility for it."

"I'm not blaming anyone. Things are complicated for her."

"It isn't Tina's fault," I tell him. "And it's complicated for me, too. If I had my way, Blake Reynolds would completely disappear."

I hadn't expected to say that. He looks at me. His eyes are wide, one eyebrow cocked. I know how stupid it sounds. I know that if I tried to explain why I wanted out of my life, he would think I was spoiled.

And—with more than a month of living Tina's life behind me—at this point, I realize that I probably am.

But he only says one thing. "Hmm."

The tinny sound of the chipper news anchor is no longer a welcome distraction. It makes me feel almost sick to my stomach. I *am* spoiled for not wanting that burden on my shoulders.

I've been trying not to think about it, but now it sinks in. I'm taking over for my dad in a matter of weeks, and I'm not strong enough. I know it, deep in my bones. When I fail, the whole world will be watching. My failure will be documented in books, academic articles, and derivative shareholder suits.

God, this is such a fucking mess.

"Things are complicated," Mr. Chen says. "People always jump to conclusions. People think I don't understand English because I don't speak loudly. They see my lucky leg and think I have a bad life." He smiles faintly. "I try not to conclude too much too early."

I turn back to Mr. Chen. "Are you being ironic when you call it your lucky leg?"

"No." But instead of smiling, his face goes blank. His eyes shift inward. "Of course not."

"Then why…?"

"When I came to America, there was another man who came with me. Chun Donghai. He also practiced Falun Gong, and was also in the same reeducation camp as me. We both left China at the same time."

I fold my hands and wait for him to continue.

"We both filed paperwork for asylum. We even had the same lawyer. When it was my turn, the man who heard my story believed me when I said I was tortured in China. After all, I had proof it happened." He points to his leg. "So my family stayed. Donghai went back to China."

I swallow.

"I call it my lucky leg as a reminder. Every time I tell myself 'if only,' I know the answer. If only I hadn't been injured, I would have been deported. If only I had a different leg, my wife would have been sent for reeducation and she would have been…" He pauses, picking among words. "Killed," he finally settles on. "Probably. Without my lucky leg, I wouldn't have a second daughter, and Xingjuan would have quit school at sixteen and worked in a factory, just like I did." He looks up at me. "So yes, I think it's a lucky leg. Do you disagree?"

I envy him his certainty. If only my dad didn't run Cyclone. The last few months have been nothing but a giant *if only*. And the main thing I've learned is that there is no escape. There are no pat realizations to be had, no giant handoffs.

"Sounds lucky to me."

"Yes." He turns back to the television. "You see, it helps me remember that there is one place I most want to be, one time of my life I most yearn for."

There is no end to my father's ambition. Whatever it is he wants, he lays out a plan and grabs it, and once he has hold of it, the only thing he can think about is the thing that is next on the horizon. If Dad heard Mr. Chen talk, he'd call it a load of crap—"bullshit hippy happiness," he'd say, something I've heard so much it's like Dad is here, rolling his eyes himself. I'm sure that whatever Mr. Chen wants, whatever place he imagines, it's somewhere tranquil somewhere like the restful retreats that my father's doctor is always suggesting.

Dad tried one once. He made it two hours before he left and went rock climbing.

"Where do you imagine yourself?" I ask.

Mr. Chen simply gestures to the room around him— to the plastic flowers, the wall hangings, to Felix the Cat swinging his tail with every second. "Where else?"

TINA

*A*fter the hearing in the courtroom, the families come together in the parking lot just outside the courthouse. They chatter and talk. It has been a while since I accompanied my mother to a gathering, and I'm immediately reminded why that is.

My mother doesn't boast about her children directly in company. That would be gauche. Instead, she practices the indirect boast/insult.

"Ah," my mother says to Mrs. Ma. "Lucky you that Annie is so consistent in school. My Mabel is all over the place. She never remembers anything except saxophone and band all the time. Practice, practice, practice—all we ever hear about is practice." Of course she doesn't mention that Annie had one ignominious piano recital years ago and has never played again.

"You're so lucky," my mother says to Mrs. Chan, "that Tommy is staying at home for school. He's there for you for support. Tina is always gone, studying to be a doctor. It's hard on me."

I stand under a cluster of palm trees, fixing my gaze on the Spanish-style courthouse beyond. If I don't react, maybe it won't hurt.

Or, my favorite: "You're so lucky to have a grandchild so early. I wish Tina had a baby at nineteen. But she isn't even dating the nice boy she brought home. Oh, yes, he's okay for a white boy. He even speaks Mandarin." My mother shakes her head sadly. "And he's going to walk away. Sometimes I think that Tina is missing out on life."

That's the one that really sinks under my skin. I make my excuses and go wait for her in the car. It's stupid to let myself get upset about things like this. I know that to Western ears the practice sounds a lot ruder, a lot more passive-aggressive, than it really is. This is my mother's way of telling everyone how proud she is of me, of boasting without really boasting. But I can't help it. I *am* westernized, and there's enough truth in those backhanded compliments that it stings.

Tina works so hard; she never has time for me.

Tina is missing out on life; she isn't even dating that nice boy.

It hurts. It really hurts. I'm here, aren't I?

My mother comes back to the car thirty minutes later, beaming and happy, filled with all the latest gossip. I'm reining my emotion in as best as I can.

"You shouldn't have left so early," my mom says as she pulls out of the lot. "You're so serious. Why don't you ever have any fun?"

"I don't know," I snap back. "Why do *you* think I never have any fun? Maybe it's because I'm the only one who has any sense of responsibility in this family."

Mom goes silent. The light turns green, but she's a few seconds too slow, and she misses her turn onto the freeway despite the angry honking of the cars behind us. "What do you mean?"

"You don't pay the electric bill," I say. "You barely make rent. Every month, it's one thing after another. You don't get Mabel's meds, you don't see a doctor until everything is at its worst. You don't take anything seriously and so *I* have to do it instead. Why do you think

I'm working all the time? It's not because I love work so much. It's because you can't afford for me to stop."

"Tina…"

But now that I've started, I can't seem to stop talking. "Do you think I *want* to be a doctor? I don't really care. But I have to do something to take care of you guys. All I want is to not worry."

Her face sets in grim lines—furrowed forehead, flattened lips.

"I wish I was fun, too," I tell her. "I wish that I *could* just forget myself and have fun with Blake. But I can't, and it's your fault. You take care of everyone but yourself, and *I'm* the one who has to clean up your mess."

My mom looks straight ahead. "I didn't know you felt that way. How was I supposed to know? You never said anything like this before."

"I don't know," I snap. "You know what everyone else needs. It's just your own daughter you never pay attention to."

She sighs. "I never asked you to do any of those things. I thought you wanted to help."

I bite back tears. I do. I did. But I also sometimes wish that I was allowed to need her instead. I wish that it was just help, that I didn't resent her as much as I loved her. I wish I could let myself relax instead of worrying, that I could stop being the responsible one. But I'm the only one who is responsible. I can't stop. We can't trade places, she and I, because everything would fall apart. But I'm not going to get my wish. And worst of all, more money hasn't made it hurt less. I still worry.

"Never mind, Ma," I say, my throat raspy. "Forget I said anything."

But she just sits straight in her seat. "I can't forget," she says stiffly. "I don't forget. You should know this about me already."

15.

TINA

I don't think the rest of the weekend could get any worse, but it does. When I ask Mabel how much a saxophone of her own would cost—as compared to the dented one she has on loan from the school—my mother interrupts me.

"That's not your worry," she says. "It's *my* worry."

Blake is still barely eating my mother's food, even though he does a valiant job of moving it around on his plate.

My fight with my mom infects everything. I thought it would be better if she didn't embarrass me, but it's not. She's silent, and that cold silence cuts more deeply than any embarrassment.

I try to apologize to her on Sunday morning before we leave.

"Did you mean it?" she asks.

And—because I did—I pause.

She shakes her head. "Don't say sorry, then, when you're not."

By the time I get in the car with Blake, I'm not sure if I'm relieved to be leaving this mess behind me or if I'm heartbroken that I've fucked things up so badly with my mom. I wait until we swap our loaned Toyota for his Tesla.

"We should stop and have lunch," I say. "And breakfast. You must be starving."

He's driving when I say this. I can see his face go still. His fingers close on the wheel.

"I'm not hungry." His tone is casual, but there's a tightness to his face. "Your mother fed me really, really well."

"Come on, Blake," I say. "You don't need to lie to me. I was watching you the entire weekend. You ate about as much as I did, and you're a foot taller than me."

"I'm not a foot taller than you."

"Nine inches. Whatever. And Dad says you went on a two-hour run on Friday when we were at the hearing. It's okay. You're not going to offend me if you don't like my mother's cooking. It's an acquired taste."

"There was nothing wrong with your mother's food," he says quietly.

"Oh, so you eat like that all the time?" I say sarcastically.

This is met with silence. His jaw sets. I rummage through my memory, looking for evidence that he's lying. But what I remember instead is…

Blake at our first lunch together, eating a handful of bean sprouts. Blake at lunch with his father, taking a spoonful of rice and some dal. Blake telling me he won't let me cook for him because it would be cheating. I can remember him eating apples occasionally. And… And…

"Oh my God," I say, this time with no sarcasm at all. "You eat like that all the time."

His eyes stare ahead. His face is too still.

"Blake…"

I look over at him.

He exhales.

"Blake. Are you okay?"

For a long moment, he doesn't say anything. He just drives, his jaw set in a hard line.

"No." When he finally speaks, his voice is hoarse. "No. I don't think that I am." His hand opens on the wheel and then clenches once more. "I have a problem. I've been…trying to fix it, but that hasn't really worked." He lets out a long breath.

"Does anyone know?"

"You."

There are now only two weeks until the launch. Two weeks and then I walk away. I'm not supposed to care about him.

Not caring, not worrying—these are not things I can do on command. And I've been lying to myself, pretending that it will be bearable to watch him walk away. No. Here's one thing that will hurt more: knowing that I had the chance to make him feel a little better, and I chose not to.

"I know." He swallows. "It's stupid. It's so fucking stupid, I'm mad at myself. I know it's stupid. I know I'm stupid. How hard is it to fucking eat more?" His voice is shaking. "But I don't. I can't. And when I try, when I make myself—I end up going out for a run."

"You need to talk to someone about this," I say.

"I should be able to fix this myself. Dad thinks I can run a company. I can't even fucking control myself."

"Blake. It's okay."

He shakes his head. "No. It's not. You know what? That day in class—that day you got so mad at me? Afterward, you said you didn't have time for my bullshit apology. And I was so fucking jealous. I wanted to not have time for my bullshit, either."

"Hey." I reach over and take his hand.

"You were right," he says shakily. "I thought your life would be magic. Like it would somehow make this better. That if I just had what you had, I wouldn't...do this. But we've never traded, not really. None of this has done a damned thing. It's not my life that's fucked-up. It's me."

I don't want to care. I don't want to hurt because he hurts. But here I am, caring anyway, and it scares me. It scares me, but still, I squeeze his hand. He glances down, as if realizing for the first time that I'm touching him. That our fingers are intertwined. That the current of electricity is arcing between us uninterrupted.

And then he lifts his head and truly looks at me. There's a raw hunger in him, something bigger than what he's just admitted.

There's a lot of truth in what my mother told me. I *don't* let myself have fun. I pull away from people who could be my friends. I refuse to let people help me. And right now, I realize that Blake and I have a lot in common—a lot more than either of us can admit.

"Do you remember when you told me that you'd bought something ridiculously luxurious, and it was a mango?" he asks. "I was so fucking jealous of you. I wished that I could feel what that was like. I wanted to want something like that. I wanted to have that so badly."

I don't have answers to any of his problems. I don't even have solutions to mine. But this one thing? This, I can handle. "Come on," I say. "Let's get some mangoes."

We pull off the freeway a few miles later and follow the computer's directions to a little grocery store. Fifteen minutes later, we're sitting in a rest stop, cutting our mangoes to bits.

"Here," I tell him. "Trade me. Pretend you're me. Let me tell you what it was like when I had that mango."

He shuts his eyes obligingly.

"I didn't have a lot of money," I tell him. "And that meant one thing and one thing only—fried rice."

He smiles despite himself. "Kind of a stereotype, don't you think?"

"Whose stereotype? Rice is peasant food for more than half the world. It's easy. It's cheap. You can dress it up with a lot of other things. A little bit of onion, a bag of frozen carrots and peas. A carton of eggs. With enough rice, that can last you basically forever. It does for some people."

"It actually sounds good."

"If you have a decent underlying spice cabinet, you can break up the monotony a little. Fried rice with soy sauce one day. Spicy rice the next. And then curry rice. You can fool your tongue indefinitely. You can't fool your body. You start craving."

He's sitting on the picnic table, his eyes shut.

"For me, the thing I start craving first is greens. Lettuce. Pea shoots. Anything that isn't coming out of a bag of frozen veggies. And fruit. If you have an extra dollar or two, you buy apples and eat them in quarters, dividing them throughout the day."

I slide next to him on the table. The sun is warm around us.

"But you get sick of apples, too, pretty soon. And so that's where I want you to imagine yourself: sick to death of fried rice. No respite. No letting up. And then suddenly, one day, someone hands you a debit card and says, 'Hey. Here's fifteen thousand dollars.' No, I'm not going to buy a stupid purse. I'm going to buy this."

I hold up a piece of mango to his lips. He opens his mouth and the fruit slides in. His lips close on my fingers like a kiss, and I can't bring myself to draw away. He's warmer than the sun, and I feel myself getting pulled in, closer and closer.

"Oh, God." He doesn't open his eyes. "That's so good."

I feed him another slice, golden and dripping juice.

"That's what it feels like," I tell him. "Like there's a deep-seated need, something in my bones, something missing. And then you take a bite and there's an explosion of flavor, something bigger than just the taste buds screaming, yes, yes, *this* is what I need."

I hand him another piece of mango. He bites it in half, chews, and then takes the other half.

"That's what it felt like," I say. "It felt like I'd been starving myself. Like I…"

He opens his eyes and looks at me.

"Like there was something I needed," I say softly. "Something I've needed deep down. Something I've been denying myself because I can't let myself want it." My voice trails off.

I'm not describing the taste of mango anymore. My whole body yearns for his. For this thing I've been denying myself. For physical affection. For our bodies joined. For his arms around me all night.

It's going to hurt when he walks away.

But you know what?

It'll hurt more if he walks away and we leave things like this, desperate and wanting, incomplete.

My voice drops. "It's like there's someone I've been denying myself. All this time."

"Yes." His voice is hoarse in response. "That. Always that." And he slides his arm around me, pulls me close, and kisses me. He tastes sweet like mango. Like he's bigger than my taste buds, like he's precisely the luxury I have been craving. I let my eyes shut and tilt my head back, falling into his embrace.

And I know, despite all the constellations placed in the sky as warning, why all those Greek maidens gave it up in the end. It's because all the pain is worth it for this one moment.

His tongue is sure against mine, touching me with insistent strokes. His hand clamps around me, holding me in place. And he holds me like I matter, like I'm the entire world.

"I can't touch you," I say. "My hands are sticky."

"That," he says, "is what washing machines are for." He reaches out and takes hold of my fingers and then, very deliberately, he wipes them on his shirt. The sun is hot against my shoulders; Blake is sweet to the taste and tempting to the touch.

I'm not sure how long we stay there, kissing in the sun and the wind, stopping only long enough to feed each other bites of fruit. Long enough for me to touch him all over, to feel his body hard and lean through his shirt. Long enough for me to lose all sense of safety.

The air smells of new beginnings—crisp and clear, untouched by any worries. He touches me like the middle of the story, strong and sure. But despite the mango on his tongue, he tastes almost bittersweet, because the end is coming. It's coming, but it's not here. Not yet.

"Let's get home," I tell him. "Let's go home and find a bed."

I won't be home until tomorrow morning, I text Maria as we turn up the freeway heading back to campus.

The answer comes back shortly. *Something wrong?*

I glance over at Blake. He's driving. For the first time in…I'm not sure how long, he looks completely calm. As if he's finally in place.

And for all the turmoil I feel inside, I sense it, too. That hint of calmness, as if in a sea of things that have gone wrong, this one thing is right.

Nothing, I text back. *I just realized you were right.*

<3! She sends back.

And for now, that's exactly what this is. A little texted heart, two characters. Fragile and all too breakable.

16.

BLAKE

We don't talk much on the remainder of the drive back. This thing between us is too new to be pinned down with words. But it's contained in the feel of her hand on my thigh as we drive. The squeeze of her fingers on mine. It's the look in her eyes, every time I glance her way—liquid, alight, as if she's filled with the luminous light of a thousand stars.

It's beautiful and unsettling all at once, because I know how she feels about constellations.

By unspoken consent, I go straight to the converted garage. She gets out when I do and comes to stand by me.

"Hi, Tina." Somehow, the moment seems to stretch. I pull her close, let her body fold into mine. She comes, molding against me. She told me once our lives fit together as well as Legos and puzzle pieces, but our bodies have no such problem. We work together.

I want her. I want *this*. Her voice is a low, sensual caress, and I'm on fire, burning for her.

She looks up at me. "Blake…"

I set a finger on her lips. Not to silence her; to feel them, soft against my skin. To sense the warmth of her breath so that when she says yes, I'll capture the feel of it on the palm of my hand. I imagine, briefly, that I can catch hold of it and keep it. Maybe if I do, I'll be able to pin it down.

"Why are we still outside?" she asks.

"Because." I take her hand in mine. "Your pulse is racing. Your hands are shaking. I want you to feel safe."

"Nothing is safe anymore." But her hand squeezes mine. "I thought I could avoid getting hurt. I thought I could avoid caring. But I can't."

She sets her other hand on my chest.

I wish I could lie to her. I wish I could tell her that this is nothing, that she'll never be hurt. I wish I could say that even though I'm going to take over for my dad in two weeks, we can still be something.

But I remember Peter's funeral all too well: the crowds. And yet…not one person from outside work. I don't even think I'll be able to hold on to *myself* when I go back. I can't promise to hold on to her.

"How can I make this better for you?" I ask.

Her hand slides down my chest. "This is going to hurt no matter what we do. It's never going to be safe. But maybe we can have something. A memory that we can keep safe, no matter what happens."

"I don't want a memory," I tell her. "I want the whole damned two weeks."

I want more than that. I want so much.

Her hand slips down another inch. Her finger bisects my chest, cleaving a line through my abs. She hooks it in the waistband of my jeans and pulls me closer.

"If we start now," she says in a low voice, "it can be two weeks and eight hours."

The night seems very dark despite the lamp lighting the street. I can hear the weeds in the empty lot rustle on a night breeze. All my senses are catching fire. The sensation of her hand, warm against my skin, inches from my groin. I slide my arm around her, pulling her close to me for a hard kiss. Her lips open to mine.

And then there is no night. There is no lamp. There are no weeds to rustle. There's just me and her and this shattering kiss. There's only our hands, wrapping around each other, touching, wanting. Our bodies, closing the distance.

She doesn't uncurl her finger from my jeans; instead, she undoes the fastening. She takes hold of the zipper.

"I'm undoing this on the count of three," she says. "So if we're not inside by then…"

I pick her up. She lets out a little gasp, but leans against me. Her weight is welcome. It's wanted.

"One," she says.

I take her across the street.

"Two."

At least she's counting slowly. I struggle with the gate. We pass the clothesline strung in the backyard, laden with shapes that are indecipherable in the dark.

"Three."

True to her word, she's unzipped my jeans by the time I've managed to unlock the door. By the time we're inside, shutting the door, her hands are on my bare hips, sliding under my boxers.

"Tina. Wait."

I can't see her face in the dark.

"Two weeks," she says. "And eight hours. I don't know what I've been waiting for." And she gets on her knees. She pulls down my boxers, and takes me in her mouth.

I go from semi-erect to sledgehammer hard in the space of a few seconds. Her mouth is fucking hot; her hands slide up my thighs. She teases me with her tongue, tracing the head of my penis, then taking my full length again.

"Holy fucking shit." My hands tangle in her hair. "Tina. Jesus."

She pulls away briefly. "Don't tell me to slow down." Her voice is shaking. "I want to do this." And then her mouth is on me, hot, sending pleasure shivering up my spine.

"I want to do things, too," I growl.

In answer, her lips press around my length. The pressure intensifies. It's so good, it takes control of me. My hips flex of their own accord. My hands tangle in her hair. My whole body tightens, tensing. I can't take much more of this, not without blowing my load. And as much as I want that...

It takes an act of willpower to set my hands on her shoulders, to step away.

She looks up at me. She's on her knees in front of me. My eyes are adjusting to the dim light filtering in through the windows.

"Tina." My voice is a growl. "Do I get to touch you back?"

Her hands clench on my thighs.

"It's easier this way. If I don't have to..."

"Be vulnerable?"

I can hear her exhale. "If I don't have to admit that I am vulnerable." But she looks up, and then, very slowly, she stands. "But I am." Her voice is low. "I am, Blake."

"Hey." I touch her lips. "You're not alone."

She reaches out and takes my hands. "Nothing is safe," she says, and slowly, she stands. She puts my hands on her. She slides them under her shirt, and my fingers find her skin, warm and soft and inviting.

"Bullshit," I say softly. "After all this time? You know how I feel. You know what I want. Maybe the rest of the world is dangerous to us. But you? Me?" I run my hands up her ribs. Her bra is soft and silky to my touch. Her nipples make hard dots against the fabric. She shivers, and I can feel her body tense all over. And then she relaxes, melting into my touch. Letting me stroke those hard points, letting that sensual desire coil between us.

"You know the truth," I say. "We're not dangerous, not to each other."

She lets out a breath. "Not for the next two weeks and eight hours."

And then we're kissing again, lips melting into each other in the dark, hands fumbling with clothing. I pull her shirt over her head. Her bra follows next. I take one of her nipples in my mouth, nibbling on it, licking. Feeling her whole body flush with warm pleasure. She lets out little gasps.

She lets me undo her jeans, and then takes my hands in hers and guides them between her legs.

Touching her, sliding my fingers through her folds in the dark, discovering the slick feel of her desire, is everything. She lets me slip a finger inside her, lets me feel the heat of her clamped around me. Then she takes my other hand and shows me where to touch her—right there, lightly brushing that hard bundle of nerves. She shows me how to make her breath catch, how to make her body writhe, how to make her throw her head back.

She shows me all the ways she's vulnerable to me.

There's a condom in my wallet. I tilt the face into the moonlight spilling through the windows, long enough to check the date briefly—it's still good—before handing it over to her.

She opens the packet and then slowly unrolls it down my length. Her fingers are warm against me, so good.

"I want you so much," I say.

She looks up at me. "Come and have me."

I pull her onto the bed with me and kiss her. She's naked against my skin; her body presses against mine. She undoes the last buttons of my shirt, pulling it off, and then there's nothing between us at all. Nothing but the heat of her breath—and then, as I take her mouth with mine, nothing at all. We're skin to skin, our bodies pressed together. She wraps a leg around me, exposing her core.

She's wet, so fucking wet. And after all this time, it's easy, so easy, to adjust myself, to slide into her inch by heated inch. To claim her body as her hands drift to my chest.

She does something with her muscles, squeezing my cock, and I let out a breath.

And then I do what she showed me—finding that rhythm of my body, that spot she responded to. I want her to know that everything she gives me, everything we have… I'll never use it to hurt her.

I try to take it slow. But when I get it right, the response is electric. There's this one angle—I hit it, and she lets her breath out. Her body tenses around mine and her hips rise.

"There," she says. "That's it." And we're both lost in the slide of flesh, the give and take. The harder I go, the more she responds, until she's gasping, until I can hardly breathe, either. Until we're both nothing but flames. Her body clenches hard around mine. She lets out a little noise and then a longer moan. I let everything go—every worry, every unfulfilled lust, every last desire. I come hard, pumping into her, and she holds me.

"*Y*ou have a tattoo," I say to her.

Half an hour later, after a little cleanup, we're still naked. We're still touching each other because I can't get enough of the feel of her. We're still kissing, long and slow. We're just recharging temporarily.

And she does have a tattoo—a little molecule on her left ankle.

"I got it a year ago," she says. "Maria and I have matching tattoos. We got them after we got through organic together."

Funny that there's still so much I don't know about her. Funny that I want to know it all, to fit it into one night together. Funny that we're not talking about the things that matter, even though we are.

"Is Maria premed too? I didn't realize that."

"Nope. She tapped out after organic. She said it was too much boring memorization for her. So she decided to be an actuary instead."

"Words that have never before been spoken: 'Organic chemistry is too boring; let's become actuaries.'"

Tina touches my shoulder and lets her hand fall down my arm. "So what about yours? When did you get it?"

"When I was eighteen." I turn my arm to show her. "If you pop open a first-generation Cyclone Tempest and take out the shielding plate, this is what you'll find. Magnified by about a thousand percent. It was the first product I really worked on."

"So you designed this?" Her fingers trace the circuitry.

"Nope. My input is higher level than circuit design. But I got this to remind myself that wherever I go, whatever I do, Cyclone will always be under my skin."

My voice falls. I'm not sure how to go forward from here. I'm not sure how to face what comes after these two weeks. Cyclone is in me—but knowing I have to go back makes me feel restless even now.

She must feel my body tense beside her, must know the direction of my thoughts.

"Blake. Just because we're not talking about how fucked-up this is doesn't mean it's not fucked-up."

"I know."

She turns to me. "I don't know if I should be shoving chocolate bars on you or getting you a feeding tube. I'm completely unqualified to deal with this."

It takes me a moment to respond. "I haven't exactly managed to deal with it well, either. When I came up with the circumference scrolling solution for Fernanda, it took me months. We looked at hundreds of possibilities. We'd actually decided on something else. And then I just had this idea when I was driving after a run—it just popped into my head. I thought this would be like that time. That if I got far enough away, I'd just figure it out one day."

"Not all problems get solved in an instant of understanding. This is completely over my head."

"I know." I take her hand. "Just... Don't let go of me yet, okay? I have two weeks. That's all I can ask for."

Her fingers squeeze mine. "I think you should see someone."

A sudden panic takes me. "Ah, well," I joke. "Since I have five dollars and sixteen cents, that's not exactly happening right now."

"Blake." She sits up. "No."

I'm not looking at her. "We had an agreement. A deal. If I break it, this ends *now*, not just two weeks from now. Besides, I don't have time to see anyone. Mr. Zhen is counting on me."

"*Blake.*" She turns to me and puts her hand on my chest. "Don't you *dare* use me as an excuse to avoid getting help."

I shut my eyes. That's exactly what this is: an excuse. There's another reason I've never wanted to see anyone. How could I look my father in the eyes, knowing that I'm keeping this from him, and yet telling a stranger? If I find a therapist, it'll be real. Right now? Right now, at least I can pretend. I can pretend it's a distant visitor, hanging out at my place for a short spell, but one who will be leaving any day.

My heart is beating hard against her palm. But she reaches up with her other hand and turns me so I'm looking in her eyes.

All along, deep down, part of me thought that if we ever got to this place—if Tina ever found out what was truly, deeply, most screwed up about me—that she'd know that our lives aren't any different. Mine's not any harder or easier than hers. Everyone has problems.

And this is the moment when I realize that's complete shit. Yeah, everyone has problems. Somewhere else on this planet, there is someone just like me— someone who's fucked-up and confused and who doesn't want to tell anyone. Someone who needs help. Someone who wants out of his head. And the only difference between me and him is that I have the money to do something about it.

There never has been a trade. I've never been able to give away pieces of myself. I carry them all with me no matter what path I take.

"I don't know what is going on with you," Tina says, "but I think anyone who can do this…" She runs her finger down my tattoo. "…Can do this." She sets her finger on my forehead.

And maybe that's what I needed to hear, because this time when I kiss her, there's no urgency. No overwhelming need. For now, there's no danger. There's just me and her. Just a silent stillness, a space where there's room for both of us.

17.

It takes three days, but I do it.

First, I tell Mr. Zhen that I have to quit. He sighs heavily, and tells me to come back and say hi anytime I have a chance. And then he calls one of the twenty applications he's been storing and replaces me in fifteen minutes.

I find someone who specializes in athletes who have eating disorders. I call. We set up an appointment. I go to her office and shake her hand and sit in the comfortable chair in front of her desk. By the time I'm sitting there, I must have had this conversation with her a million times in my head.

"Hi," I tell her.

She doesn't act like she knows all about me, even though she probably does. She doesn't raise an eyebrow. She just folds her hands and tells me about patient-client confidentiality. And then, even though I already filled out a lengthy intake form, she asks me, "So, Blake. Why are you here?"

I take a deep breath. "I'm here," I say, "because I have a problem."

By the end of the day, I don't just have a therapist. I have a nutritionist. A food diary. And I have something else from her: a promise that this has happened to other people, but that they have gotten better.

For the first time, when I tell myself that I have a problem but that I'm going to fix it, I believe it.

TINA

I try to call my mother. I figure that I can tell her that Blake's my boyfriend now, that she was right and I was wrong. I want it to be an olive branch. Something to try to put us back where we used to be.

But she's stiff and formal when she answers the phone.

"Tina." Her voice sounds disapproving.

"Hi, Ma. How are things going?"

"Well," she says. "Very well."

"How is work?"

"Fine," she says. "No need for you to worry about it, okay?"

I exhale. "And is everything okay otherwise?"

"There's nothing for you to do," she says stiffly. "I'm responsible for myself. So don't worry. Go be a student."

I hang up, dissatisfied. Isn't that what I wanted? For her to take care of herself? For me to not have to worry?

I pull up the utilities website anyway. But when I try to log in, an error message appears. *Email and/or password is invalid or incorrect,* the site tells me in red letters.

I try again, and then again. But I can't get in. My mother has changed the password, locking me out.

I never realized that the thing I most wanted would feel like a slap in the face.

"*I* think I'm dating Blake." I set the plates on the kitchen table later that night. It's a dark glass table, round, big enough for two. It's not dark yet, but the sun is beginning to set over the Bay, coloring the view with hints of pink and purple. Dinner tonight is simple—rice, steamed fish, spicy green beans—but the scent of sesame oil and fresh ginger, combined with a generous handful of cilantro, still feels luxurious to me.

Maria does not look surprised by this revelation. Instead she pulls her plate toward her. "Duh."

"No, I mean…" I fumble for words. "I don't think we're just hooking up, okay? I think we're dating."

Whatever that magical division is between having sex and having a relationship, we crossed it. We crossed it a long time ago; I just wasn't willing to admit it. And more than anything else, that scares me.

"I'm sorry," Maria says. "Am I supposed to be shocked?"

"Yes. You could at least pretend."

She turns to me and widens her eyes. "Oh my God, you're dating Blake Reynolds? How is that even possible? It seems so *unlikely*, what with you two lusting after each other and spending all that time in each other's company. I would never have imagined it, *especially* after you spent an entire weekend with him and then boned him all night.

Who would have thought that two people in their early twenties would have functional hormones?"

"I think you could be more sarcastic."

"You're right." She eats a forkful of fish. "Let me try harder. To think that this happened on a college campus, of all places. Nobody *ever* gets horny in college. I'm shocked. This is my shocked face." She gestures to her nose with her chopsticks. Unsurprisingly, her shocked face looks dryly amused.

I throw a green bean at her.

"Show-off." She frowns. "You know I can't throw with chopsticks."

"I'm being serious," I say. "I'm dating Blake Reynolds and I'm freaking out here. We don't make any sense. This is going to be over in a little more than a week, and what am I doing? I'm letting myself get all wound up in him. It's getting worse."

"Okay," Maria says with a roll of her eyes, "is there a real reason this is going to be over in a week, or is that just dramatics on your part?"

He's going back to his father's company in a week. He won't have time for me. He won't be here. I look over at Maria—and I realize that this is not yet public information. Dating Blake Reynolds, absurdly wealthy college student, is ridiculous. The prospect of dating Blake Reynolds, interim CEO of Cyclone Systems, is unfathomable.

"Okay," I say. "Remember how I had to sign a huge stack of papers to get Cyclone prototypes? I have this vague memory of something that said something like, 'WARNING: YOUR CONDUCT IS BLAH BLAH LAW BLAH BLAH SOMETHING SOMETHING

TWENTY YEARS OF JAIL.' This is the point in the conversation where I think I need to talk to a lawyer before I tell you anything." I don't know what constitutes material, nonpublic information, but the fact that a twenty-three-year old is about to take over for his father is probably material. And it's certainly not public.

Her eyes widen.

I spread my hands. "*Now* do you understand why I'm freaking out? I'm dating a guy where, if I tell you what's going on, I might go to *jail*. His family puts their private business up for public consumption to sell products. Tell me honestly, Maria. Do you think this is going to last?"

She blows out a breath. But she doesn't answer. She doesn't have to.

Some things are obvious from the start. I knew this; I knew I had to protect myself.

I didn't. And the fact that I know that this will hurt Blake as much as it hurts me? It doesn't make me feel better. Not one bit.

BLAKE

*H*ope is a curious thing.

Sometimes, the reason you can't figure out the solution to your problem is that your problem and your solution are all tangled up, knitted together so firmly that you can't excise the problem without blowing the solution to bits.

It's exactly five days before the launch when I figure this out. My therapist asks me the one question I don't want to answer. I look into her eyes and I know—I *know*—why this is a problem, and why I've been so stymied. I know why I haven't been able to find the answer.

I go to Tina's afterward. My house, I suppose, although I don't know what it is anymore. She waves at me when I come in. She lets me kiss her. And then she goes back to reading over the launch script one last time. I can see it over her shoulder. I've read it myself a dozen times now.

All this time I've been telling myself I can find a solution, that now that I'm seeing someone, I can fake it once I get back. I've been telling myself that I can actually be the person that my dad needs me to be and still not disappear. I've even been telling myself that maybe I'll figure this out—figure out how to keep Tina, too.

Tina reaches out and makes a tiny change to the script. I put my hand on top of hers.

"Hey," I say.

She looks up. "What's going on?"

"There's something I need to tell you."

For a second, her eyes widen. She moves back, ever so subtly.

"It's about Peter."

"Peter Georgiacodis?"

At this point, she's read every launch script. I don't know how much she's managed to infer. His comments are all over the scripts before his death. She's seen our last launch. She knows—she has to know—that he wasn't just a coworker. That he mattered to me, to Dad.

I sit down next to her. "I must have met him for the first time when I was a kid, even though I don't remember it. I don't remember when he started meaning so much. Maybe it was because he never suggested to Dad that I should be in daycare instead of wandering around a major corporation. Maybe it was because he was always there. He would stop whatever he was doing to walk me through my algebra homework when my dad didn't know the answers. It's fucked-up, I guess, to say that one of the most important people in my life was my dad's CFO. But…he was."

She looks over at me. "There's nothing fucked-up about love."

"No?" I can't even look at her now. "Do you know what it's like to run a place like Cyclone? Peter and my dad… I can't even guess how much time they spent working. Eighty, hundred-hour weeks, again and again without ending. Year after year. Peter was the strongest person I knew. He was the only person who could make my dad back down when he was wrong. Peter was twenty-eight when he took over as CFO." I take a deep breath. "He died of a heart attack at forty-five."

"I know." She stands up and runs a hand down my shoulder. "I know, Blake."

"Since then, even my dad has begun to lose it. He doesn't say it, but I know it. There's only so much he can take." I look over at Tina. "If this broke Peter, if it's breaking my dad… What chance do I have?"

She doesn't say anything.

"All this time, I've been telling myself that once I fix this little problem, once I figure out why I'm so fucked-up, I'm going back. I'm taking over. I'm going to be there for my dad. But that's why it's not going away. Because I can't let myself go back." Every time. Every time I thought it was going so well. Every time, I'd talk to my dad, and he'd tell me to come back, and it would all get fucked-up again. "If I take over," I tell her, "I really will be killing myself. At least this way, I choose how I go."

She folds her arm around me and pulls me close. It's fucked-up. I know it's fucked-up.

Tina inhales. "Blake. You have to tell your father."

"I know," I say. I've never wanted to tell him the truth I've known deep down: that I'm not the person he thinks I am. That I can't do this. "I know."

---

*T*ry to tell him. Really, I do. I plan out what I'm going to say. I write it out. I visualize it. I use every trick my therapist has to get me ready to deliver.

But there's no time. When I call my dad a few days before the launch, he looks...relaxed, for the first time in months. That edgy energy, crackling around him, has subsided into almost softness.

"Hey, Dad."

"Hi, Blake." He smiles at me. "How are you doing? Enjoying your last few days of freedom?"

I can't make myself smile at that. I can't make myself joke. I just look in his eyes. I've imagined telling him a thousand times: *Dad, I have a problem. Dad, we need to talk.*

But he's smiling, really smiling. I haven't seen him smile like this since Peter passed away. "You know, Blake," he says quietly, "I'm proud of you."

That's the thing. If Vader had really raised Luke Skywalker, this would be the moment when he could have asked anything of his son, and Luke would have done it. No questions asked.

"I know." My throat hurts.

"I'm proud of you for telling me to go to hell because you wanted to go to school," he says. "I'm proud of everything you've done. I'm proud of the launch you've come up with. And I'm really proud of Fernanda. She's going to make a huge splash. The media is going crazy with speculation."

"I know," I say.

"I just wanted to say that. I'm proud of you, asshole."

It's all I've ever wanted. And maybe that's why I can't make myself say it. *Dad, I have a problem.*

I don't want him to know. I don't want him ever to doubt me. I'm stuck between two things I cannot do, and in the end, my dad's strength of will is going to win out.

"You're going to kick everyone's ass," he says. "Hell. Maybe I won't bother coming back at all."

I manage a smile.

And as soon as I cut the video, I go for a run.

When I come back, Tina doesn't ask me what I was thinking. She doesn't berate me. She doesn't tell me I'm an idiot. She doesn't say any of the things that I'm thinking to myself.

She doesn't even look at me, as if she knows our time is already over and she's just waiting it out. She bends over her laptop, frowning at the launch script.

I'm losing everything.

I slide by her into the shower. I'm marshaling my arguments, getting everything in order. *We're good together,* I should tell her. *I'm only fucked-up half the time. Chances like this don't come along very often, and I'm not about to give this one up. Don't make me lose you, too.*

The soapsuds sting my eyes. I can't tell my father what I need to say. Maybe I can tell her.

But when I come out of the shower, she's sitting cross-legged on the bed. She's wearing yoga pants, and she's holding a single sheet of paper.

"I have something for you," she says.

"What's going on?"

"Your life." She swallows. "You promised me we'd trade lives through the launch, right? That means your life is still mine for the next two days. And I've realized the launch is completely wrong." Her chin goes up. "The Adam and Blake show is not what it needs to be. You want a true construct? To hell with everything I've written so far."

She hands over the paper. "I don't have a whole lot yet. This isn't a script. But what I do have starts like this."

I take the paper from her hands.

She's right. This isn't a script. It's a single line of dialogue.

Blake: Dad, I can't take over for you. I have a problem.

Fuck. I can't breathe. I can't do this. I can't say those words to him.

But Tina taps her watch as I'm struggling. I don't know who she could be calling—not at first, not until the person on the other end answers.

"Hi, Tina," my father says, as if they video chat all the time.

"Adam." Tina doesn't look at her screen. She looks at me. "We need to come down the night before the launch. Blake needs to talk to you."

Dad pauses. When he speaks again, his voice is low. "Is this urgent?"

"It is," Tina says calmly. "It's going to take a little time, too."

And this is my dad, so he doesn't question. He doesn't complain. He doesn't say that the night before a launch is always taken up with a thousand little details, all of which require his attention. He doesn't ask to reschedule. He just says, "Fine. I'll make it happen."

"Thanks." She pauses. "Asshole."

"Ha. He told you about that?" My dad laughs. "God, I corrupted such a nice kid."

"Shut up, Adam. We'll see you tomorrow." She cuts the connection. "There." She presses her lips together and looks at me.

I should be mad. I should tell her she has no right to interfere. And I would—except that what I feel is not anger, but the complete absence of weight. For the first time in a year, I'm experiencing the unbearable feeling of *not* being crushed, of seeing a light at the end of the tunnel.

It's dim, but I can see it. If I can tell my father the truth, I can tell her. There are a lot of things Tina and I haven't said to each other. With the end of the relationship assumed, there's no point in saying them. But there are a lot of ways that you say you care about a person. And that? That was definitely one of them.

I take her head in my hands and kiss her.

I don't know what she's thinking. I don't know what she's feeling as our hands caress each other, as we strip to nothing. As she climbs on top of me.

I can only guess from the clench of her fingers on my shoulders, from the catch of her breath, from the way she looks at me.

From the bedroom window, I can see the scattered grid of the city lights below. They spill out onto bridges, stretch into distant buildings across the water.

She takes me and I hold her. I pour out everything into her. And I think about the stars.

18.

*M*y father has conquered the world.

It's all I can think about when he hugs me at the door. He's conquered the world and I'm not even master of myself.

"Hey," he says roughly, punching me on the shoulder. "It's good to see you."

He won't be saying that for long. I punch him back. "Good to see you, too."

I know my dad loves me. I know he's proud of what I've done. I know he thinks the world of me—and I know I'm not worth a quarter of the value he's assigned to me. But somehow, I manage to operate on autopilot. I joke. I shove him out of the way. I let him and Tina carry the conversation, and I remark that whatever it is in the oven smells good.

"It should," Dad says smugly. "I had Fred make your favorite."

It's easy to fall into our old routines, even with Tina here. It's like nothing is wrong, and I almost want to keep up the pretense forever. Almost.

I'm setting plates and forks on the table. Tina is shuffling through cabinets, finding glasses. Dad takes a dish out of the oven, looking surprisingly domestic with a cherry-red oven mitt. He sets it on the counter, a polished black marble that could double as a mirror, and then spoons pork, apples, and shredded, buttered Brussels sprouts onto plates. It smells amazing, and I can't do this. I can't sit here. I can't eat. I can't tell him.

He's as neat as ever, fastidiously wiping up a drop of gravy the instant it hits the counter, rinsing out the dish and setting it in the dishwasher, putting the oven mitt back in place. I've missed him so much.

And yet, if I could, I would walk out the door and just leave. But Tina takes my hand, as if she knows I want to escape, and she anchors me.

She pins me back to reality: I can't let tomorrow happen. I can't take over for him. I'm about to let him down—but I have to do it.

I find napkins and fold them under the silverware. Dad brings over three plates, balancing them like a waiter.

We have no ceremony. Dad sets the plates down. "Eat," he directs.

Tina glances at me, but she sits.

I can't eat. My throat is dry. The back of my throat tickles with incipient nausea. My hands curl.

"Dad."

He pauses, fork halfway to his mouth. That was the easiest word. I can say that and still not spill my secrets.

But I take a deep breath and force the issue. "We have to change the back end of the launch." I don't know how I'm managing to get these words out, but they're coming. "I can't take over for you."

I brace myself for the coming storm. Sometimes employees joke that Dad named the company *Cyclone* because he's like a tornado: You never know where he's going to land or how much damage he'll do. He might rip the entire house off its foundation. He might leave a feather untouched on a windowsill.

I don't know what will happen.

Dad slowly sets down his fork. It's coming. I can feel it coming. It would be okay if he just yelled at me. That, I could stand. But once I tell him the truth, once he knows how weak I am, how fucking ridiculous this is…

"What's going on?" His voice is quiet.

I spread my hands. "I can't do it." I won't even look at him. "I keep thinking about…Peter."

His nostrils widen and he glances at Tina.

"Peter was the strongest person I knew aside from you. But *he* couldn't do it. And you can't do it. And you're both stronger than me."

He makes a disapproving noise. "You're stronger than you think," he says.

It won't be over until I say it. "Dad." I take a deep breath. I feel raw all over, like I've been dragged through gravel naked. "I'm not." The words I've imagined saying for so long slide out. "I have a problem."

I feel like I've entered dreamspace. I'm light-headed.

"Go ahead, Blake." My dad's voice is even. "It's okay."

It's not okay. It's so not okay. After this, after he knows he can't rely on me, it's never going to be okay again. That thing my dad and I have… I'm about to break it for good.

"What kind of problem?" he asks.

And I make myself look into his eyes across the table. I make myself stone inside. I may be weak, but I can be strong enough to tell him.

"I have an eating disorder."

He lets out a long breath. His hand clenches on the tabletop.

"It's complicated," I say. "I run too much. I'm not eating enough. If you want to read more about it…"

"Fuck." The word out of his mouth is almost a primal growl, and I flinch away. "Fuck," he repeats.

But I can't stop talking now. "I'm going to be okay," I say. "Eventually. I'm seeing someone." I can't look away from his eyes, no matter how much I want to. "I have a nutritionist. There hasn't been any permanent damage. But I need to get away from everything that sets me off until it's better. And—I'm sorry. I never wanted to let you down. But I can't do this. Cyclone makes it worse."

Dad pushes his chair back from the table and looks up at the ceiling. His face is white, and I can see all the lines that age has left in his visage. They seem suddenly dark and deep.

"Fuck," he says for a third time.

"I'm sorry," I say again.

He slams his fists on the table. "Fuck me."

"I know I'm leaving a hole in the launch," I say. "I know my timing couldn't be worse. I'm sorry. And I know this just makes it worse for you. I've been telling myself I can do this for weeks. But I can't. I just…can't." I start to stand up.

Dad points a finger at me. "Sit the fuck down, Blake. Sit down and eat." His pointing finger falls slowly, clenching back into a fist. "Shit. You've been telling me for months and months that you can't do this, and did I listen? No. I was so fucking self-centered that I never let it register. I didn't see it." His voice is shaking.

"I wanted to be someone you could rely on," I say. "I wanted it so badly. I'm just not. I'm sorry, Dad."

"Why the fuck are *you* sorry?" He looks at me. "Goddammit, I know I'm an asshole. But I never, ever wanted to be an asshole to you. It's just… I've been stuck in my head, seeing only my own shit this whole time." He inhales. "No. No excuses." He stands and crosses over to me. "Blake. I'm so sorry. I never, ever wanted to…"

He bows his head and clears his throat.

And that's when I realize he's choking back tears. My dad. I've only seen him cry once before in my life, and that was horrifying.

"I should have realized," he says in a low voice. "I failed you."

I thought nothing could hurt worse than my dad being disappointed in me. But he looks ravaged right now.

It turns out I was wrong. There is one thing that's worse: the look on his face when he's disappointed in himself.

I stand up. "No." I put my hand on his shoulder. "Don't you dare. You've been the best dad I could have asked for. It's not your fault. I didn't want to tell you. I just didn't want to disappoint you."

He puts his arm around me, pulling me close. "Never," he whispers. "Never, ever, *ever,* Blake. I'm proud of you. Now and always."

"Don't fucking lie to me."

"Hell. You think I'm lying? It took me until I was fifty to realize I needed to get out. You figured it out at twenty-three. Good for you."

He squeezes me hard and I squeeze him back. We hug each other like we're afraid to let go. I'm afraid that if I look at him, this will all disappear.

"What are we going to do?" I finally ask.

He sighs. "Well. Let's break this down. I obviously have to rethink tomorrow."

"You mean, *we* have to—"

He holds up a hand. "Not your worry now, Blake. I've got it."

He says it so calmly, so precisely, that I know it's true. He's got it.

"But—"

"This is why God invented caffeine," he says. "Don't worry. I've made bigger changes on less notice. Only wusses need twenty-four hours to craft a major international announcement. I'll manage this one."

"But—"

"But for now…" He gestures to the table. "For now we're going to sit. And we're going to eat. And we're going to have a normal fucking conversation like a normal goddamned family. Because I'm still trying to convince Tina I'm not a complete fucking barbarian."

"Give it up," Tina says. "It will never happen. I know too much about you."

Dad sits. He picks up his fork again. "Tina. Did you—were you—" He stops short, shaking his head. "Never mind. Stupid question. It's obvious you knew. And that you helped him…get here." He picks up his fork, cuts off a piece of the roasted tenderloin. "Thank you."

That's all we say about it for the rest of dinner. Dad tells a story about a hilarious translation issue that arose in our Singapore office, and we all laugh—a little too hard, more than the story deserves, as if the universe has earned our mirth. As if we've had one too-close escape, and we have to smile in the teeth of the future that could have been.

The food has grown cold, but I don't pause between bites. I don't have to ask myself if I want this food to turn into me. For the first time in months, I know the answer.

I don't want to vanish. It's going to be okay.

I look over at Tina, and I let myself feel all the wistfulness that I've been harboring. God, I just want it *all* to be okay.

TINA

After dinner with Blake's dad, after a leisurely dessert and coffee where we sit in the living room and Adam Reynolds tells me stories about Blake that embarrass him, but which I can't help but find adorable—Blake stands.

"Still have something you want to show Tina tonight?" Adam asks.

Blake glances in my direction. "Yep."

Adam waves a hand. "You kids have fun."

"Are you sure? Because I can—"

"Fuck off, Blake." He says it with a smile. "Seriously. I can handle this. I'll have it figured out by midnight, tops."

"Well, then. Wait here, Tina."

Blake disappears. I glance at Adam, who shrugs as if to say that he has no idea what his son is up to. I don't either. We had agreed that once Blake took over at Cyclone, this would end. Now he's not going back, and I suddenly don't know what we are. *Where* we are. I don't even know what I want to happen. The future is an unknown, looming frighteningly over us.

When Blake returns, he has our coats. He hands me mine, takes my hand. "Come on."

He leads me outside. Blake's father's house is near the top of a hill in a wealthy residential neighborhood. Palatial houses with wide windows line the streets, separated by fancy gates and stone walls. It's dark out, but the night is lit by the golden glimmer of street lamps, of welcoming windows shedding warmth onto dark asphalt. Indirect lights catch the curve of a neighbor's statuary, illuminating a dark silhouette corkscrewing up to the sky. Little LEDs embedded in walkways down the street scatter their own warm glow.

"Where are we going?"

"We're going to look at constellations," Blake says. He takes my hand and starts to walk down the road.

"That sounds…" Awful. I glance at him. But I already know what he's going to say. I can almost imagine.

He doesn't want this to end. He's scoured Greek mythology and found me the one tale out of a thousand that doesn't end in girls being turned into trees or chained to rocks. He's going to show me *that* constellation, as if it will make everything better.

In other words, he wants to sell me a lottery ticket—and I'm so crazy about him at this point that I might be stupid enough to buy it at these long odds.

But instead of getting in his car, Blake starts walking down the street.

"We're not driving?"

"Nope."

I don't know what we are. I don't know what will happen. But I know one thing: For tonight, we're still together. And so I take his hand and I follow him.

"Are you honestly expecting to see anything?" I look up. A thready overhang of clouds shifts dark blue against the heavens. That close cloud cover makes patches of dark against darker. Even in those spots where the night sky comes through, I can't see any stars.

The swiftly moving, blinking lights of an airplane. A bright glow that's almost certainly a satellite. Maybe a few dim pinpricks that might be from another galaxy.

"I think there's too much light pollution."

"Oh ye of little faith." He just keeps walking. The street twists and turns, undulating with the contours of the land. A patch of darkness opens to my right—a park, I see, as we come closer and the shapes of picnic tables resolve themselves.

He enters and pats a picnic table. "Come here."

I sit, and he slides next to me, putting his arm around me.

"There. You see?" He gestures with his arm.

The view *is* magnificent, even at night. From this hill, the signs of civilization are spread out before us—streets, houses, laid out in a net of sparkling lights, interrupted by the dark emptiness that is the Bay.

"It's beautiful," I say, "but I think I can see exactly one star."

"I never promised you stars. I promised you constellations."

I don't know what he means until he points down, to the right. "There. You see that, right there? That round thing and those things coming off it?"

I examine the twinkling lights. "Is that a stadium?"

"No," he says with mock solemnity. "That's Grood the zombie, the mightiest of all his kind. He ruled this place once, eating the brains of all who dared defy him. But one day, Pebble, the giant centipede, dared defy him. Long did they battle. Epic was their fight."

I tilt my head toward him. "Reversed was their word order." But my heart has begun to thump.

"Reversed word order is a time-honored storytelling device that makes everything sound more epic." Blake's fingers twine with mine.

"I see." I squeeze his hand back. "Then apologetic am I for interrupting."

"When Grood finally slew Pebble with a shard of bone, loud were the shrieks of the many-legged worm. But Pebble had managed to lash him with his tentacles—"

"I thought he was a centipede. Where did he get tentacles?"

"The tentacle store. Stop interrupting."

"Sorry." I subside and lean against him.

"As everyone knows, no venom is more fatal than the poison let off by the razor-suckered tentacles of a mighty worm."

"Wait. How can everyone know that if he got his tentacles from a store? Is this a tentacle store with only one kind of tentacle? What is the point of having a tentacle store without a diverse selection?"

Blake sighs. "You know what you are?" He hasn't let go of me. "You're a story interrupter. A no-good, dirty…"

He pauses, and his voice deepens. "...sexy, clever, amazing story interrupter."

"I'm sorry," I say in a smaller voice. "I'm sensing a real market opportunity here in the tentacle-selling retail world. That's all. Carry on."

It's more than that, though. I'm afraid to let him tell his own stories. I'm afraid to write mine.

"As I was saying, the zombie got smacked with venomous tentacles. I mean, smacked was Grood with tentacles of venom. Even as Pebble lashed the earth in his death throes, Grood knew he could not last. So he drove his shard of bone deep into the earth, deep into the marrow of time itself, thus pinning himself and Pebble in a timeless struggle. Now, every night, they battle it out."

I look at the lights he's indicating.

"Before you ask me about that," Blake says, "yes, if you puncture the earth's crust deep enough, you do find a store of time. Not magma. That's a myth started by the great geology conspiracy. And before you start making snarky comments about how companies are going to start mining it and using it, I want to point out that Cyclone is already doing just that. How do you think we stay ahead?"

I take a breath. He doesn't tell me why he's telling me this story. He doesn't have to. My mouth feels dry. "Sounds legit." I try to sound unaffected. "It's not any less plausible an explanation than a hunter and a scorpion."

"Precisely. It's like they always say. Never let a little thing like light pollution stop you from finding constellations."

"They always say that?"

"No?" He glances over at me. "Then what do they always say? You tell me."

I want to believe. I want to think that there are other stories. I want to believe that we could be one.

I take a deep breath and then I point, far out over the water, to the lights of the Dumbarton Bridge.

"There," I say. "That's Ling-ling. She's a dragon. Many years ago, she made a bargain with the residents of the land."

"You need to say 'a bargain she made.'"

I bat at his hand. "Am I telling the story or are you? I'll let you know when we get to the epic part."

"Sorry. Back to the bargain."

"She would carry them on her back for a period of fifteen years. But if anyone forgot the end of the contract and crossed after the bargain ended, that person she would devour."

"Do Chinese dragons even eat people?"

"She lives in the Bay Area," I say severely. "She eats a Westernized diet."

"Good point."

"In any event, Ling-ling fell in love with a college student named Kenesha Walters. Kenesha's mother crossed the bridge with her daughter every day, and when Kenesha graduated, she started working at the same place as her mother. Ling-ling can't bear to be parted from her love, so for now she stays in place. But one day, Kenesha is going to find a job closer to home. And then, Ling-ling will feast."

"I love it." He turns to me. My body hums as he slides his arm around me. And then, very slowly, very methodically, he sets his lips on mine. There are no stars, not a single one visible. Still, I can feel the light of constellations, of things born out of our imagination. Of epic fights to the death. Of a dragon-love so powerful that it transcends species and time.

His kiss makes me think that this can be real, that we could be a story. His hands come around me, sliding underneath my T-shirt to hook under my belt. We could be there, two lovers set in the constellations below us.

Tina and Blake, placed by the gods in lights, constantly reaching for each other and never quite touching.

"That's just the thing," he says. "Maybe all the stories have been written about the stars. Fuck the stars, then. They're light years away, and they don't give a shit."

We're touching now. His hands are warm against my skin; his lips devour mine. I run my fingers down his chest, past his waist, letting them rest on hard thighs. I disappear into his kiss. Into the give and take, the cycle of tongue and breath. He lights me up, setting me ablaze until I'm breathing hard. Until my hands brush the hard rod of his erection through his jeans.

His breath breaks. "God, Tina." His hands slide up my ribs, the fingers of his right hand brushing against my breast—lightly at first, and then with more fervor.

"This can be anything we make it," he says.

There's no relief, not from the want that floods me. I want him—his body—hard inside me. But I want more than that. I want this evening, all of it. I want to forget how close we are to the end. I shut my eyes and kiss him harder.

He takes a fistful of my shirt in his hand and pulls me on top of him. Our lips meet, hungry.

"Want to go back?"

"Your dad. Is your room soundproofed?"

"Actually, no. But he'll be occupied. And he won't hear a thing, so long as we're quiet." He finds my mouth again, kissing me hard.

I pull away breathlessly. "Is that a challenge?"

Blake considers this. "Hell, yes. It is."

And then we're going back, running in the dark, pelting through the front door. A light to the left signifies that his dad is still working even though it's now past midnight, past the time he predicted he'd finish—but Blake doesn't call out in greeting. Instead, he grabs my hand and leads me up the stairs. He stops halfway, pressing me into the wall and kissing me harder. His hands clench around my hips; I can feel him hard against my belly.

I'm not sure how we manage to make it to his room, but as soon as we're in, we're kicking off shoes. As soon as mine are gone, Blake grabs hold of my jeans by the belt buckle. He undoes it and then slowly, slowly, slides my pants down.

Before I can even think to return the favor, he pushes me onto the bed.

"Remember," he growls, "we have to keep it quiet."

Then he's over me, spreading my legs wide, settling his face between my thighs. Licking me. After more than a week together, he knows exactly what I want him to do with his tongue. Where to go. How to hesitate just long enough for the anticipation to build—and how to surge forward. I have to grit my teeth not to moan aloud.

He's relentless and I'm so close to the edge. I slide my fingers through his hair, guiding, urging him on. I'm close, so close. Pleasure sweeps in, so undeniable. When I come, my hands clench against his scalp. I grit my teeth to keep from crying out, and the orgasm goes on and on and on in endless surges. And when the tide finally recedes, Blake lifts his head.

He gives me a self-satisfied grin. "My turn."

"My second turn," I tell him.

"That's what I said." He strips off his jeans and underwear in one smooth motion. His shirt comes off. He pulls me to my feet and takes off my shirt, undoes my bra.

Then he kisses me. We're naked, skin to skin, and I can taste myself on his lips. I should be boneless with pleasure, but I can feel my desire rising.

His has already risen. I run my fingers down his length, feeling him, listening to the change of his breath. God, I'm going to miss this. I'm going to miss this so much. I'm feeling too much, too much more than just the physical. Blake is an ache deep inside me.

"On all fours," he whispers in my ear, and I comply.

I hear the wrinkle of a condom wrapper, feel his hands on my hips. Then there's the brush of him against me from behind and the swell of want. He enters me, hard and sweet. I bite my lip, refusing to cry out.

"God, Tina." His hand rests against my behind. "God. This is so fucking good."

It's more than good. I can feel every stroke of him against my sensitive flesh, can feel the tension in his body as his thighs slap against mine. I take him, feeling him in me. Feeling the tide rise in both of us. My orgasm rises as his does; I crest just before he does. My throat feels hoarse from the effort of *not* screaming.

And then his thrusts get harder, firmer, faster. I feel a burst of heat as he comes, and I'm so sensitive by now that I moan.

He laughs. He's breathing hard.

He pulls out. I turn to look at him—at his wide, blue eyes, his hair, tousled by my hands. I try. I try so hard not to care, not to want, not to love.

It's too late. I've been lying to myself for weeks.

God, this is going to hurt.

19.

There are times when you find yourself in perfect harmony with another being. Like after you've taken a risk, faced your biggest fear, and found yourself blinking in the dust as a wall crumbles in front of you. Like after a perfect evening of constellation watching, followed by the best sex of your life.

It's more than just a moment. The past and the future join hands in a clasp that cannot be loosened. My fingers trail through her hair. Our bodies tangle, warm with exertion, comfortable with each other.

She looks into my eyes. Tina isn't smiling, and I know why—because she's scared, because she's feeling vulnerable. Because, like me, she doesn't want this to end.

I lean in and find her lips with mine. I don't know how this will work. I can't see any details. The only thing I know for certain is that I'm holding her now and I don't want to let go.

She looks up at me. The moon filters through the blinds, casting zebra stripes across her face. I don't want to ruin this moment, don't want her to pull away when I tell her the truth. But I can't stay silent.

"Tina." I lean in, pulling her close, and she comes to me. Her body is soft; she settles against me, her head resting against my shoulder in an act of complete trust.

There is no way I'm letting her go. Not today. Not tomorrow. Hell, no.

"We need to renegotiate." My voice feels hoarse. I wait, searching for the right words, but they don't come. The house is dark around us. I can hear the muted hum of a server in a nearby room, the occasional creak as the wood settles overhead. "Not just the end date of us—the existence of an end date at all. I don't want to let this go. I don't want to let us go."

I can feel her muscles tense. But she doesn't turn away.

"I don't know how this will work," I say. "But…it's working now."

Her hand clasps mine.

"I don't want this to end," I tell her. "I don't want to walk away from you."

"I don't know what to say." Her voice is low. "I'm not good at taking risks, Blake, and you're the biggest risk there is. I'm scared."

I can't tell her not to be scared. "I know," I say. "But I think you're wrong about the stars. There are no gods here. There are just mortals. There's just you and me. We make our own light, and we can make it say anything we want."

She turns away. And as she does, outside the edge of my consciousness, something registers. Something that draws me away from a moment that I didn't think I could be drawn away from.

A chill runs down my spine. I don't know what it is, why I give a quick shiver. I just know that something just changed—something big. *There are no gods here.*

"I don't...I'm not sure," Tina starts to say.

"Wait." I set a finger on her lips. "Something is wrong."

I hear another noise, this time coming clearly from downstairs: the shattering of glass. That, and then, a stark nothing.

It's my dad. I can explain the noise. It's well after midnight now, and despite his boasts earlier, he's not finished yet. He was getting himself some coffee and he dropped a mug. It's nothing.

But even though my mind is telling me to dismiss it, my body refuses. The hair rises on the back of my neck. I can feel it overtake me. My life just changed, and I don't know how.

"Blake," Tina says. "I..."

It's nothing, I tell myself. I turn back to Tina. But that sense of wrongness is too strong, too powerful, like my subconscious is reaching out and shaking me awake.

Fuck.

"Hold on to whatever you were going to say."

And that's when I hear something else. It's a low sound that I can't classify. I try to tell myself that it could be anything: a raccoon in the backyard or a coyote slinking through from the hills.

But I know it isn't any of those things. It's instinct operating here, but I grew up in this house. I've fallen asleep listening to its creaks and moans all my life. And right now, the sounds all *feel* wrong. The moment isn't just gone; it's smashed to irretrievable bits. I push back the covers and pull on a pair of boxers and then jeans.

"Blake?" Tina's watching me, her eyebrows knitting into worried lines.

"Something's wrong," I tell her, and that sounds right, even though I have no idea what is going on.

She doesn't ask what. She doesn't say anything. She just scrambles into jeans and a shirt and follows me downstairs.

A light is on in the kitchen; it casts a warm glow on the stairs, but for some reason, it just chills me. Something is wrong; I know it, even if I don't know what. I hurry. Tina's slippers slap on the stairs behind me, but I rush ahead.

Shards of ceramic greet me, spread over the marble floor. That's when I realize how my subconscious knew something was wrong. There was something I didn't hear. Dad's a neat freak. If he dropped a glass, I should have heard him cleaning up afterward.

I didn't. And I don't see him now. Not at first.

Then I hear him. It's a repeat of the second noise I heard—a low moan, followed by the catch of breath. I pick my way among the mug shards, making my way around the gleaming island of black marble. My heart is pounding. I don't want to think what is happening. I can't.

Dad is there. He's lying on the floor.

For a moment, it doesn't make any sense to me. Why the fuck is he on the floor? What's going on? And then I see his hand, clenched hard. Beads of sweat are popping out on his forehead. His skin is pale; his teeth are gritted.

"Dad?"

Behind me, Tina comes into the kitchen. She looks around, slowly. "Oh my God," she says. "Blake. Call 911."

"Don't." Dad grates the word out.

She's already looking around for some kind of a phone. "Don't be an idiot," she snaps. "Something's obviously wrong." Her gaze lands on his phone on the counter. She grabs it and swipes at the screen. "What's your passcode? Oh, wait. Never mind. The emergency call still works."

"No. Call my fucking doctor." Dad pushes up to a sitting position. "He's handled this before. There's an emergency contact screen—you should be able to find his contact info without the passcode…"

"What the fuck, Dad?" I ask. "What do you mean, *before?*"

"I had a little arrhythmia a few weeks ago," he admits. "Bad enough that I was a little shaken. Nothing like this, though."

I stare at him. "You've been having *heart problems* and you didn't tell me?"

"Your doctor is Kevin Wong?" Tina is asking.

"Yeah," Dad says to Tina, ignoring me. "Kevin. That's him. He lives two streets over. He can be here before the paramedics. And he'll make sure we get in front of the narrative. God knows what the fucking ambulance drivers will say if they get here before Kevin can tell them what to think."

"Narrative?" I say. "You're having a heart attack and you're worried about what the public will think?"

But inside I'm screaming. This is exactly what happened to Peter—*exactly*. Heart attack. Just before a launch. I can't lose Dad, not like this.

Dad shakes his head. "It's not what you think."

"What," I ask him, "you're *not* having a heart attack?"

Tina speaks swiftly into the phone. I tell myself it's going to be okay. Someone will be here soon, someone who will be able to fix this. They'll make it all better.

"That's exactly what I'm doing." He shuts his eyes. "I'm *only* having a heart attack, Blake. That's all that's happening, right? That's what we have to make sure everyone thinks."

I don't understand what he's saying at first. Tina sets the phone down. She doesn't look at me. She looks at my dad, looks at him as if she's seeing him for the first time.

"How long…" Her voice shakes. She lets out a long breath. "How long," she finally asks, "have you been doing cocaine?"

For a second, I don't know what to say. It's fucking ridiculous to even consider. My dad wouldn't…wouldn't…

I lift my head. It's on the counter. A fine dust of white powder glistens in poisonous contrast to the gleaming marble. It sits next to a plastic bag filled with a white substance.

On the floor, Dad shuts his eyes. "Oh, you know. On and off. For ten years or so."

Ten fucking years? He has to be shitting me.

"More on than off these last six." He blows out his breath. "I was losing my edge. I had to do something."

"Christ." I can't breathe.

"Blake." He motions me close. "Look. I was going to tell you. I meant to."

He was going to tell me? I don't even know what to say to this. The thing he's talking about—it's just not possible. I don't believe it.

"When I was twenty and thirty, I didn't think anything of doing ninety hours a week. But then I hit forty." His hand curls around me. "It was like I hit a wall. I needed something to keep my edge. And Peter and I…"

"You're fucking kidding me," I say. "*Peter* knew about this, and he let you do it?"

And that's when Dad breaks. He doesn't cry. He doesn't moan. But his face collapses.

"God, Blake. Why do you think I couldn't tell you? You think Peter had a heart attack at forty-five for no reason? He didn't just *let* me do it. He was doing it with me." He gasps for air. "How could you live with me once you knew I killed him? I can't even live with myself."

I don't even know what to say. "You told me you wanted to go on vacation."

He shakes his head. "Vacation. Rehab. Whatever."

"What about tonight? You just shrugged and told me not to worry about you. You didn't *tell* me."

He opens his eyes, meeting mine. "I killed Peter." There's a stark coldness inside him. "You think, once you told me, I'd kill you, too? I'd rather fucking die."

He just might.

It's weird. All this time I've been telling myself that my father is stronger than I am. That the last thing I want is his disappointment. That I can't tell him that I have a problem, because if I do, I might lose his respect.

I was right. There are no gods, just us shit-stupid mortals.

I take hold of his hand. "You stupid fucker," I say. "I'm never going to stop being proud of you. I'm never going to stop loving you. So live. Live, you stupid bastard."

I hear the door open in the distance. I hadn't even realized that the doctor was here. Tina must have let him in. Dr. Wong comes in at a half jog and leans down beside my father.

I expect him to take his pulse or examine him, but apparently that's old school. He pulls out a phone and snaps a little plastic alligator clip on my dad's finger.

"Are you experiencing chest pain?" Dr. Wong has a soft, sweet voice. It's almost instantly calming. I can already tell he has a great bedside manner.

"It's cliché, but...it's like there's a damned elephant sitting on my chest."

"There you are," Dr. Wong says in his quiet voice. "I told you to stop doing cocaine."

"Hey, asshole," my dad snaps back. "This is a heart attack, not a fucking teachable moment."

"Technically," Dr. Wong says, "I won't know it's a heart attack until I see an EKG. Until then, my official diagnosis is teachable moment."

"Shit," Dad grumbles. "You're fired."

Dr. Wong ignores this. "Once I get an EKG, it turns into a *fucking* teachable moment."

No wonder my dad likes this guy. I can hear the ambulance now, a dim wail in the distance.

Dad grabs my wrist. "Hey." His voice is getting softer. "About the narrative..."

I look up. His bag of cocaine is still sitting on the counter. I want to tell him to fuck the narrative. But he's clutching at my sleeve and he looks even more desperate now.

I stand up and pick up the bag. "I'm throwing out all your stupid cocaine if I have to come through the house with a fucking dog, do you hear me?" Dad shuts his eyes in relief.

"Live," I say, "because when you get back from the hospital, I'm throwing your stupid ass in rehab."

The front windows fill with flashing red and blue lights. The ambulance is here. "Live." I swipe my hand across the counter, gathering up the remains of the dust that sent him into this latest attack. I slide the plastic baggie into an oven mitt, obscuring it from prying eyes.

"Love you too, asshole." His voice is weak. "Check my bathroom cabinet. And the nightstand."

The EMTs are hustling through the front door, pushing a gurney before them. Dr. Wong meets them at the front and directs them as they strap my dad in. It doesn't seem real. None of it seems real. Their boots crunch on ceramic. Dr. Wong hands me a card and tells me that my dad will be at the hospital, that I'm free to follow along.

I walk beside them, bringing him to the ambulance.

"Live, you stupid fucking bastard," I tell him, again, leaning over the cot. "I love you."

"Love you, too." His eyes are shut. But the EMT grabs his head and slips a breathing mask on, and that's the end of the conversation. I tell myself that it can't be that bad—that if he's talking and cracking jokes, this can't possibly be the end.

I'm pretty sure I'm lying to myself. I wait in the cold night air until the EMTs slam the doors shut, until they strap themselves in their seats, until the lights seem to flare all the more brightly, and they let the sirens blare, briefly, warning the night that they're coming. And then they're gone.

20.

I'm standing in the driveway. The lights of the ambulance are receding; a moment later, they slip around a corner and are swallowed by the hill. My awareness of the circumstances seeps back in slowly. It's almost like waking up from a nightmare: First, there's a sharp shock of consciousness, where physical reality sets in. My feet are bare. The concrete underfoot is wet and cold. I'm wearing nothing but a pair of jeans, and my skin is so cold that I've begun to shiver.

Next, memory floods back. Except when you wake up from a bad dream, you have to remind yourself that everything is okay—that nobody has died, that there are no monsters.

This is exactly the opposite.

Dad is doing cocaine.

No, scratch that.

Dad *has* been doing cocaine. For years. My father has been killing himself. He's been begging for my help, and I was too blind to understand how much he needed me.

I'm the worst son ever. Somehow, the cold feels appropriate. It pinches my flesh, robs me of feeling. I could put on a parka and I would never feel warm again.

Footsteps sound behind me. I turn around to see Tina holding a broom. Apparently, she's cleaned up the broken mug. She's watching me with dark, clear eyes.

Twenty minutes ago, we were in bed, closer than close. Twenty minutes ago, I knew I couldn't go on without her. I know that even more strongly now. I have never wanted anyone like I want Tina.

"Come on, Blake," she says, gesturing me in. Her voice is gentle. "You need to come in and get dressed. I'll drive you to the hospital."

"I don't even know where they're taking him."

"You're holding the card in your hand," she points out. "Dr. Wong just gave it to you."

Shit. So he did. I'm not thinking very well right at the moment.

She comes up and takes the card from me. "Here. He's being taken to…the Reynolds Foundation Emergency Department? Huh. What a coincidence. For some weird reason, I'm going to guess that they'll take good care of your dad there."

I look down. It's drizzling, and I'm wet enough that my jeans are plastered to me. Have to hope that the EMTs didn't have a camera. I can imagine what it would look like if *these* photos hit Twitter. For the first time, I can see how I must look: sparse and still too scrawny. The entire world just landed on my shoulders, and I've been dicking around.

I take a deep breath. "All right," I say. "But I have to get a few things ready."

I don't just get dressed. I get a bag. I tell Tina that I'm putting a few things together for my dad. I am getting a handful of things, because he will go crazy if he doesn't have at least a tablet if—no, *when*—he wakes up. But it's not just that. I send her off to find a blanket—I tell her it's for me, while I'm waiting for him to come to—but the truth is I don't want her to see this.

I ransack his room. I find a bag of white powder in the bathroom, another in his nightstand. I'm in a cold fury now—angry at him, furious with myself—as I toss it in a duffle alongside the stash from the kitchen. I gather up his personal items—computer, tablet, phone, headset, and, on second thought, a razor and a toothbrush—and throw those in a separate messenger bag.

Tina meets me downstairs. She's packed up my bag as well as her own. She throws these all in the car, and then slides into the driver's seat.

I can't look at her yet. Instead, I pull out my phone, slip on a Bluetooth headset, and look out the window. The streetlights slide by between dark houses and dark trees. I glance at my phone, choose a number, and dial.

The phone rings three times before a voice on the other line answers. "Blake?" The voice of Amy Ellis, our head of public relations, is blurred by sleep. But she doesn't complain about the time. She knows that if I'm calling, it's urgent. "What's going on?"

"We need a press release," I tell her, "and we need it in five minutes, because chances are someone is going to squawk soon." I don't know how I manage to sound so calm.

There's a pause. "Your dad told me things were being rearranged a few hours ago."

"Fuck what my dad told you," I say. "This is bigger than that."

She sighs. "You know I have to have your dad's approval to release anything. But hit me with the damage."

"You're not getting his sign-off on this." I shut my eyes. "We need a press release saying that Adam Reynolds had a heart attack this morning."

It's easier to say it that way. *Adam Reynolds,* not *Dad.* As if I can pretend he's the distant owner of some distant company. As if I'm not bleeding inside.

I hear her intake of breath. "Oh, God. Blake. Is he okay? Are *you* okay?"

"He's in stable condition," I tell her, which I hope is true. "I'm on my way to the hospital where he's being treated now."

"Which hospital?"

"Don't release that." I shut my eyes. "Not that they won't figure it out anyway. Still. The most important thing is to get the message out, to get ahead of any of the aftershocks. I'll have more details in an hour or so."

There's a long pause. "What about the product launch today? This is short notice, and the press will kill me. But do we need to cancel?"

I look down at the clock. It's one in the morning, and yes, the product launch is this afternoon. I imagine my dad, larger than life, striding across the stage with a knowing smile. He has such a flair for these things. How the fuck am I supposed to take his place at the launch? It's ridiculous, that's what it is. It's the most ridiculous thing in the world.

And yet.

I watch the streetlights slide by on an empty, deserted world.

For the first time in a long time, I don't feel like his shoes are too big to be filled by me. I don't feel like he's impossibly strong, unbowed by any problems. His weakness is equally my strength.

One thing at a time. "I'm doing the launch," I say.

I hear Tina suck in air beside me.

I should feel like I'm disappearing now, like my life doesn't belong to me. But now, for the first time, this doesn't feel like it's taking me over.

I still feel all my grief shut up inside me. But now it has a cause, an outlet. I know the name of the thing that killed Peter, and it wasn't Cyclone and it wasn't the job. It was not being able to walk away when it got to be too much.

I can do this, because I am going to walk away. For the first time, this feels like a winnable battle.

"It's better if I run the launch," I continue. "It'll give the investors a sense of continuity. It'll give the community a sense of belonging. And I'm the only one who can tell jokes about my dad." I can already sense it. If I tell jokes, everyone will believe it's not serious. And they *have* to think it's not serious—the less serious it seems, the better things will go. I shut my eyes. "Speaking of which. Amy, I need someone out there to make up some jokes about my dad."

"Are you serious?"

"Yeah." I shut my eyes. "We need to minimize this as best as we can, and that means I need to tell jokes. I'm not really in the mood to make them up right now, though. So that's on you."

"*Is* this serious?" Her voice is subdued.

My father has been doing cocaine. He's been doing it even after he watched it kill his best friend. If this isn't serious, I don't know what is.

"I don't know," I lie. "I hope not."

Tina is pulling into the hospital parking lot.

I shake my head. "I have to go. I'll talk to you later." I end the call.

Tina finds a spot. But instead of grabbing our stuff and going, we sit there in the car. She's parked right under an overhead light; it washes us with a pale, fluorescent light.

There are a lot of things we need to say to each other.

I put my hands on the dashboard. "I know we're supposed to end this when I go back to Cyclone. But...don't. Please." I glance over at her. "Stay with me."

She shuts her eyes. Her fingers curl around the edge of the steering wheel and she bows her head. "Blake. This isn't the time to have this conversation. Your life has just been turned around, you—"

"It's exactly the time," I tell her. "This isn't temporary, Tina. I care about you. I care about you a lot. And you know that."

Her voice breaks. "And I care about you. But—"

"Don't tell me that this can't happen." My heart is beating roughly. "Don't tell me that this isn't the time for you to break up with me. Don't tell me that you don't fit in my life. Whatever it is you're thinking, don't tell me that."

She raises her head and looks up at me, turning her face to mine.

"All I'm saying is that this is not the time to work out those details. Your dad is sick. Let's just..."

"No," I tell her. "If you're going to come into that hospital with me, I don't want it to be because you think I'm too fragile to handle the truth. This isn't hard. If you walk in there with me, if you're there for me through this, I don't know how I can make myself let you go. If that's not okay with you, walk away. I won't even feel it if I lose you now. There's too much else that hurts. Don't wait until tomorrow or the day after. Do it now."

She doesn't say anything. Her fingers clench around the wheel. She makes a little noise in her throat. I want to reach out and put my arms around her. I want everything to be okay.

We don't get everything we want.

She looks at me in mute, pained agony. But she doesn't reach out to me. She doesn't say she'll be there for me. And that means she won't. One more ache in my heart—I can scarcely feel it.

"That's that, then." I open the door.

"Blake," she says.

"I know," I tell her. "I know you care about me. We both have to keep ourselves safe. I know you. It's okay. I'm going to be okay."

"*Blake.*"

"Stay in my house as long as you want." I cast her a glance. "I'm probably not going to be back anytime soon."

"Blake…" The last iteration of my name. Her voice trails off. She looks over at me. There's a hint of tears on her lashes.

But she doesn't say anything for a long time. She doesn't lie. She doesn't tell me she wants us to keep going.

"Take care of yourself," she finally says.

"Yeah." I hoist my overnight bag and look over at her. "Take care of yourself, too."

Then I'm pushing off.

It's better this way. My heart aches with an almost physical pain. I feel hollow and empty and bruised. But I would feel hollow and empty and bruised even if she were by my side. I'm half-unconscious as it is.

I raise my chin and walk forward. The hospital doors slide open automatically as I approach, and I step inside.

I don't look back.

TINA

I don't know how I manage to get on the freeway. My hands are shaking. My tears give haloes to the streetlights, turning them into avenging angels frowning at me over three lanes of asphalt.

I drive. I can't do anything else—just drive, drive, and even then, I still can't push myself to go above forty, even on a deserted highway. When the freeway bends north, I get off. Not because I have somewhere else to be, but because if I continue on, I'll end up back at Blake's house in Berkeley and that will break me down.

I don't have any idea where I am, and I like it that way. I pass signs in Spanish advertising hair salons. There are residences with cinderblock walls and steel gates enclosing modest yards. I punch off the map displayed by the car. I want to lose myself.

The road slips away behind me. My hands squeeze the steering wheel; I stare straight ahead over slick asphalt.

It wasn't supposed to end like this. I knew it would hurt. I knew I would miss him.

It wasn't supposed to feel like love.

But it had tonight. It *had*.

And I don't know what to do with that.

I'd seen the rest of the day in one long rush. I'd go into the hospital with him. In a few hours, his staff would converge on him, and I'd be there—holding his hand while they coached him through the altered launch, offering him the comfort he so badly needed. I'd be there when he was at his most vulnerable, his most hurting. I'd be there in the audience when everything would broadcast to millions around the world, translated into seven languages simultaneously. I would be there, and when it was over—when press from the entire world converged on him to ask about the future of Cyclone—he'd make his way to me.

It's one thing for us to comfort one another in private, but in public, I'm the daughter of a Walmart baker and a janitor. I don't know how to be with him—him and his media training and his SEC regulations and his private jokes with his father, born from corporate sensitivity training.

I don't want to love Blake. Loving him will never be safe.

The road I'm on narrows from two lanes to one. Sidewalks give way to rough gravel roadsides. I turn right just before the street peters out in a residential neighborhood nestled against foothills.

After a few minutes of winding hither and thither, the new road I'm on begins to climb the hills in earnest, hairpinning up slopes that I can't see in the darkness. My headlights illuminate only in flashes: a house, huge, hidden behind an ornate gate; the glimpse of orange rock where the road has been carved into a steep incline. Eucalyptus branches stretch overhead as the road continues twisting up and up.

It's a road that finally matches my speed, a road where my thirty miles an hour seems safe. I keep going, glimpsing the scenery only long enough to leave it all behind: Grassy banks covered with oak leaves shift into moss-covered fallen logs. A private gate comes up on the right and then disappears in dark fog.

Eventually, the private homes I catch sight of turn into farmland. I glimpse a stile to the right, the arched sign of a ranch home on the left. The road takes on a meditative quality, something quiet and unending. It fits what I need right now.

I can go slowly. I have to, here. One flubbed turn and I'd be careening off the hillside. This is my life: I have to play it safe.

I *have* to play it safe.

My eyes are stinging and for a moment, I have the strange impression that the windshield wipers aren't working properly. But of course it isn't the car. Blake would never own a vehicle that would dare malfunction. I'm the thing that has broken down, my vision blurring with tears that I refuse to acknowledge.

I always play it safe. What choice have I had?

That's what dries my tears. Not words of wisdom or comfort, but a deep-seated anger.

I always play it safe. I have to. I've chosen my future as if it were a blown-glass artifact, whorls and loops that needed to be packed away in tissue paper, put up high to keep it safe. I don't go out. I don't take risks. I never know when my parents will need an extra ten dollars. It's an illusion that Blake and I could trade lives. Because he's always known that he'll get back to his—and I've always known I'll fall back into mine.

He's always had someone to catch him. And me? Unless I'm careful, I can lose everything.

The higher I go, the wilder the landscape becomes. I pass through a spooky forest. Wizened wizard trees reach many-fingered branches to the sky. Moss drips from their branches like tattered scarves, and they look down on me like judgmental aunties.

Look at that girl there. Can't even drive a car safely, let alone manage her life.

Fuck them. Fuck them all.

My tears come back, blurring the forest. I pass a cluster of buildings that are labeled as some kind of observatory. Only fitting; here the stars are out in force, burning down on me, letting me know exactly where I belong.

I start on the descent.

The road lies before me like a skein of snarled yarn. I untangle it the way I untangle everything else: at thirty miles an hour.

When I first started on this road, its contortions felt comforting—a reminder that it was okay for me to go slowly when the conditions demand it. As it goes on and on and on, it begins to feel like a cage.

Maybe that's why, as I descend past pinyon pines, as the land flattens out into wide meadows, I let myself accelerate.

Thirty gives way to thirty-five; thirty-five slides into forty. The car is utterly silent; only the tires make noise as we move forward. It's shockingly easy to get used to speed. So easy I can't believe I've never done it before.

It feels like an act of defiance to watch the speedometer go up, like I'm flipping off the entire universe. Maybe I can't have Blake—but just for a little bit, I don't have to play it safe.

It's still dark, but the brights on the car illumine the road on the way down. The car grips the road, turning without a single squeak of complaint.

I don't have to play it safe.

There's something powerful about going fast in a car that's built for speed. Instead of feeling out of control, I feel like I'm finally in charge. The car whips around a turn, and then another. Gravel spits up on the side of the road, but I don't care. The turns are getting broader as we head down. The foothills give way to long lazy curves, barely even descending, and then, finally, the road spits me out onto an empty highway, a long, straight shot heading into the dark.

I pass through a silent town in a matter of minutes and find myself on a wide road, vacant this early in the morning.

I'm going to give up this life in a few days. Why *not* let it all go? Why not find out now, after all these months, all these *years*, of being careful, what I can really do?

There's nobody around to hurt, nothing nearby. Nothing but orchards, fields green with plants reaching tentative leaves toward dark-gray skies.

It's a straight road, a road that was made for sixty-five.

Hell, sixty-five doesn't hurt. In fact, it seems natural. So natural I almost feel angry. All this time, I've been going thirty when I can do *this* instead?

Sixty-five turns into seventy and then eighty. Orchards whip by. There's a single railroad track running parallel to the road. I push harder. If this car had wings, I think I could lift off.

With no vibrations from the engine, I can't even tell how fast I'm going. I whip by a speed limit sign; it accusingly reminds me that I shouldn't be going above seventy miles an hour. I'm at ninety-five.

Fuck it. You only live once. I'm out of that cage of a road. I'm never going to have the chance to live this way again. And suddenly, I'm so goddamned sick of being safe.

I slam my foot on the pedal and the car surges forward smoothly, as if everything until now has been mere child's play. The acceleration slams me back in my seat; the world whips by. At this speed, I don't have to think. I don't have to feel. I don't have to hesitate or wait. I don't have to be a good daughter or a good student. I don't have to be good at all. I can just be *me*, whoever that is.

You need to be careful, Xingjuan. There are some words that are embedded in me, like a fishhook stuck in my heart. I can tug at them, but they don't come out. I shake my head, trying to deny it.

But I know the truth. I'm only speeding down this unknown road because I'm trying to escape the truth. I've been falling in love with Blake, and I don't know how to do it. I don't know how to be careful with him, and I'm scared of getting hurt. I couldn't even open my mouth tonight. His dad had a heart attack; he's taken on a burden so tremendous that it's been eating him alive this last year. I knew how much he needed me, but I couldn't even speak up. That's how scared I was.

You need to be careful, Xingjuan.

Those tears I've pushed away come back in full force. I'm *tired* of being careful.

It's funny that I hear my mother's voice telling me to be careful, because my mother is the least careful person I know. She throws her heart into her work. She loves every person she assists. She believes them with all of her heart, works with all of her soul, weeps when she fails and rejoices when she wins. She's the opposite of careful, and I don't know how she ended up with me as a daughter. My mother has never told me to be careful in her life. She just laughs and tells me to make my boyfriend wear two condoms.

And yet: *You need to be careful, Xingjuan.*

That's when I remember where I heard those words—the one and only time my mother ever spoke them to me. The memory hits me so hard, it's almost physical. I can feel it. Her hand on my wrist, yanking me close. The air is dry with a hint of sand on it. Her mouth hovers down near my ear, my heart beating fast.

Don't say those things out loud, my mother is saying. *You need to be careful, Xingjuan. You don't know who will report you.*

And with that piece restored, other bits come floating back. I'd been playing with other children. I'd mentioned—unthinking—that my dad had gone to the park to practice after the government had banned Falun Gong. I was just six, too young to understand what I was saying.

My mother grabbed me by the hand and told me to be quiet, that someone could hear. That if they did, they might take my father away.

By the time we got home, it was too late. The authorities had picked up my father at work, and I didn't see him for months.

I don't think I ever really did forget that. Not really, not deep down. All this time, I've been telling myself that I have to try harder, that I have to give my parents everything. Every time something has gone wrong, I've wondered what I did wrong, how I could have prevented it. I've always known that I failed them, and I've been trying to make up for it ever since. Maybe I've hoped that if I do, that one day I'll make up for ruining everything.

I imagine telling my mother that. She would look at me with one eyebrow raised, shaking her head. And for the first time in my life, I hear the actual words my mother would speak rather than the ones I've held onto in my head.

"Don't be silly," she would say. "Whoever said you ruined anything? Take the best you can, and don't look back."

I can't stop crying.

It's too much. I've been stupid, so stupid, afraid to embrace the best thing that has happened to me simply because I was afraid I didn't deserve it, because I was certain it would be yanked away from me.

Maybe I am just setting myself up for heartache—but maybe, just maybe, I deserve to give myself a chance.

I look down at the speedometer. I'm going…a hundred and thirty? Holy fuck. What am I doing? What was I thinking? I tap the brakes once, and then again, slowing, slowing. The speedometer drifts down. One twenty. One ten.

I hit a hundred, and that's when I hear it—the slow wail of a siren springing to life behind me. I glance in the rearview mirror. Red flashing lights reflect into my face.

It shouldn't be funny, but somehow it is. I'm laughing as I hit the brakes, laughing as I slowly maneuver the car to the side of the road.

It just goes to show. All this time, I've been holding back, afraid to drive at a reasonable speed, trying so hard to be careful for fear that something would happen. It always does to us mortals, doesn't it?

I drove fast. And here I am. Something has happened. And somehow, it doesn't seem that bad.

21.

The cop took my license ten minutes ago. He hasn't returned yet. Instead, his car sits behind Blake's Tesla, red lights strobing across my passenger seat. The sky is still dark; the moon has set, and out here, the stars make a glimmering net overhead.

I wonder what my mom would say if she could see me now. Her advice for dealing with police is…legally sound, perhaps, but not conciliatory. Not ever conciliatory. I'm pretty sure that what I need right now is more than conciliatory. Something closer to abject as hell. I don't know how fast the officer clocked me, but it was probably over a hundred.

That may well be enough to push me into the "arrest for reckless driving" band, and *that* is the last thing I need right now.

When he comes up to me, I'm going to apologize.

I plan what I'm going to say. The officer will be back any second now. He'll give me a whopping fine and a huge lecture. But another minute passes while I hyperventilate, wondering what is going on. Then two. The officer finally gets out of his car again and I breathe a sigh of relief. But he doesn't come toward me. He faces away from me, looking down the dark road.

A moment later, a second police car pulls up. Shit. I *am* going to get arrested. I'm wondering if I should call someone. Blake? No, definitely not Blake. He has enough to deal with this morning, and I just left him. His father's in the hospital. He has a product launch this afternoon. If he's not seeing to his dad or preparing, he should be sleeping, not sorting out some sordid police matter involving the person who is, at the moment, *definitely* not his girlfriend.

The longer I sit, the worse I feel about what happened. I wasn't ready to hear his words. I didn't let myself believe that we could be anything together. I didn't know how to look at him and think that he would do anything other than break my heart. So I broke his instead.

I *still* don't know how we can be anything. All the old arguments apply.

But one thing has changed: I want to figure it out.

As I'm considering this, the second officer gets out of his car and then opens the back door of his vehicle. How cute. They brought backup for me. I almost feel important.

But the backup that jumps out of the backseat is not an officer—at least not a human one. It's a dog, an adorable yellow lab with big brown eyes and one ear that flops down. It has a goofy grin and its tongue hangs out. It's so far removed from the typical authoritarian-looking German Shepherd that the police dog harness looks like a Halloween costume.

Not good, something whispers in the back of my mind. I brush this aside.

The officer guides the dog to the car. They start to walk around and then, right by the rear door, the dog sits.

It's an absurd thing; for a second, I entertain an idle notion that the dog has gone off the clock. Despite my racing pulse, I smile. Maybe cop dogs aren't as perfectly trained as the TV shows indicate.

But the dog doesn't do any of the things you'd expect a dog to do when it sits. No scratching, no licking, no curling up in a little ball. It just looks up at the officer holding his leash, its tail waving back and forth. Absurdly, instead of ordering the dog back to work, the officer hands it a treat and scratches its head. It's cute, but it's over too soon. The new officer puts the dog back in the car.

Maybe the dog decided I wasn't dangerous.

Maybe...

I swallow. The first officer unholsters his gun, comes abreast of the car door. My pulse was running swiftly before. It starts hammering now. I can't think. I have no idea why he'd pull a weapon now, but there it is. Dark, lethal metal. The morning sun reflects off its edges.

He raises it in my direction. "Get out of the car with your hands up."

My hands shake as I open the door. I have no idea what just happened. I can't think. I don't understand. This is all going so wrong.

He gestures to me to turn for a pat down.

I place my hands on the side of the vehicle. As I do, I look into the backseat.

Blake took his bag with him when he went into the hospital. But he left something in the car when he went— a duffle bag scarcely the size of a backpack. I was so upset it didn't even register. I've been so upset that I've been smiling at the dog, not realizing what I know all too well in the back of my mind.

But it registers now. It registers with cold, icy clarity. I can almost hear the promise Blake made to his father. *I'm throwing out all your stupid cocaine if I have to come through the house with a fucking dog.*

That wasn't an attack dog; it was a drug dog. And when that cute, sweet Lab sat down, it pointed a doggy paw at me and said, "This one!"

This is not something I can simply talk my way out of. Abject won't do it. Conciliatory won't do it.

I've just been pulled over by the cops while driving one hundred and thirty miles an hour in a car that doesn't belong to me, and I have an unknown quantity of cocaine in my backseat.

I am so fucked.

---

*T*hey let me have one phone call. I entertain the idea of calling Blake, but he'll find out—or his people will find out—eventually.

But, I realize on the drive into the station, the only defense I have to offer is this: *No, sir, this cocaine doesn't belong to me. It belongs to Adam Reynolds. Arrest him instead.* I'm not even sure Blake and I are on the same side anymore.

Hell, even if Blake were willing to help, he has enough on his mind right now. He doesn't need me bothering him.

I tell myself all those things, but there's one fundamental reason I'm not calling him. Maybe the stars have it right. Maybe mortals dabble with gods at their own peril. But then, those Greek gods of old? They never met my mother.

I think she could take them.

T can envision my mother getting out of bed. Walking to the Felix-the-Cat phone she loves so much and frowning at it, wondering why it's ringing at this hour of the morning. I can envision her putting her hand out.

And somehow, just as I imagine her lifting the receiver, she picks up.

She no doubt hears the recording warning her that the call is coming from a police station and that unless the other party is a lawyer, it will be monitored. I can hear her breathing. She's probably wondering which of her friends is calling her this time.

"Mom?" I say. My voice sounds thin.

"Tina?" She's shocked.

I inhale. "Ma. I've been arrested."

She doesn't say anything for one fraught second. Any other mother would be sputtering at this point. *What did you do? How could you? What's wrong with you?*

My mother switches to Mandarin. "You remember what I told you?" she tells me. "Never tell the police anything, not for any reason."

"Mom, I—"

"No," she interrupts. "Don't tell me anything that happened, not even in another language. I'm not a lawyer.

They're going to record this. Don't you know anything about the law? Don't talk, not where they can hear you."

"I know," I say. "Put it on my next birthday cake."

"Where are you?" she demands.

I tell her. She doesn't ask how I came to be in a police station near Modesto. She doesn't ask what I'm doing. She doesn't demand any explanations at all.

"I won't let anything happen to you," she says. "I'll be there as soon as I can."

"You have to be at work in an hour." My protest is halfhearted.

"This is what I do," she says in English. "If I can't do this for my own daughter, what good am I?"

Maybe that's what I wanted—no, needed—to hear. That I matter. That it will be okay with her if I fuck-up, that my mother will still love me.

"Don't talk to the police, heh? They tell you lies."

This is my mother in fight mode—the way she is for all the people she works with. This is what Mom does. She's there for people who need her. All those interrupted nights—she's been someone's first phone call.

If there is one person I could have on my side against impossible odds, it's her.

22.

BLAKE

"Hey, Dad." I sit by my father's bed. "Are you coherent yet?" The room is finally empty of doctors, nurses, and other helpful personnel. Dad has his own room in the ICU decorated in industrial gray. There's a clip on his finger, attached to another machine nearby.

"Huh." He turns his head and rubs at his eyes. "I'm pretty fucking muzzy. What do they have me on?"

"Some kind of painkiller. I can find out exactly what it is."

He struggles to sit up. "I don't want it." His hand finds the IV coming out of his arm. "Is it coming through here? Fuck. Make it stop. That shit's addictive."

I stare at him. "Are you shitting me? You're worried about that, *now*?"

"Come on," he says with a roll of his eyes. "Don't be a stupid asshole. Cocaine isn't addictive. It's just habit-forming. Medically speaking." He frowns.

"That's reassuring," I say dryly.

But he stops short of ripping the IV out of his arm. "I guess I should ask. How fucked am I?"

"They shot your arteries full of dye and made a little video of it circulating through your heart. You should make Dr. Wong show it to you. It's pretty cool. No blockages anywhere. They didn't even have to put in a stent."

Dad's hand creeps over his heart. "Huh."

"The only reason they're keeping you in the hospital is because you have a giant hole in your thigh where they put the dye in, and they don't trust you not to open it up. Congratulations, motherfucker. You're not going to die unless you keep trying to kill yourself."

His gaze falls inward. "Better than I deserve."

"Better than we both deserve," I say. "It turns out that the back half of the product launch practically rewrites itself. We've got about five hours until we're on. Think you'll be up for a two-minute video check-in from the hospital?"

"Yeah." He shuts his eyes. "You know, Blake. I can't...I don't want you to take over. Not if it's going to..." He doesn't finish his sentence. He doesn't need to.

"I already talked to the board. They've agreed that David will take over temporarily. And I told them we're going to have to restructure the corporation—you obviously need to cut back. Even after rehab."

He nods. "You?"

"Give me a year with a therapist and we'll talk about me and Cyclone again."

It really is that easy. I can say no. I can tell him I have a problem, and it becomes just a...thing. An obstacle. Something I can attack. It was only silence that made it insurmountable.

"And Tina?"

I shut my eyes. "I don't want to talk about Tina."

"That bad, huh?"

I'm saved from answering by a knock on the door. My dad's administrative assistant comes in.

"Hey, George." My dad does his best to look comfortable in a green hospital gown. "Is something going on?"

"I'm sorry to interrupt," George says, "but I'm not sure if this is important. Blake, the police contacted us."

We do not want the police involved in this. Not now. Not ever. "What about?"

"They have your car." He clears his throat.

I begin to feel light-headed.

"And they want to know if they should charge the driver with theft on top of everything else. Normally, I'd have told them to fuck off—but the driver's Tina Chen. I've seen that name on Adam's schedule."

"Shit." I shut my eyes. "It's not theft. Wait. What do you mean, on top of everything else?"

George starts to talk.

It turns out, my father and I are going to have to talk about Tina anyway.

TINA

My mother arrives six hours later. I know because I'm conducted from the prison cell where I'm staying to an interrogation room.

"They say I can talk to you," she says. "Just the two of us." She's still speaking Mandarin. I'm still in handcuffs.

"Why would they let you do that?" I wrinkle my noise.

"Because I acted like I was stupid," she says with a smile. "'Oh, let me talk to her, I'll make her apologize. My daughter is a good girl, I promise, I'll make her tell you what happened.' They got greedy. They're recording everything. They think all they need to do is get an interpreter and boom, easy conviction." Her smile is sharklike. "DA says he'll think about bail. Your father will figure that out, and then we'll walk away, leaving them with nothing."

I have to smile at that.

"So, tell me," she says. "Talk about anything but this. What is going on with you?"

"I broke up with Blake."

"Ah ha!" Her face lights. "I *knew* you were dating him. Trying to keep things from your mother? Never works." She frowns. "Wait, why break up with him? He seemed so nice. Did he do something wrong?"

"No." I shut my eyes. "Mom, do you remember China?"

She stills. "Yes. But you don't much, right?"

"Only little things." I look down. "A doll. Grandma." I swallow. "And I remember that one day, I told someone that Dad was in the park with the others. They took him away and shattered his kneecap and we didn't see him for two months." Now that the words are spilling from my mouth, I can't stop them. "I remember that it was my fault, my fault he got taken away. My fault that—"

"Shh!" My mother leans forward. "Never say that. Never. It was not your fault. Not anyone's fault, except the Communists'."

"All this time," I say, choking, "I've been trying to make it up to you guys, to make things right. I've been scared, so scared, and so convinced that I had to do anything I could to stay safe."

My mother rubs her eyes. "When I got on the plane leaving China, I promised myself that I would never be afraid again. That I would never be quiet again. I have never done so."

"No. You haven't."

She looks over at me. "Maybe I should have promised that my daughter would never be afraid, too. I should have realized. I should have asked."

"No, Ma. Never."

She leans over and sets her hand on my shoulder.

But at that moment, the door opens. I expect the officer to gruffly tell us not to touch. Instead, he saunters in and undoes my handcuffs.

"You're free to go," he says.

"What?" My mother stands. "Why? No bail?"

"You," he says to her with exaggerated slowness, "can go." He demonstrates with two fingers walking.

"I understand *what,*" my mother snaps. "Just not why. Explain why."

The guard shrugs. "The DA made other arrangements."

My head is spinning. I don't know what that means, what will happen with me.

But I'm not about to question my good fortune. I elbow my mother and frown at her, and then stand up and follow the guard to get my things. Which is good; even though the launch is today, I don't want to think about leaving my prototypes in the hands of the police.

They're keeping the car, the officer tells us as he leads us down a long hall. Apparently, that's evidence.

Fine. I'll let Blake deal with that.

I see another policeman coming our way. A man is following him. I don't even register who it is until we're almost on top of them.

And then I do. His sandy hair is tousled; his eyes are bright blue and he's wearing glasses. But the man being led down the hall is most definitely Blake Reynolds.

"Blake?" I come to a stop. "What are you doing here?"

He gives me a long, slow smile. "What do you think?"

I can't think anything at all.

"We've got twelve minutes until the launch," he says. "Everything we agreed on together? It's still on. Come on, Tina. Trade me."

My eyes go wide. My heart starts to thump. "What? Blake—your dad, the product launch—no, I can't let you—"

"Too late," he says. "I already signed the papers."

"*Blake.*"

"Have fun, Tina." He winks at me. "And, oh, if you have a chance, do watch the launch. For me, okay?"

23.

"What is going on?" My mother grabs my arm as we head to the car. "What is Blake doing here? Why is he staying? Is he dealing drugs? What did he mean launch? Is it a rocket launch? Why is the DA listening to him?"

"It's a long story."

My mother looks at me sidelong. "We have a long drive."

I glance at my watch. "Um. Not yet. We have to watch the product launch."

"Product launch. What is this product launch? And how do we watch it without a TV?"

I'm not going to get around this one. I take a deep breath. "Okay. Here's the deal. Blake is…"

"I know, your boyfriend. Don't you know you can't lie to your mother?"

"He *wasn't* my boyfriend when we came down," I mutter. "Really. That came afterward. And we broke up this morning." I frown. "I think."

"Huh. Didn't look like a breakup to me back there." We arrive at her car. She unlocks my side of the car and I open my bag. I take out a tablet and check the reception. It's complete crap. "Drive north," I tell her. The launch has already started.

She starts her car. "Fancy gadget." She frowns at it on my lap. "*Very* fancy gadget. Are you selling meth or something? I was only joking when I said you should deal drugs."

"Ma! *No.* Of course I'm not."

"I had to ask," she says mildly.

"Look. I didn't lie to you about Blake being my boyfriend. I did imply that he had...not a lot of money."

"Oh?" My mother perks up. "He's rich? Is that a present from him?"

"He's Blake Reynolds," I explain.

She frowns. "Who? Some kind of actor?"

"His dad is the CEO of Cyclone. The company that makes these." I tilt the tablet to her. "This is a preproduction model."

"Hmm." She frowns.

I stick to the basics. "Cyclone is launching a new product right now. Blake was supposed to be running the launch. His dad had a heart attack last night." I inhale. "If Blake is here, getting me out of this, he's not *there*. So if he wants me to watch the product launch, I will." I keep my eye on the reception on the way back, and once I have four bars, I motion my mother into a supermarket parking lot.

She parks next to a flock of shopping carts. I navigate to the Cyclone website. It's twenty-two minutes into the launch by the time I get the feed working. David Yu, the chief product engineer, is finishing the demo on the updated tablet and the new video app, to massive applause.

The screen behind him goes black and a spotlight falls on him.

"So," he says. "Internet: We have to talk about your gossip problem. Apparently there are rumors out there that we have a new, undisclosed product codenamed Fernanda. The top three claims are…"

He does a quarter turn, and as he talks, bullet points appear behind him. They're familiar to me. They should be; I wrote them. I can't help but feel a sense of pride.

"One," he says. "Fernanda is a flying smart drone that will mix drinks and deliver them." A cute little animated video plays, demonstrating this, and the audience's laughter can be heard over the feed.

"Get it straight," he says without cracking a smile. "That's next year's product line."

The laughter doubles.

"Two," he says, "some of you think that Fernanda is an injectable microchip for people that allows you to pay for things without using your wallet or a phone."

There's a clip of a woman waving her hand in front of a credit card reader.

Yu wrinkles his nose. "That's disgusting. Where do you get these ideas?" He pauses. "No, don't tell me. Do I look like I want to know? We don't mind if you write Cyclone/microchip fanfic. Just don't show it to us. Thank you."

I can't help myself. I grin and lean back.

"Three," Yu says. "Some of you apparently think that Fernanda is a watch. Come on, internet. How unrealistic can you be? Even though smartwatch technology is relatively new, the field is already crowded. And the challenges of producing a truly excellent watch are enormous. You guys know that Cyclone doesn't get into a field unless we can leave our competitors in the dust.

Unless we can put out something that is easier to use and more robust than anything on the market. Come on, people. What are the chances that Cyclone would be getting into the smartwatch business?"

There's a long, dramatic pause.

Yu smiles. "Actually, one out of three isn't bad."

The audience erupts in applause, and despite myself, despite the fact that I wrote that last little section, I find myself smiling along with them.

"I want you to meet our newest product. She's been codenamed Fernanda, but now she's ready to be called by her launch name: the Cyclone Vortex." The watch practically sells itself, and as Yu goes through its features, he does a good job of snarking on the competition without ever mentioning them by name.

"Of course," he says, when discussing the health monitoring features, "if what you want is to have a GPS record of your run, you'll do what every athlete does. You'll put on your watch. And then you'll strap a tablet, a phone, a printer, and the complete works of Shakespeare to your back." He grins. "Oh, wait. Nobody wants to do that. That's why the Vortex has a built-in GPS chip, so it's not dependent on any of our other technology."

The crowd oohs over the circumference ring scrolling.

"But the Vortex has another amazing feature," Yu says. "Remember how I told you earlier that we had updated our computers with the newest, the best video app ever invented? One that could follow your face as you walked around the room? Well, the Vortex is the first fully video-capable watch in the world. Let me bring up Lisa, our product management specialist."

He taps the watch, and Lisa, a smiling brunette, answers. They show how the watch automatically adjusts the video to stay on his face, even when he gestures, waves his hands, and then—to tumultuous applause—performs a handstand. The video of his face is jerky, but it's video.

Lisa on the other side of the call smiles. "It's amazing," she says. "I only wish…"

Yu clambers to his feet. "Yes. We're trying. But it's not the same thing without them." He doesn't say who *they* are.

From here on out, this part of the launch is new. It was going to be Adam and Blake, but Adam's in the hospital and Blake… I lean forward.

"Some of you found the patents last night," Lisa says, "and so you know that Blake and Adam had their hands on the Vortex the way they do all Cyclone products. We're told that Adam is in the ICU and active at the moment, and that he'll make a full and complete recovery. We're sorry that they can't say hi in person and introduce the Vortex to you themselves, but Adam's health has to come first."

Yu shakes his head, looking sad. "After all, it's not like we made a portable device that allows people to make three-way video calls over a cellular network."

There's a single second delay—a moment of breathless silence while everyone processes this—and then a beep.

Incoming call, the projection of the watch screen behind them says. *Adam Reynolds.*

"Oh, wait." Yu grins, taps his watch, and a little icon of Adam's face projects onto the screen. "It turns out that we did."

The video rearranges to show Adam in a green gown, a slice of gray wall and an IV pole visible behind him. "Hey David," he says. "How's the launch going?"

The crowd screams in appreciation, and I can't help but smile. Adam has been the public face of this company since its inception. They're happy to see him. He looks tired, but he has a smirk on his face.

"Good, good," David says. "But the crowd voted for a drink drone as our next new product and I told them they could have it next Christmas."

"Man, who put you in charge? What were they thinking?" Suddenly Adam frowns and points at the screen. "Wait. Who *did* put you in charge? Isn't Blake running things over there?"

Yu frowns. "Blake? Blake isn't here. I thought Blake was with you."

I feel a cold little chill.

"No," Adam says. "He's not." The two fall into silence.

"Wait," my mother says. "Doesn't he know where Blake is?"

"Of course he does." I'm reassuring myself as much as I'm reassuring her. "These things are fully scripted." They almost always are. Blake wouldn't have told me to watch the launch if it was going to end up a complete clusterfuck. Right?

"If he's not at the launch," Adam says, "where is he? Dang it. If only we had built a video-capable device that handled robust four-way calling."

The *dang it* convinces me this is scripted. *Dang* is not the word Adam Reynolds would reach for on his own.

On cue, the watch beeps.

Incoming call: Blake Reynolds. "Oh wait," Adam says. "We did."

The audience laughs, playing along, and the new video resolves into Blake.

He's taken off his glasses, but his hair is still disheveled. He smiles broadly. "Hey, Dad. Lisa. David. Internet."

"Blake, where the hell are you?"

"About that…" Blake smiles. "So, there's this really cool feature we haven't shown you yet with the Vortex video. We've shown you that the camera will adjust to follow your face, no matter how you move your hands. But it turns out, um." He grins. "Sometimes a picture is worth a million words. Before now, when someone asked you over the phone where you were, you'd have to answer with a description." He beams at the screen. "For instance, I could say, 'Hi, Dad! I'm in jail!'"

The audience laughs disbelievingly.

"Or," Blake says, "you can tap the edge of the watch, telling the camera to go into scenery pan mode. And then you can show everyone where you really are."

His video shifts to an all-too-familiar view of a bare cell.

"Which," Blake's voice continues, "it turns out is…still jail. Sorry."

There's a single high-pitched gurgle of laughter, quickly curtailed as it becomes obvious that Blake is serious. I'm leaning forward. I don't know where this is going, what they're planning to do with it.

"Dude," Adam says with an exaggerated clap of his hand to his heart, "are you trying to give me a heart attack?"

That draws a wave of laughter.

"Well," Blake shoots back, "at least if I do, I know you're in the right place to get the very best of care."

Another wave of laughter.

"After all," Blake says with a grin, "you *are* wearing a device with real-time heart-rate monitoring."

"You can't say that." Adam holds up a finger. "The FDA has not approved that statement. Also, I pulled up the record of my heart rate during the attack. It doesn't show a single useful thing." He sighs. "That would have been good publicity."

Blake shakes his head. "You must be getting old. You can't even have a heart attack right."

"You see that?" Adam points a finger at the screen. "Shifting the blame back to me already. You're not off the hook. Want to explain what you're doing in jail?"

"It's a long story."

Adam raises an eyebrow and points to the IV pole behind him. "I'm not going anywhere."

There's another wave of good-natured laughter.

"Fine." Blake sighs. "It started because my girlfriend broke up with me."

Someone in the audience lets out a protracted *Awww;* someone else yells something that comes out indistinctly over the feed.

"I heard that," Blake says. "Don't talk about her that way. I know it *looks* like she broke up with me just before a huge launch when my dad was in the hospital. But I don't blame her for it, and by the time I'm done here, neither will you. Let me set the scene for you. It's two in the morning. My father has just had a heart attack. The ambulance lights are receding in the distance. And I am doing what any good son would do under the circumstances."

Adam doesn't say anything.

And me? I hold my breath. I know these things are supposed to be true constructions, but I also know that Blake won't tell the *real* truth. They aren't going there. They wouldn't.

"Which," Blake says smoothly, "is this: I'm gathering up my dad's cocaine."

Holy fuck. They did. There is dead silence from the crowd. I set my hand on the screen, my head spinning.

True construct is one thing. This? This is too real. I'm not sure if I'm looking at the truth or a fake. I'm not sure what I'm looking at, and I'm living it.

"This might be a good time to mention," Adam says with a growl, "that I have a problem."

I don't even know what to think.

"So I put all this in the car, my girlfriend drives me to the hospital, and I am distracted by the fact that my dad had a heart attack, and also happens to have a cocaine problem. So I leave, and um." Blake shrugs. "Yeah. There's still cocaine in the car. Which wouldn't be a problem, but she gets pulled over by the cops, who find it. She spends six hours in handcuffs." He makes a face. "See? I told you not to blame her for breaking up with me."

"So it *is* his fault," my mother says beside me.

"That is so not how it went down," I say to the screen. "Blake, you idiot."

"In any event," Blake says with apparent good cheer, "this leaves me with two choices. First, I can keep quiet, stick around for the launch, hire lawyers, and let my girlfriend take the fall. Or…" Blake shrugs. "I can strike a bargain with the DA to get her out."

"Well," Adam points out, "she *did* break up with you, so I vote for door number one." The audience laughs.

"I kind of think that announcing this on a live stream with—what are we at, David?"

"A hundred and six million viewers," Yu puts in.

"Yeah. I think I've kind of shut that door." Blake smiles. "Jokes aside, there was never any choice about what I was going to do."

"There is that," Adam says softly.

I have always been confused by Blake's relationship with his father. It is, in so many ways, not remotely ideal. They swear at each other. They milk their friendship onstage for corporate good will. Blake's dad put him in a commercial when he wasn't even two years old. The first time I met Adam Reynolds, he offered me fifty grand to leave his son.

I told him I'd settle for sixty-six billion. In this moment, I realize that he would take that—that if it came down to it, if the choice was between Blake and his company, between Blake and those sixty-six billion dollars, he'd choose Blake every single time.

It may be fucked-up, but it's love.

"But that's between me and her, not me, her and one hundred and six million viewers," Blake says.

"You know," Adam puts in, "we could make it between you, her, and a hundred and six million viewers."

Blake shakes his head. "No. Seriously. This we did not talk about."

But Adam just looks up at the ceiling. "If only," he says with a smirk, "we had made a video-capable smartwatch that could manage robust five-way video calling over a cellular network."

"Dad," Blake says sharply.

But time seems to have slowed for me. There's no way I should be able to call in. Their tech automatically blocks all unauthorized calls to devices during the launches. But... Adam is looking calmly at his screen. I feel like he's looking at me.

This is a true construct, truer than anything else. It's a risk, a huge risk. If I make that call, everything will change. Adam Reynolds has just put in his sixty-six billion dollars.

The only question is if I'm willing to match him.

Without thinking, I pull up Blake's contact information on my watch and hit call.

On my tablet, on the live stream, I see my name show up.

Incoming call: Tina Chen.

"Oh wait," Adam Reynolds says. "We did."

And then I'm on screen. There's a horrible noise.

"Tina," Blake says, "turn off the sound on your live stream or there'll be feedback."

I flick the mute on my tablet with shaking hands.

"This is not scripted," I say. "I was in jail literally an hour ago. You people are crazy."

"That's not true," Adam says smoothly. "It was scripted. I just didn't tell you and Blake about this part. Thanks for playing along. Internet, meet Tina."

"Hi." My voice is shaking a little. "I didn't get my part, and so I'm going to tell you that Blake is a huge liar."

Now that I'm not looking at my tablet, Blake's face takes up a mere quarter of my watch face. Tiny Blake raises his eyebrows.

"I broke up with him before I was arrested," I say. "I broke up with him because I didn't want to fall in love with him. And before anyone tells me how *stupid* that is, I want to point out that his family broadcasts everything about themselves to their hundred and six million viewers. That is really screwed up, if you think about it."

"Wait just one minute," Adam says, sounding wounded. "That's completely unfair. According to internal statistics, we're up to a hundred and eleven million viewers right now."

"Oh," I say on a shaky laugh. "Well. That makes everything better."

"Tina," Adam says, "has a little sarcasm problem. She fits in. We're trying to keep her."

"Also," Blake says, "we don't broadcast *everything* on the internet. That's a myth. I think we may have two or three secrets left. We're holding those for a later launch."

I can't help but smile. "Still screwed up."

Adam smiles. "Welcome to the family, Tina. We may be a little off kilter, but we have the best gadgets."

"A little premature, Dad," Blake says. "We're still broken up."

I take a deep breath. "Maybe we should talk about that," I say, "when there's a hundred and eleven million and three fewer people around, give or take."

Blake smiles at me. The video is tiny. The sound isn't great. But that smile…it comes across, even with all those millions of other people watching along. It fills me up.

"This video interface sucks," I say. "You're this small. Do *not* buy the Vortex, people, not unless you want one of the more romantic moments in your life to be compressed to the size of a sugar cube."

"Hey." Adam frowns. "That is totally uncalled for. Don't listen to her. Buy it. Buy three."

"I'm out." I hit end, and then unmute the sound on my tablet.

Blake is smiling and shaking his head.

"You know," Adam says thoughtfully, "possibly we should have gotten her in on the script from the start."

Blake just smiles. "Ah. That's one we should talk about later, too."

24.

TINA

$\mathcal{M}$y mother drives me back to the Bay Area. This time, though, we take a proper freeway instead of going through winding mountain roads.

We don't say much. Her only commentary on the whole matter is this: "If Blake's dad is so rich, can I make him pay for the gas money I spent to come up here?"

For months, I worried about precisely this: my mother discovering I have a source who could fund her hobby to an extreme she's never discovered before. I thought I would be embarrassed. Ha. *Adam* got me thrown in jail. He owes me.

"Soak him," I tell her. "Hell, don't stop with gas money. You don't know how rich people think. Make him fund a nonprofit center for you. You can quit your job."

She wrinkles her nose. "What, and let that bossy pain-in-my-butt tell me what to do with my time? Ugh. Gas money, and he can pay for my hours today."

She doesn't ask me any other embarrassing questions. She doesn't make horrible demands. She's just there for me.

I look up Cyclone's press release halfway through the drive. It came out concurrently with our conversation. This release lays out the facts of what happened last night in startling clarity. It mentions Adam's cocaine habit and his subsequent heart attack. It says that he'll be going into rehab.

There's more, too. Sometime this morning, the board of directors had an emergency meeting. Cyclone will be undergoing a reorganization. The CEO position will be split in three, going forward: a chief product officer, a chairman, and CEO. They don't say anything about the deal Blake cut with the DA.

The news is confused. Half of everyone thinks the whole thing is a stunt. The other half doesn't know what to think. Some law firm is already talking about a derivative shareholder suit, but Cyclone stock is up—way up.

Still, I'm out of jail. And he's apparently out, too, since he's done at least one interview since the launch. It just goes to show: You really can't trade lives. There's no way I could have managed that, not even with all Blake's money. But that realization no longer makes me feel bitter. It just…is. There's nothing I can do about it. No matter what happens, everything he does will always be easier for him in every way.

Except when it isn't.

I come home to find Maria waiting for me with pad thai.

"You know," she says as we spoon food onto our plates, "you may end up the most famous Tina Chen of them all. You could be the first Google result for your name."

"Fuck that," I say. But for the first time in years, I don't know for sure that I will be invisible. I don't know what my future holds. All of the things that I had planned, every stepping stone I had imagined... I'm not sure that I actually need them. I don't know that I'll do what's safest.

I don't have to anymore.

9:15 PM
Hi Tina.
Sorry this has taken so long.
The day's been kind of crazy.
Can we talk?

> *9:15 PM*
> *Sure. When? Where?*
> *Don't take this the wrong way but I kind of want to see you in person.*

9:16 PM
Is there a wrong way to take that? ;-)
Meet me here in 45 mins

---

*H*e sends GPS coordinates. When I check, they're a ten-minute walk from his home in the Berkeley Hills. I'm not sure what to say to him. I'm not sure how any of this is going to work. But after I take a quick shower, I go to my closet. Ever since that day in the parking lot long ago, ever since Maria got my favorite sweater dry-cleaned, I've been afraid to wear it.

I've been afraid to believe in what it once represented: the hope that maybe today, everything that can go wrong, won't.

I'm not afraid any longer.

I put it on.

B L A K E

I'm waiting in the park when Tina walks up. She's wearing jeans and a white sweater. It catches the light in all this darkness, makes it easy for me to chart her progress up the street.

I stand. I can't keep myself from going to her. My heart is pounding; my head feels odd.

Her hair is dark around her shoulders, cloaking her in the night.

"Hi, Blake." She walks toward me. Her head tilts back as I come close, and the light from a streetlamp nearby spills across her face. I want to hold her, touch her.

"Hi, Tina."

She's the one who reaches for me first. She takes my head in her hands and then pulls me down to her. I wrap her in my arms and kiss her. And for a moment—or maybe an hour—I don't do anything else. I just hold her close and kiss her in the dark, let our lips, our hands, our bodies melt into each other. They say all the things we could whisper. We kiss and kiss, first, like there's no tomorrow, and then—when we've made our way past that, when our lips and tongues are acquainted once more, we kiss like there is one.

We end up on a bench.

From up here, we can see the lights of two bridges, the shimmering skyline of San Francisco against the dark night sky. We see no stars—not a single one—and I like it that way.

First, there are truths to be exchanged. I gesture south, into the darkness. "There," I say. "Dad's still in the hospital down there, and he's already impatient to be out."

"He's really okay, then?"

"He's fine." I smile, despite myself. "One of the DA's conditions was that Dad write an op-ed telling people not to do drugs. I read the first draft. I think…the DA will regret that one. But too bad. They already signed off on the deal."

"How did you pull that off so swiftly?"

I sigh. "How do you think? Money. If they agreed to do a deal, we agreed not to contest the seizure of my car. It was basically a six-figure bribe."

Tina shuts her eyes. "Shit. I'm sorry."

"Hey. You may recall that *I* left my dad's cocaine in there in the first place. You have no business apologizing to me."

"Yes, I do. It's just…" She points far out to sea, past the distant lights of an offshore rig, into nothingness. "There," she says. "Years ago. In China. I remembered early this morning that when I was six, I said something that got my father in trouble. All my life, I've been remembering my mother grabbing me, telling me to be careful. And all my life, I've remembered what happened when I wasn't. That's why I walked away this morning. That's why I tried to keep you so far away. Love is never safe."

I think about my father, still in the hospital. I think about Peter, who I never thought I could lose. I think about Tina checking the electricity bill for her parents.

"Love is never safe," Tina repeats. "It's weird. It's magical. It's the moment when you break through the dark shell that protects your heart and say, this, this person. I'm going to let this person in, let him come so close that he can hurt me more than I can possibly imagine. I'm going to let him hurt me." She inhales. "Love is never safe."

"And yet," I say, "we do it anyway."

"We do it anyway." Her voice is a quiet echo of mine, but her hands close on mine.

"What do you see now?" she asks.

From here, we can see the skyscrapers of the city, the lights of the Bay Bridge. Behind it, there's a dark silhouette—the old decommissioned bridge still being dismantled. We can see the darkness of ocean, and to the north, the scattered lights of the Marin Headlands.

"I'm not sure," I admit. "I'm not sure what comes next. But whatever it is, I want you with me for it."

We're kissing again, bathed in the light of the streetlamp overhead and the constellations we have yet to name below us. We're writing our own script. And the light we're going to build together will drown out every million-year-old star that insists we cannot be.

Thank you!

Thank you for reading *Trade Me*. I hope you enjoyed it.

Is this the end for Tina and Blake?

No. You'll see more of Tina and Blake in the next books in the series. *Hold Me* is up next, and it will be about Maria Lopez, Tina's best friend. *Find Me*, the book after that, will bring you even more of Tina and Blake.

What about Adam Reynolds? When do we get to find out more about him?

Adam Reynolds is getting his own story. I say *story* instead of *book* because What Lies Between Me and You will be five books long, and will span twenty-five years. It's a behemoth.

Ooh. Will it be about Adam getting together with Blake's mom?

No.

When will these books release?

I'm not the fastest writer and I don't like making promises when I'm not sure I can keep them. I hope that *Hold Me* will be out sometime in 2016. If you want to get an email when it's available, you can sign up for my new release e-mail list at www.courtneymilan.com, follow me on twitter at @courtneymilan, or like my Facebook page at http://facebook.com/courtneymilanauthor.

I don't want to wait that long! What can I do in the meantime?

Luckily, I have written many other books. If you haven't already done so, you can try my historical romances. I suggest starting with *The Duchess War*— it's free on most platforms right now. There's humor, there's angst...there are no smartwatches, but in the course of the Brothers Sinister series, you will get primers (they go from A-Z), pretty gowns (and some intentionally hideous ones), pink snapdragons (except there is no such thing as a pink snapdragon), and exclamation points (necessary for proper pronunciation). Give them a try. If you've already read all my books, I have a list of recommendations for other authors on my website.

And if you're looking for more in the Cyclone universe, there are two shorts you can read. The first is from a few years before *Trade Me* starts, and it's a snippet of life at Cyclone from Adam Reynolds's point of view. The second is a cross-over story between the Brothers Sinister series and the Cyclone universe, set initially in the year 2020...until Adam accidentally time-travels back to Victorian England. You can find them linked on my website at http://www.courtneymilan.com

Is there anything else you can tell me?

Many of my historical romance readers already know that if you continue past the end matter, I have author notes and extra stuff. I'm sure some of you are wondering what kind of anti-drug op-ed Adam Reynolds would write. After this page, you'll find Adam Reynolds's anti-drug op-ed. I hope it's everything you imagined.

An op-ed by Adam Reynolds

Don't Do Drugs

*H*ey, kids. Don't do drugs.

That's what I'm supposed to tell you, isn't it? I've already seen myself held up by disapproving pundits as a tarnished example of what might happen to you if you screw up. Kids, don't do drugs. You might have a heart attack. You might die. Even Adam Reynolds suffered the consequences, so drugs have to be bad.

The problem with this line of argument is that kids, unlike adults, aren't stupid.

Hey kids. Don't do drugs. You might win the Tour de France seven times in a row. You might make tens of millions of dollars off endorsements. But—hey—after reigning over the world as undisputed champion for decades, you might suffer a momentary embarrassment on national television when you're forced to admit the truth.

So definitely, kids, don't do drugs.

Kids, be careful with drugs. They might give you the edge you need to take your company from great to mind-boggling. Between 2004, when I first started using cocaine, and 2015, when I had my heart attack, Cyclone's market capitalization went from $223 to $413 billion. So kids—beware of drugs; they might make you and your shareholders $190 billion. You might rule the world. You'll be on the cover of *Time*.

But you never know. Late one night, you might experience a momentary crushing pain in your chest, one that decent medical care will soon alleviate.

Definitely—whatever you do, kids—do *not* do drugs. They can lead you to the pinnacle of the world. They can give you everything. But beware, because…because…because…

Yeah, that's ringing a little hollow, isn't it?

So let's stop with the pretense and tell kids the truth.

Hey, kids. Drugs are like every other risk you could take in life. For instance, you could save your money, get a loan that you'll have to personally guarantee, and start your own business. If you do, chances are—sorry, kids— you'll fail. Yeah, I started my own business in my parents' garage at nineteen. But my parents backed me with three hundred grand, and that might have had something to do with my subsequent success.

You? You'd never get out of the garage.

You could go to college. Go ahead, kids. Take on a hundred grand in debt. Graduate. And then ask yourself why the kid in your class whose parents paid for everything has a better job than you, advances faster, goes further. Watch him twenty years later—the year you're making the final payment on your own education, when your kid is signing up for a million bucks in educational loans (gotta love inflation, kids—it will never be on *your* side), and *his* kid is going to school with everything paid for.

Drugs are like everything else in life: they're a roulette wheel that is slanted precipitously toward those of us who are already predisposed to win. We have golden tickets, and everything we do turns out all right.

So here's the truth, kids. If you're not already winning, don't do drugs. They'll eat you up and spit you out. *You* won't win the Tour de France. You won't make a hundred and ninety billion dollars. You'll lose. And when you lose, it won't be at the petty cost of a few days spent in the hospital. You won't suffer through an embarrassing interview with one of the most powerful women in the world.

You'll lose everything and nobody will even notice. Your tickets are aluminum. You weren't born holding gold, and chances are, you'll never touch it.

Now, as it turns out, I promised to write a soul-searching opinion piece telling people not to do drugs. But let's face it. Drugs aren't—and have never been—the real problem. (Except for heroin. Nobody ever accomplished anything on heroin, not even with a golden ticket, so kids, if you have any sense at all, you will leave that crap right where you found it.)

And so I have to question the utility of browbeating small children about using drugs. I think that instead of telling them what they should do, I should let them tell me.

Here I am, holding this ticket made of gold. It bought me the world. If I wanted to, I could keep cashing it in for a higher score. It's a little tarnished, yes—but gold is gold.

Given everything I've just told you, kids, what do you think I should be doing?

Adam Reynolds announced his permanent retirement as CEO of Cyclone Systems early this morning. He doesn't know what he's going to do next.

Hold Me: Teaser

Eighteen months ago, Maria Lopez felt an unexpected spark with Jay, a hot, tattooed, motorcycle-riding bad boy who checked off every item on her fantasy list. But "too good to be true" never ends well. So when he asked for her number, she walked away.

When she runs into him again, she discovers that Jay is a different kind of trouble than she's imagined. He's a demanding, driven genius, and once he's set his sights on something, he does not give up. Now that their paths have crossed once more, he's not going to let her get away until he knows exactly what's on her fantasy list...and figures out how to make her embrace it.

Want to know what happens? You can find out more about *Hold Me* at:

http://www.courtneymilan.com/holdme.php

Other Books by Courtney

The Turner Series
Unveiled
Unlocked
Unclaimed
Unraveled

Not in any series
A Right Honorable Gentleman
What Happened at Midnight
The Lady Always Wins

The Carhart Series
This Wicked Gift
Proof by Seduction
Trial by Desire

Author's Note

$\mathcal{T}$he ideas that formed the backbone of this book go way, way back with me.

When I first consciously had the idea for this book, I realized that in order to make the premise work, I would need to have a huge company—the kind of company that had a market capitalization of several hundred billion dollars. As you can imagine, companies that meet that criterion are few in number: Apple, Microsoft, Oracle, Google… There are more, of course, but it's just not a very large list, all things considered.

Add in that the plot also required the company be run by someone (or, rather, someones) who had acquired something of a cult of personality, and the number of similar companies gets even smaller.

And so I want to go on the record as saying that despite the inevitable comparisons that will be drawn, I really, really, did not set out to make Cyclone sound so much like Apple. When I first got the idea for this book, it was sometime in early 2013. Apple had not yet announced a smartwatch, and while there were rumors, they were distant rumors.

I said in the beginning that any similarities are coincidental. A more accurate statement is probably that the similarities that do exist are the result of the dictates of reality. There are only so many believable ways to set up a company that large, and even fewer to have one that is dominated by a particular personality. Adam Reynolds is my own invention. He's not supposed to be a stand-in for any particular CEO, and to the extent that he has traits that may remind you of someone (dropping out of college, for instance), those are traits that are widely shared (Steve Jobs, Bill Gates, Larry Ellison, Mark Zuckerberg) by multiple entrepreneurs.

I invented the fundamental traits of Fernanda/the Cyclone Vortex before Apple announced their own smartwatch. I, personally, would rather own a Vortex (sorry, Apple!) but then, I have the benefit of being able to make things up without having to solve any engineering difficulties.

I made up the details of Fernanda on my own. But as completely awesome as Blake's car may sound, I did not make up anything about it. It's all true. The car is quiet. The handles extend out toward you. It turns on automatically when you sit in it. I could add several hundred other details. I test-drove a Tesla to get a feel for it, and this was a dangerous thing to do. I had to actively restrain myself from turning this book into a Tesla love-fest. A friend of mine told me I should ask Elon Musk to sponsor the book, and I considered pitching the idea for about two seconds, which is two seconds longer than I have ever considered any potential sponsorship idea before. (This book is not sponsored by Tesla Motors.) (I have no desire to ever have my books sponsored by any corporations, whether real or imaginary.)

If I had 1.4 billion dollars, I would absolutely buy a Tesla. (You don't need 1.4 billion dollars.)

T say I got the idea for this book in 2013, but there are aspects of it that have been around for longer.

I don't discuss the precise contours of Blake's eating disorder in the book, mainly because this is not a book about eating disorders; it's a book where a character happens to have one. But for those who are wondering, Blake is not anorexic: He's not obsessed with either his weight or his figure. And his particular eating disorder has a different presentation than anorexia normally would.

I got the idea for an athletic protagonist with an eating disorder in late 2012, when I was reading Tyler Hamilton's *The Secret Race*. The book talks a great deal about the Tour de France and the many ways that athletes attempted to win. Obviously, much of it is given over to a discussion of Lance Armstrong. But he also talks about weight. At one point in the book, he states, quite plainly, that he thought all the cyclists around had eating disorders. This stuck in my head, and I've been mulling it over ever since.

Eating disorders in male athletes are not well understood. For female athletes, there has been a lot of research on what is called the Female Athlete Triad, an eating disorder that arises when an athlete (typically an endurance athlete) does not take in enough food to cover her training. This often results in a loss of bone mass, a reduction or even a cessation in menstrual periods, and other energy deficiencies. Overtraining in this way does not always result in significant weight loss—that's why it's a little harder to detect.

Female Athlete Triad is obviously something that people initially assumed only applied to women. In recent years, however, there's been a growing discussion of whether there's a similar presentation for men (many think there is) and how to discover it (it's harder, because men don't have periods, and so they're lacking that particular canary in the coal mine). In Blake's case, his symptoms include the stress fracture he suffers at the race he runs in Spain, among other things. It's complex, with multiple psychological factors that need to be addressed. Luckily, he's going to be seeing a great therapist.

---

*A*nother piece of this book—Tina's background— came from a time much earlier than Tyler Hamilton's book. Anyone who has ever had to read any number of immigration cases has probably run into a case involving someone who practiced Falun Gong. Falun Gong is a series of exercises, coupled with some teachings, that was popular in China in the 1990s. It was, in fact, potentially too popular, and the Communist government banned it.

Protests followed; one of those protests involved ten thousand practitioners showing up, unannounced and unexpected, in Beijing. Needless to say, this freaked out the central government, and they quashed the practice with greater vigor.

The torture that Tina's father suffered is actually mild compared to what has been reported. The U.S. State Department issued a report describing some of the practices; you can read it here. If anything, I've understated what could potentially happen to practitioners of Falun Gong in China. Some of the worst reports suggest that those who refuse to recant are not only executed arbitrarily, but their organs are harvested for medical purposes.

The immigration problem with Falun Gong, on the other hand, is a little more difficult. Anyone who has studied immigration law knows that it is a harsh business. Potential asylum seekers are expected to corroborate their stories—but it's hard to get evidence that the government has put you in a secret camp. (I've seen it go down both ways—person A gets deported because there's no evidence that he was tortured in a secret Communist reeducation camp; person B presents evidence that states that he was held in a reeducation camp, and then the immigration judge decides the evidence is fraudulent, because why would the government admit that it held someone in a secret camp?)

(I also want to point out that this cuts both ways: the fact that there is rarely evidence of horrible government shenanigans means that unscrupulous people seeking asylum may choose to claim that they're practitioners of Falun Gong simply because their stories cannot be easily disproven.) The end result is that a lot of people who have claimed to practice Falun Gong have been deported.

I first heard about Falun Gong when I was working on the Ninth Circuit, where a substantial portion of the docket is composed of immigration cases, and for some reason, that inherent dilemma—damned if you don't have evidence, damned if you do—has stuck with me.

There's another piece of Tina that goes even farther back.

I have a lot of memories of Berkeley. One of my strongest ones, though, is this. My fellow physical chemistry GSIs in the chemistry department all taught Chem 1A in our first year as graduate students.

Teaching Chem 1A, at least the year I did so, was an exercise in helplessness. Our sections were scripted; the class skipped some very basic concepts in chemistry— things like balancing equations and dimensional analysis—that are foundational, on the theory that anyone going to Cal would already know.

Well, they didn't all know. The students of mine who *didn't* know those things were—inevitably—the ones who did not come from rich areas. They had science teachers in high school who taught gym class (nothing wrong with that—except if the gym teacher doesn't know science). Our sections were scripted; instead of covering those basics as instructors, we had to do terrible things like show our students pictures of random things and have them talk about what they meant.

(To this day, these pictures still make me want to beat someone over the head. Y'all, any one-state system has the same entropy as any other one-state system. Stop teaching our kids lies in lieu of balancing equations! Obviously, I still feel a fiery rage when I let myself think about this.)

All the GSIs talked about it: The students who were at the greatest risk in our classes weren't the ones who worked the least, or even the ones who most lacked aptitude. They were the ones who didn't come from school districts that had money. They were poor and more likely to be immigrants or people of color.

Perhaps the greatest stretch of my imagination in this whole book is the one that nobody but me will notice. To this day, my deepest regrets are for those students who were set up to struggle from before the day they enrolled. The playing field was never equal. I wanted to write someone who succeeded despite the fact that everything in the system was set up against her.

I wish I'd been able to do more.

Acknowledgments

*T*hank you to everyone who listened when I told them about my idea for this book, and told me it was not a horrible idea to write it: Ann Aguirre, Tessa Dare, Sherry Thomas, Brenna Aubrey, Rawles Lumumba, Carey Baldwin, Leigh LaValle… I'm sure there are others who belong on this list. Writing in a new subgenre is a scary thing, and this book terrified me on many, many levels.

I'm grateful to the many people who helped me get this book together on a tight turnaround: Robin Harders and Briana Lambert for editing, Martha Trachtenberg for copy editing, Julie Naughton, Rawles Lumumba, and Rebecca Hill for last minute proofing. And Rose Lerner for being the absolute best and proofing even when I didn't ask her to do it. Thanks also to Professor Robert van Houweling, who sent me his syllabus for PS 1, and the City of Berkeley, for not giving me a ticket when my meter had totally expired when I went to do my campus walk around.

I pulled on years of listening to people in my family talk about living in China to write this book. Tami, TJ, Mom, and Dad were all ridiculously helpful. Tami answered last-minute questions about Mandarin at…um…seriously, the last minute.

Mr. Milan was very excited to finally know something about legitimate medical procedures that would actually be used in the book, and to be able to have actual input other than suggesting that everyone get chlamydia or syphilis. He thinks the cath lab (where they stick a catheter in your femoral artery and pump you full of dye so they can observe what's going on in your heart) is awesome and you cannot imagine how excited he was that someone actually got cathed in the book. He answered lots and lots of questions. Like: how long does it take to cath someone? How can you tell if someone's having a heart attack? At what point would you suspect and/or not suspect cocaine usage? What signs do you have that someone is using cocaine? I did not ask him all of these questions, but he answered them all anyway. Seriously, you have no idea how much he likes the cath lab. He is reading this over my shoulder as I write, and he wants me to drop a link to this YouTube video about cathing people. He thinks it's *hilarious*. I, as a normal citizen, find it frightening.

Usually I thank people and say that any mistakes are my own, but I'm married to Mr. Milan and told him all these details three times, so if he missed something and it ended up wrong, it's because he wasn't paying attention. Feel free to blame him if something is off. (I'm kidding.) (I'm not kidding.)

Sean B. at the Denver Tesla not only let me test drive the car even though I told him that I was never going to buy one, he answered innumerable weird questions that nobody else had ever asked. Questions like, "What happens if I'm driving down the road and I throw my electronic key fob out the window?"

And as for my AK co-clerks…you know that I can never thank you guys enough. This book is dedicated to you for a reason.

Finally, if you've gotten this far—thank you for taking a chance on a new book in a new subgenre for me. I hope you enjoyed the ride.

38215504R00202

Made in the USA
Columbia, SC
16 December 2018